Blood Runs Deep

To the Good doctor [illegible]

[illegible]

7/17/23

Blood Runs Deep

From Blood on the Capitol Trilogy

Bill Halamandaris

Bill Halamandaris
Blood Runs Deep

Published by Spines

ISBN: 979-8-89691-196-8

Spines

For Angie

Contents

Acknowledgments

This was written largely as an homage to John D. MacDonald, who is my favorite author. I have read everything he has written, going back to when I stumbled on one of his early books in our public library. I was twelve.

I was hooked deep enough that I looked for his works for fifty years, delighting in each discovery. When Travis McGee came along, I couldn't wait for the release of the next title in the series. I read them all – sometimes several times.

When MacDonald passed away, I felt like I had lost a friend. I also mourned the loss of my favorite fictional character. Through the many years that have followed, I have often wondered what happened to Travis McGee. Where would you have gone? What would he have done if his story had not been cut short?

This book suggests an answer to that question. It comes with gratitude to John D. MacDonald for the many hours of enjoyment he provided and his continuing inspiration.

In addition, I am grateful to Spines, the publishing team, Dr. Kim Enders for her technical advice, and Paulette Lawing, Marielle Jones, Capt. Todd Gilroy and Beth Raymond for their editorial assistance. Here and everywhere in my life, I'm grateful to my wife, Angie, for her encouragement, patience, and support. It's not fun being the spouse of a writer, particularly in the days of COVID when this project started. You can never be quiet enough, and there is nowhere to go.

There are those who will read what follows with doubt and suspicion. They will swear these events could not be possible. Others will swear they were there and remember these events in specificity and great detail. Where you sit determines what you see. There is truth enough to support either persuasion.

The Call

It was strange.

Someone I didn't know called the United States Senate looking for me.

He said an uncle I had never met had left me a boat in Florida. The man said his name was Meyer – just Meyer.

It was 2:30 PM on a fine Friday. It was a perfectly ordinary day. It's not the kind of day you would expect anything life-changing. The sun was shining. The temperature was soft and inviting. It's all rare for Washington. It was the kind of day that made you think about packing it in early and getting a jump on the weekend. And that's what I was doing when the Capitol switchboard patched the call through to PSI – the Permanent Subcommittee on Investigations.

Two of the four people on my team – John Fine and Dick Broadbent – had already gone home. Fine is an Ivy League lawyer out of Northwestern and Yale. He was already in place when I was hired. He is supposed to report to me, but we both know that there isn't much I can do about it if he doesn't. And at least he had an excuse – such as it was. He was home helping Pam, his wife, prepare for her coming-out party. In his defense, he didn't have much choice. It's no secret she is high maintenance. She is a Macklin, as in Macklin Magazines.

Dick never needs an excuse to leave early and to be candid, he is rarely missed when he does. He is a paper-weight. The only reason he is there is because the Ranking Member called in a favor to get him out of Colorado and away from his daughter. A former Deputy Sheriff, Dick knew next to nothing about the Senate when he arrived and hasn't bothered to learn much since. Like Fine, I didn't hire him, and I can't fire him. They report to me, but they answer to the guy who got them their job.

Bill Christoff was my hire, which probably explains why he was still there. If Dick is a paperweight, Bill is a paper-eater, and – if experience is any guide – he would be there long after everyone else had left. He is a lawyer, CPA, and former chief of staff for the governor of New York. Bill has the look and intensity of a rabbinical scholar and wears in rotation the same suit in three colors. The shirt is always white. The tie is always solid. The shoes are always Johnston & Murphy – one of three pairs he owns. As you might imagine, he has almost no social life. All he cares about is his work.

I was standing next to him when the receptionist announced the call. I dropped my shoulder bag on the desk nearest the door and picked up the phone, wondering who would be calling so near the end of the day and why the caller hadn't dialed directly instead of calling the

Capitol's main switchboard – (202) 224-3121. That number gives you access to everyone on The Hill.

Out of the thousands of possibilities, the caller had asked for me by name – Theo James Alexander. In my years on The Hill, this was the first time that had happened.

Meyer said he called the main switchboard because he didn't know how else to reach me. Who was he? I wondered. What was he talking about? My father had two brothers, but both passed away before I had a chance to get to know them – one in Vietnam, the other in Iraq. So, who was he talking about? How did he know he could find me at the Senate? And what was all this about a boat? I have been on my share of fishing boats, but boating in and of itself is not something that has ever interested me all that much. I have always been inclined to agree with those who say a boat is a hole in the water you throw money into.

So, it was strange.

The Hunter

The call may have been strange, but the timing was excellent.

To be honest, I was bored. I am not one who idles well. I need action. I need movement. I have a lot of energy and am, by nature, an aggressive animal. I cloak my aggression in ways that are considered socially acceptable, but at heart, I know I am a hunter.

Most men – and a lot of women – are, on some level. The species hasn't evolved all that much. The only difference is what we hunt. Broadbent hunts the blossoms, the young and tender conquests. Fine, a poor boy surrounded by rich men, hunts the things thought to be essential for The Good Life.

I view one with disgust and the other with indifference. I need a sharper edge, a finer focus, and a more compelling purpose. Put it this way: some people run just for the fun of running. I need something to chase and something to catch that makes the chase worth the effort.

I need to feel it matters. I need to be able to justify what may otherwise be unjustifiable with the knowledge that it serves the greater good.

God help me. I believe in justice. I need something to do that feeds my sense of righteousness. I live on the rush that comes from rattling a predator's dish, shooing away the vultures, and turning over the largest rocks I can find to watch the maggots squirm, shrivel up, and die in the bright, unforgiving light.

The last investigation had been a big one. Half a dozen corporations were ripping off the taxpayer to the tune of a billion dollars a year. It had taken me more than a year to bring them down and put a stop to it. When that was over, my adrenaline dropped. I was spent – exhausted and aimless.

Six months later, I was still coasting, cleaning up the loose ends and recharging. But I was increasingly aware I was going through the motions, wasting time and energy. I was getting restless.

So, the timing was good. I needed something to do and someone to chase.

It sounded like that was what Meyer was handing me. His voice was flat and emotionless. He said he had not seen or heard from my uncle in over six months. He said he had been instructed to call me if that ever happened and that there was more than a boat involved, but he didn't know about all that. I would have to talk to the lawyers and see for myself.

He was able to clear up one thing before he hung up. The uncle was on my mother's side. That required some thought.

So, I put in a call to M. J. – Senator Colgate's handler. Colgate is the Chairman of PSI and my boss. He persuaded me to return to The Hill when he took over the Committee.

I have to say it was a tough sell. I don't think anyone else could have done it. I have been on The Hill most of my adult life. I have done just about everything there is to do there, from running elevators while in college to working on the committee and personal staff of several Senators before finding a niche at PSI.

I was reluctant to go back because I knew it so well. PSI suited my talents and instincts, but the process had become so polluted it was getting hard to get anything done. The Senate had changed. Members had changed. Personal interests and the pursuit of power now prevailed, cycling back and forth in an endless, progressive loop like a carnival ride that no one seemed to want to get off. Somewhere in all that, the public's interest was getting lost.

It had gotten to the point where I had to begin every major inquiry by investigating my own Committee. By then, I knew some Members would be connected to whoever or whatever I was investigating. I had to find out who that was what their interests were and seal them off if I was to have any hope of success. The saddest part of all this was that it was likely to be a different Member every time. My best friend and advocate on one issue were likely to be my worst enemy on another.

It got to be frustrating and disheartening. After a while, the juice just didn't seem to be worth the squeeze.

By then, the real estate investment company I began while I was in college was firmly established.

That had started simply enough. I began by buying properties on The Hill that no one else seemed to want. It got to be a bigger deal than I ever expected. The business seemed to grow organically, largely because – for a while at least – the supply far exceeded the demand.

The Hill is the largest residential area in the District of Columbia. It started with shanties erected south and east of the Capitol, which were built to house the men working on the Capitol Building and the Washington Navy Yard. During WWII, it developed into a community for members of Congress and others employed on The Hill, but it fell out of favor when people started migrating to the suburbs. I bought against the tide, betting it would come back – and it did.

All of a sudden, it seemed people got tired of fighting traffic for an hour and a half every day to get to work. The Hill became an "in" place to live, and everybody seemed to want properties you couldn't give away a few years before. In the process, I wound up with more money than I knew what to do with. That made it easy to walk away. I told myself I didn't need the ego and self-promotion pervading the Senate. I could live without it – or so I thought.

But it wasn't long before I realized I missed the hunt, and it wasn't something I could easily replicate somewhere else. I kept busy managing and maintaining my properties. I worked off my excess energy by doubling down on my exercise routines, running down the Mall to the Lincoln

Memorial and back every morning, and working out every afternoon in the gym I created in the carriage house behind my townhouse. Still, it felt like I was just killing time.

So, when Colgate called, I was ready.

Colgate is the heir to the Colgate Company and carries the name of the grandparent who started it all – J. Carlson Colgate. When he was elected to the Senate, he seemed natural for assignments to the Finance and Commerce committees, but leadership failed to take into account his ambition and his love of combat. While Colgate looks like he came from corporate central casting – tall, dark, and handsome, with a boyish smile – the core is as rough as the exterior is smooth.

When a man who has everything runs for public office, they often say it is because he has a desire to serve. While that is undeniably part of Colgate's motivation, I think the real draw is the competition – a desire to find a game worth winning and test himself against the best the field has to offer. They say he has the double Y chromosome. True or not, he is the most aggressive animal I have ever seen.

That makes our instincts very much aligned. Still, I turned him down three times. I had to make sure our interests were aligned as well. He was candid and open about that, saying he wanted me to help position him for a run for the White House. He knew his wealth and business experience would guarantee him the backing of the established interests, but that wouldn't be enough. He would have to broaden his support if he were to succeed. He needed to identify himself with the interests of the common person.

Looking back, I would have to say my resistance was largely due to inertia. I have always found it difficult to go back to anything I have left behind. Colgate prevailed by insisting I come in and sit down with him. He listened to my objections and said, "OK." He would make it easy for me. He said if I came back to work with him, I would be given a free hand, report directly to him, be attached to PSI, have complete access to and control of the Subcommittee's resources, and be paid "WAE."

The latter is perhaps most important. WAE is the While Actually Employed schedule. It is a handy device often used by Members to hide people they don't want to show on their personal staff. While WAE employees are listed in the Green Book, a public report published by the Secretary of the Senate identifying all staff and their compensation, there is no detail or explanation. No one knows who these people really are or what they really do. You will find relatives, political consultants, and girlfriends listed there, along with people like me with specific expertise or a price tag too high to advertise.

In short, Colgate gave me everything I wanted – freedom of operation, the authority of the Senate, backup when I needed it, and his support. The latter includes a Black American Express card. It forwards my expenses directly to him and saves me the aggravation of filling out reimbursement forms justifying what I am doing. It also avoids unnecessary questions from bureaucrats and clerks who can slow you down and turn you off. In return, I give Colgate what he wants – wall-to-wall press, a horse to ride, and targets to skewer.

MJ – Mary Jane Matser – picked up my call on the second ring.

"Where's the Chairman?" I asked.

"Pittsburgh," She said. "He is huddling with his political advisers. You saw the Congressional Times cover last week – "Ten Members to Watch." Thanks to you, he is a player now. People are coming at him from every direction. The brain trust is trying to separate the wheat from the chaff."

"Spoken like a good Pennsylvania Dutch girl."

A quick laugh.

"I could have taken you home and said they are swarming on him like maggots on a bleed."

I feigned disgust.

"Ugh. Please don't."

"Sorry. I guess I already did."

"Yes, you did, didn't you? I am deeply offended… Anyway, it sounds like he will be busy for a while. If he is looking for me, let him know I'm going to take a few days off to deal with a personal matter."

"Something serious, Theo?"

"I don't know. It's strange."

Max

From the air, the Capitol looks like a wedding cake surrounded by shoeboxes. Over the years, the shoeboxes have multiplied - Senate Office Buildings to the North, House Office Buildings to the South. The Committee on Government Operations is on the first floor of Dirksen – the middle box on the Senate side – just past the elevators, two-thirds of the way down. The Permanent Subcommittee for Oversight and Investigations occupies the last office in that suite.

I walked out of Dirksen's south entrance and headed east, awed as always by the reality of where I was and the beauty of this place. The Capitol was across the street, and the Supreme Court was a block south. Union Station is three blocks north, surrounded by the flags of the states. All picture perfect if you ignore the parking lots, the Capitol police headquarters, and other assorted service buildings. It's even more impressive when you realize how far the City has come.

George Washington was underwhelmed when he heard the location of the city that was to bear his name. He said, “That Indian swamp in the wilderness?” He was not suggesting that the City was only fit for reptiles - though you can make that case. He was being accurate. Washington was built on marginal land no one wanted, carved out of the least desirable parts of Maryland and Virginia.

For a couple of weeks in the spring and fall, Washington can be delightful, but winter can be biting, and most of the summer is stifling with the heat of the 90s and the air being so thick you can bite it. Until 1939, when air conditioning was installed in the Capitol, legislators took every opportunity to escape The Hill for the relative comfort of other places.

Before then, it was often said that good Americans went to Paris when they died while the rest went to Washington. It was “Hell on the Potomac,” devilishly uncomfortable, miserably boring, desolate, and devoid of satisfaction. It was a place where, as Dickens said, “Few people would live who were not obliged to.”

That has largely changed. On days like today, it is hard to imagine a place you would rather be. It felt good to be out, and I enjoyed the short walk to my home on Constitution Avenue. It’s three blocks east of the Capitol, sandwiched between a federal townhouse and a 19th-century manor house. The cherry blossoms had made their celebrated brief appearance a month ago and were long gone, but the azaleas, tulip trees, apple trees and redbuds were doing their best to compensate. Blossoms lined the street all the way to the Capitol and down the

Mall, coloring the sky pink and white in the fading light of the blue period.

My residence is the last of my properties on The Hill. It has two floors and an English basement, is wide and deep with ten-foot ceilings, and has a covered courtyard in the back leading to a carriage house.

The self-contained nature of its design and its proximity to the Capitol are the primary reasons I kept it when I sold everything else to Denton Real Estate. Denton was as happy to take over my holdings as I was to let go. The sale established Denton as the biggest player on The Hill while giving me that measure of freedom that comes with the knowledge that I have the resources to do anything I might want to do if my experience with Colgate doesn't pan out.

When I arrived home, Max was waiting at the front door. Max is a minister - licensed to preach the gospel in California - a doctor and a lawyer. He has a Ph. D. and is listed in several indices of prominent Americans. He is also my dog.

Max is a purebred Lhasa Apso, twelve pounds or so, depending on the length of his cream-colored coat. I inherited him from a long-gone girlfriend. She wanted a lap dog. While he looks the part with a button nose and large dark eyes, he lacks the disposition. Picture a dust mop with teeth. Try to pick him up, and he'll take your hand off.

At one time or another, he had snapped at every member of her household. She gave up on him after he tried one of her dinner guests on the kitchen table. "It's either you or the pound," She said when she dropped him off. "I thought of you because you are a lot alike."

I've never been quite sure how to take that, but I must admit there are times when I see a resemblance. Max was sitting on the floor halfway to the stairs. Most dogs would have come running. He barely acknowledged my presence.

He tilted his head in a look of recognition and then walked toward the back of the house. The door to the staircase leading to the English basement was open, telling me Sam had given him the run of the house.

He stopped halfway through the living room and looked over his shoulder, making sure I was following. He was hungry and expected to be fed. Inside the refrigerator, I found a six-pack of coke, some chips, half a bottle of salsa, and something that looked like it might once have been cheese. The cupboard was bare. All we had were canned goods and some dry dog food for Max. He hasn't touched that since he got his law degree.

His dish is near his bed in the corner of the kitchen. Framed diplomas and certificates of achievement decorate his wall. His J.D. says, Harvard. The Ph. D. is from Georgetown. The Doctor of Divinity says Stanford, while the medical degree is from Yale. They surround a framed certificate from the American Kennel Club.

This probably says more about me and my sense of humor than anything it might say about Max. While standing in a supermarket line one morning, I found myself struck by a tabloid advertisement I saw over the shoulder of the person in front of me. For a small amount of money and minimal effort, the ad promised anyone could acquire an advanced degree.

The ad made it sound so easy, so I decided to respond and see what would happen. Since I already have several degrees, I used Max's formal name instead – B. B. Maxwell.

I filled out the form and sent them a money order for $75. Two weeks later, Max received a diploma certifying he was a Doctor of Divinity. There were also instructions on the tax advantages of setting up your church.

This amused me enough that I started looking for more opportunities to extend Max's pedigree. Before long, the project took on a life of its own. Max began receiving more mail than I did. He was receiving solicitations for everything from medicine to mail-order brides.

Mixed in with all this, a year or so after it all began, came a letter from the American Biographical Index. They indicated they chronicled prominent Americans, said they had become aware of Max's achievements, and invited him to apply. I filled in the form for Max, listing his occupation as a security specialist and his age in months. The plaque came a month later. Along with it was an invitation to buy a memorial copy of the Index for $299.

That led to further honors and invitations, which are increasingly mainstream. When I saw how seriously people who should have known better were taking Max's phony degrees, the project took on a new dimension. It seemed reasonable to suppose that not everyone who answered these ads had a pet and shared my sense of humor.

On that assumption, we opened a formal Congressional investigation and began systematically clipping and responding to questionable ads. The further we got into it, the more outrageous it became. Before long, it was clear the problem merited the attention of law enforcement agencies. We invited the U. S. Postal Service and the FBI to join us, conducting a sting called "Dipscam."

The FBI concluded its investigation by finding that some 50,000 professionals were operating in the United States with phony credentials. One diploma mill in Oregon had conferred 2,300 phony degrees to people who wanted to be doctors, chiropractors, psychiatrists, and engineers. Another had sold 3,000 phony diplomas, including 200 to federal employees.

One of these people was an anesthesiologist at Fort Dix who failed to notice a patient's heart had stopped during a routine operation. The patient suffered irreparable brain damage as a result. Another of these individuals was masquerading as a surgeon in Nebraska. Not only had he not gone to Medical School, but we learned he had not even gone to college.

Ultimately, more than a dozen Congressional hearings spun out of this process. Businesses were closed. People were jailed. Laws were changed, and Max became celebrated enough that ABC wanted to feature him as their Person of the Week. Max modestly declined.

I poured some of the dry food into his dish, added water, and waited for a reaction. There was a chance he might eat it, I thought, but my hope was short-lived. Max walked to his dish, sniffed disdainfully, and then looked up at me as if to say, "Surely, you don't expect me to eat this."

When nothing better was offered, Max walked to the eight-foot sliding glass doors at the back of the house and settled into his guardian position – shaggy head up and alert, looking like a miniature of the sphinx, paws forward, tail curled back like a bow on his butt – eyes fixed on Sam. I opened a Coke and joined him, taking a seat on a stool at the kitchen counter.

Together, we watched Sam wearing out the Stair-master on the second floor of the carriage house. She was moving with fierce determination, pushing herself and punishing the machine. Bruno, the Great Dane next door, was patrolling his yard, pacing up and down the six-foot fence that separated our properties, waiting for her to come out. A massive beast, coal black, bred and trained to work as a police dog, he provided security for the immediate world. He was always outside - rain or shine - probably because there was no room for him inside. His head is as big as Max's body.

While we watched, Sam, formally Samantha Jean Hough, finished her workout, switching from the Stair-master to a series of floor exercises, twisting her body into one unlikely position after another. She says it's not yoga, but it looks enough like yoga to make it hard to tell the difference.

She came out of the carriage house half an hour later and walked toward us, stopping to turn on the heater for the hot tub. She moved confidently and deliberately.

There is nothing dainty about Sam. She is more the Amazon, built to scale, coming in at five foot nine in her stocking feet. She has the kind of figure that made Hefner rich. The narrowness of her waist accentuates the fullness of her hips and exaggerates the differential with her chest, giving her figure almost cartoon dimensions.

She came up the stairs and opened the sliding glass door. A grey t-shirt that looked like it might have been snagged from my laundry basket hung loosely over her black Under Armour. Her arms and shoulders glistened with perspiration. Her damp hair hung close to her face.

I couldn't resist a wise remark.

"You look like you rode hard and put to bed wet."

"Not yet," She said, tossing it off. "But the night is young."

We are friends without privileges, though she often reminds me privileges have been offered. A couple of years back, when we were both between relationships, she invited me to see Springfield in concert at the Kennedy Center. Halfway through "This Gun's for Hire," she grabbed my arm tightly, brought her lips close enough for me to feel the heat of her breath on my ear, and whispered, "I sure hope he's not starting something you can't finish."

I didn't. Later that night, and often after that, I have wondered why I didn't.

"Show me a beautiful woman," Halle Berry said, "And I'll show you a man tired of fucking her."

Maybe she's right. If that's all there is, it can get old fast.

The last one was the worst. Sam thought he was "the one." They were engaged and living together when he announced he wasn't attracted to her anymore. He had found someone slimmer, someone younger, someone new.

She arrived on my doorstep in pieces. After holding her until she had cried herself out, I invited her to stay in the English Basement while she figured out what to do. That had evolved into a lease of convenience. She enjoyed having a place three blocks from work, a friend she could talk to, and a friend she could use as a doorstop. I enjoyed having someone around to take care of Max when I wasn't there and watch the house when I traveled. I charge her enough rent to protect her pride and give her the run of the house when I am gone,

At first, she couldn't talk about what happened. Then that's all she could talk about. Finally, she started pulling out of it. When she asked if she could use the exercise equipment in the carriage house, I knew she had turned the corner and was facing forward.

"Why do you take so much crap from those mopes you date and never cut me a break?" I asked.

"I don't know," She said. "Maybe it's because I'm not sleeping with you."

There it was. She had finally said it.

"You're probably right," I said after allowing a moment for her comment to register. "I think I would remember that."

"You would never be able to forget it," She said firmly.

I let her have the rhetorical victory, but I knew the bigger battle was before her. She would come back to our conversation, probably in the still of the night when the ghosts of bad relationships surface, and ask that most persistent of all questions – Why?

Maybe it had already started. She paced the floor before me and stopped to look at me with earnest eyes.

"What is it with you, anyway?" She said.

It was a question she had hesitated to ask in the past, and from the tremor in her voice, she wasn't sure she wanted answered now.

"What do you mean?" I said, buying some time.

"I get the full-court press from most guys in a fast five. I've been living here for more than a year, and you haven't begun to make a pass. Most people wouldn't believe that was possible. You couldn't persuade anyone who knows us there isn't something going on between us… So, what's the deal?"

I wasn't about to tell her that things only have the value we give them. Besides, I had good reason to know how fragile she was. There are too many cracks left by years of what psychologists call "inconsistent stimuli" – attraction then rejection, a constant reversal of direction.

I knew I had to tread carefully. The last thing she needed was another reason to follow Alice down the rabbit hole.

"Maybe it's just bad timing," I said. "You were involved with someone when we met. Then I got involved with someone. I counseled you after your breakup. You returned the favor. By the time we got through all that, we were pretty far into the friend zone. Once you get there, it's hard to go back."

"All right," She said after a thoughtful pause. "Not sure if I buy it, but alright."

Her eyes dropped. She used her fingers to comb her damp hair, pulling it back away from her face.

"But it is more than that," She said.

Her eyes were back. Hard on me.

"What do you mean?"

"I just don't understand you. You and all your weirdness."

"Like what?"

"What's with this mania you have for putting your back to the wall? How many headwaiters have you freaked out by insisting they hold the table while you get behind it? And why can't you stand anything in your pockets? I mean, what are pockets for, anyway? Why can't you ever do anything like everyone else? Why do you always question everyone you meet? You stop and talk with everyone – people you know and people you don't. Why do you have to have a reason for everything you do? Have you ever, just once, done something – anything – simply because it felt good?"

All good questions, I thought. There was no simple answer.

"I am what I am," I said.

"You and Popeye."

She wrinkled her nose like a doe pulling a scent out of the forest.

"But that's what I meant about the friend zone," I said. "You already know a lot about me. There are things a friend will tolerate that might be too hard for anyone else to understand."

The look on her face said it all. It was one I've seen many times before. How do you tell someone that pretty is not enough?

It is such a waste, such a tremendous waste, I wanted

to tell her. They undervalue you, and worse, you undervalue yourself. You are so obviously attractive; everything else you have to offer is neither needed nor wanted. It is an unnecessary complication. Can you understand, Samantha Jean? You are more than this.

All this I should have said, but I didn't. I'm not sure why I didn't. I guess even a brave man can be a coward at times.

Instead, I handed her the towel she had left on the counter, and I told her I was going to be gone for a few days. I didn't elaborate, and she didn't ask. When she left, Max followed at her heels. A few moments later, I heard the shower kick on downstairs.

I poured myself a shot of Metaxa, checked the mail, and sat down to think.

Meyer's call troubled me. I knew my father's family well. They were a big, hearty bunch that didn't hold anything back. If they had a long-lost relative, he wouldn't be lost long. They would have found him, embraced him, and drawn him in.

My mother's side of the family was something else. I realized I knew nearly everything about one half of my family and nearly nothing about the other. I knew my mother's mother died when she was seven. I knew her father wasn't much of a man. From what I'd heard, he seemed ill-prepared by either nature or interest to raise a child, and that was the least of his failings.

My father found my mother working in the family bakery on Main Street just below Church Circle in Annapolis. He was finishing a tour of duty at Ft. Meade and was smart enough to see her for what she was. Six months later, they were married. When Dad was discharged, they made their way west to the family ranch in Colorado and never looked back.

I never had the impression my mother left anyone or anything that mattered behind. I had only a vague memory of hearing about a brother, someone older and distant who had never really been part of the family.

Who was he? What became of him? How did he even know of my existence? Why had he surfaced, apparently asking to be part of my life from death when he never wanted to be part of my life while still alive? And what was all this stuff about a boat? I knew less about boats than I did about him.

My Mom was two years gone. There was no way to ask her now. Dad passed away a year before Mom. They are buried beside each other on the ranch where they always wanted to be. If Dad were alive, he probably wouldn't have much to say anyway. He never spoke about her family. There was no one who could fill in the blanks, and there were about thirty years of them.

But if Meyer was right, I had an uncle, and something had happened to him. I knew not what, but I intended to find out. We might not have been close, but he was kin of my kin. I knew I would not stop until my blood could rest in peace.

I went to sleep with that understanding and the overwhelming sense of release that came with it. My malaise was over.

I had promised John I would attend their party – what staff was calling Macklin's Big Reveal. His wife, Pam, would never forgive either one of us if I skipped the unveiling of their new home, but there was nothing to keep me in Washington after that. Not when I finally had something compelling to do.

It was time to find out something about myself. It was time to find out about my uncle. It was time to answer Meyer's unspoken questions. His message and manner suggested foul play. If that were the case, someone would answer.

The People

Before we get too far along, you should know who I am and where I come from. Start with the fact that I hate the categorical imperatives. The question of race, in particular, gives me the heaves.

I find those bureaucratic forms that ask you to identify with some slice of humanity insulting. There is no room for percentages, of course. You can't say you are 50 percent Caucasian and 50 percent African American, 25 percent Asian and 75 percent Latino, or any other combination. One must choose to identify with one group or another.

Ironically, these forms capture the great truth buried in what they are trying to deny: The human race is one piece. As the National Geographic Society has now thoroughly documented, we can all trace our DNA back to the verdant valleys of Africa. From there, we migrated into groups and tribes and populated the world, developing identities specific to the places we populated. But the differences we see are distinctions without a difference. In every meaningful, measurable way, we are the same.

When pushed to choose, I mark the box for Native Americans. It has as much to do with where and how I was raised as anything else. If I had been raised in New York or Los Angeles, I might have felt differently about it, but I was raised in a high country on the western slope of the Continental Divide, and my paternal grandmother was Ute. She was the granddaughter of Chief Denali, known to his people as "The Great One." Nature and nurture combined to give her heritage a disproportionate influence over who I am and how I see the world.

In southern Utah and western Colorado, the Utes are looked down on and despairingly called "garbage-can" Indians. They are not. They were not. The Utes are the oldest residents of Colorado. Two thousand years ago, they ranged over the entire Colorado Plateau, covering much of Utah, Colorado, Arizona, and New Mexico before separating into tribes that became the Paiute, Shoshone, and Comanche people. In Shoshonean – their language – the Utes are "The People," the mightiest and most valiant.

Their world changed when gold was discovered in Cherry Creek, at a place we now call Denver. Miners and settlers rushed in, as they were inclined to do, tearing up the land and following the trail of precious metals through the mountains, pushing the tribes back as they advanced.

These men did not come to the land to cherish it and care for it like my grandfather did. For these men, the land was something to be conquered, something to be plundered. For these men, one piece of land was like another. They came to take what they could from it. It's the difference between loving the land and raping it.

To The People, this is a sacrilege. The People are *of* the land. We do not own the land. We are only given the right to use it and care for it for a short period. After we are gone, that right passes beyond us. We see the Great Spirit in the woods, the rivers, and the lakes. We hear it in the wind. We know we are not one thing and all of nature another. We know we are all part of the great river of life.

The People know we come from the land and will return to it. It nourishes and sustains us. We live off the land, but we take only what we need. Women gather berries and fruit, amaranth seeds, wild onion, rice grass and dandelion – all things that grow naturally in the high country. Men hunt, but they never kill more than they need, nor do they ever kill in the name of something called "sport."

The white man does not understand this way of life. He does not see himself as part of the natural order of things. He sees himself as separate and apart. He sees no need to nourish and protect the earth and its creatures. He kills whatever and whenever he can. He tears up the ground, poisons the water, and pollutes the air.

Lately, this breed of man has developed a new subspecies – a fact-resistant, science-denying variant. There are many viruses in this world, but none so deadly as this pretentious, vicious virus that feeds on the deadly combination of arrogance and ignorance, marching head-first and proudly into the darkness of the unrepentant, never knowing the cancer it is, killing its host as it advances.

If you doubt me, look around. We're not just warming the world; we're cutting down the rainforest. We're not just cutting down the rainforest; we're moving invasive species into the rainforest. Doing just one of these things would precipitate a mass extinction. Put it together, and we are looking at the worst extinction of species since the days of the dinosaurs.

Humankind is the asteroid now, and there is no cure for its inherent and deadly narcissism that would have us believe we are at the center of the universe. Unfortunately, there is no vaccine for stupidity. We have put more than forty thousand species on the Red List. The only reason we haven't joined them there is because we compile it. If we stay the course, 30 to 50 percent of the planet's species will be extinct within thirty years.

The People do not understand this. They have lived naturally in the valleys of the White and Yampa River systems for generations. In the fall, family units begin moving out of the mountains into sheltered areas for the winter along the White, Green, and Colorado Rivers. In the spring, they follow the melting snow line, and in summer, in the high country.

Two thousand years of this history changed when Nathan Meeker moved into the White River Valley. Meeker had a firm opinion about how other people should live their lives. He came to Colorado to start what he said would be a utopian colony. It never occurred to him that he might be destroying one.

Along with Horace Greeley, Meeker conceived the Union Colony – now Greeley, Colorado – in the foothills of the Rocky Mountains. To pay the debts he accumulated, Meeker sought and obtained a political position – the job of Indian Agent at the White River Indian Reserve. It didn't seem to matter that his contact with Indians had been minimal. He knew nothing about them or their culture and had little interest in learning.

Meeker moved the Indian agency to Powell Park, building his headquarters on the Indians' traditional grazing ground. He wanted to farm the area and tried to press The People into service. He got frustrated when they resisted. Why should they resist, after all? All he wanted was to take their land and change their way of life.

Meeker's response to the Utes' resistance was to do what the white man has always done. He sent for the cavalry. One hundred and fifty-three soldiers arrived from Wyoming in 1789 to help him tame the savages and bend them to his will. History – written by the white man, of course – remembers the Utes' response as the Meeker Massacre.

The People won the battle and lost the war. Newspapers of the day demanded the removal of Utes from any land that could be "mined, farmed or ranched," and it was commonly said, "The only good Ute was a dead Ute." To the white man, Indians were subhuman, kin to coyotes, snakes, and other vermin. Within a year, the U. S. Congress had the tribes forcibly removed from what had always been their land.

The People were pushed out and confined to arid land in Utah that no one wanted. Chief Ouray, head of the southern tribes, was appointed their leader largely because he was known to favor peace and compromise. In Ouray's defense, he knew the Utes could not win in a war with the white man. The White Man had too many guns, too many soldiers, and too little understanding.

But one band, led by Chief Denali, refused to give up its traditional life and be confined. The Great One took his tribe and headed for the high country near Hahn's Peak. If they wanted him, he said, they would have to come and get him.

His instincts were good. No one wanted him that bad. No one followed. The area was too forbidding. A lot of soldiers could be lost in that rugged terrain before even seeing an Indian.

The only white men living in that area were mountain men, a handful of a hearty breed who had learned to live like natives. One of these men was Robert Baxter. Baxter was 5' 6", stocky, and tough as nails. He had a broad face covered with a full beard. He was a third-generation mountain man, a quarter-breed Apache and did not see The People as an enemy. They took nothing from him. He welcomed their presence.

Baxter lived in peace with The People, married The Great One's youngest daughter, Dayani, and settled down, filing the first claim for a homestead in the White River valley. It helped that his Indian bride came with an extended family that could help herd the sheep he hoped to raise. By the time my grandfather came along, Baxter had a thriving ranch, two daughters and a son. One of his daughters, Kaiah, was to become my grandmother.

Grandad Theo Alexandropolos became Theo Alexander on Ellis Island. Theo is the diminutive of Theodore. I'm told it signifies someone fearless and strong. True or not, it certainly described my grandfather.

To this day, I don't know where he found the courage to venture into the high country alone.

Occasionally, I got a clue when I overheard friends talking about the remarkable things they had seen him do, morphing his name and referring to him as the "Therio" – a slang expression in Greek meaning "beast." It was a tribute to his strength and relentless will.

He was a huge man at a time when there weren't many. His body had been hardened by years of working in the steel mills in Pittsburgh and then on the railroad going west until a stop in Utah, where he found work in the coke ovens down south near the Colorado border. They said he wore a size 52 jacket and used to stop at the blacksmith shop on the way home from the coke ovens to lift weights for fun. They said he was able to lift 500 pounds after a hard day's labor. I wasn't there, but given my size and what I know I can do, I wouldn't be surprised if that were true.

When he had put away enough money, Grandad went looking for a place of his own. He found it in the high country northwest of Steamboat. To this day, I don't know how. It's not easy to get there even now. What I know is that he came in on horseback, riding up the western slope of the Continental Divide from Grand Junction, past Aspen and the Flat Tops, until he found the place that was to become his home. He said he just knew it when he saw it. He was like that.

Grandad built a small shelter to stake his claim and went back down to file under the Stock Raising Homestead Act of 1916. The Act provided settlers with a full section – 640 acres – for ranching purposes. Through the years, he extended south and east until his ranch abutted the Baxter's on the East and the White River on the South, more than tripling the size of his original spread. Cattle require 1-2 acres per head. He had enough land to run nearly a thousand head, along with a small flock of sheep, some goats, chickens, and pigs.

The White River Valley Ranch is now one of the largest family spreads on the western slope, twice the size of the average ranch in Colorado. Wildlife abounds. The ranch and the forests surrounding it provide lush habitats for nearly every critter you can name – deer, moose, elk, mountain lions, bears, mountain sheep, mountain goats, lynx, coyotes, porcupines, beavers, foxes, rabbits, and many varieties of birds. You can't take a ten-minute hike into the woods near our home without seeing wildlife.

While it's not clear how Grandad found the White River valley, it's no mystery how he found Kaiah. Baxter was his nearest neighbor. He found her there. She was fierce and fearless, as small as he was large, and probably the only thing on earth he was afraid of. She was tough, unyielding, and completely devoted to him. He was tall and broad like the oak. She was tough and hearty like the willow.

Every 4th of July, Grandad hosted a celebration to show his appreciation and his love for this country. He would roast a lamb on an open spit, barbeque a side of beef, cook bread and chickens in the beehive oven he had built near the house, and break out some of Kaiah's home-made wine. Sometimes, he would have a hundred people there. People came from miles around, often staying the night to sleep it off before heading home.

One of our guests the year I turned ten was a man from Craig, a little weasel of a man with a thin face and scrawny body. The kind of guy that feels cheated at a free lunch. The more he drank, the more obnoxious he became. After a few drinks, he started making snide comments and began talking about my grandparents and their relationship. I heard him, and I know my grandfather heard him, but Grandad said nothing until the little man made a disparaging remark about my grandmother. Then "Therio" emerged.

Grandad said not a word, but his face clouded up, and I knew a storm was coming. He walked a few feet to the corral, grabbed a corner fence post and yanked it out of the ground. He shook the slats off and held them in his hands like a six-foot baseball bat. He went after the weasel. The man from Craig cut and ran, and it was well that he did. Granddad was ready to hammer him into the ground.

It's the code of the West. Show up at the front door and say you are hungry, and my family will welcome you, feed you, and offer you work until you are back on your feet. Come in through the window in the dead of the night, and you will go out feet first. The county sheriff is a full day away down a rough and rocky road. It is a lot of trouble when a shovel will do just as well.

My father, James, was one of three boys. All three enlisted in the Army when it was their time. It was expected. Grandad felt service was an obligation we owe this country and those who came before us. Only one of his sons, my father, came home. His brothers never had a chance to marry or start a family, so when I came along, the weight of our family came down on my shoulders and raising me became everyone's responsibility.

My mother handled the academics, teaching me, as well as the Baxter children, the essentials. She was the valedictorian of her high school and wanted to become a teacher. We became her students. When I wasn't inside working with her at the kitchen table, I was outside working with my father and grandfather. They taught me how to live in a high country and what it meant to be a man.

Kaiah taught me the ways of The People. She was a quiet, intense woman with dark, watchful eyes. As a child, I thought she was always watching me – and she probably was. She taught me how to read the forest, feel the forest, and harvest the forest – gathering chokecherries, wild raspberries, gooseberries, buffalo berries, amaranth seeds, wild onions, rice grass, and dandelions.

We lived off the land, and we lived simply. Good was anything that produced whatever functioned. Wickedness was a waste. My grandparents had no use for anything or anyone that didn't contribute and would not tolerate parasites.

Kaiah kept cats, for example. Cats were fine because they killed vermin in the barns and stables, she said; they earned their way. Grandpa had dogs to help work the stock, but neither one had any use for house pets or lap dogs.

I learned that lesson the hard way. The Baxter's gave me a mixed-breed puppy. He was small and cute, the runt of the litter, with one mangled leg. I brought him home, nursed him, and tried to sneak scraps and pieces of bread from the table. Even so, he didn't last a month. He couldn't compete with the working dogs. Maybe that's why I took in Max.

That same summer, coyotes took a calf and two lambs in less than two weeks. It was during that time when I felt manly enough to start using swear words, the ones I knew. I filled out my hand during those two weeks.

Granddad was a walking storm cloud. He would swear through the night. In the mornings, while Dad worked the stock, he would fetch his rifle and go hunting. On an open range, coyotes can take down 5-6% of the herd unless controlled. It's a bigger problem than you might think. Some forty percent of livestock lost on the range is lost to coyotes and other predators. Granddad wasn't going to stand for it.

Several times, I remember waking to shots. As the killing went on and Granddad got madder, the swear words got bigger with fewer spaces in between. One morning, he came home with the hindquarters of a calf. All that was left, he said. He wasn't muttering anymore. He was a long way away in a place I didn't want to go. He was in beast mode.

Grandad hauled out the traps. Not the new cyanide traps, but the old-fashioned wicked-looking things Dad had said he never liked to use because the damn livestock were so damn stupid, they'd likely ruin themselves in one. Granddad cut the hindquarter into strips, loaded them and the traps with some wax and pegs into an old burlap bag, and rode off.

When he came back, he said he had put down traps because he knew where they were. The last kill had been so near the den he had been able to track them to it. A big kill, he said, makes for a lot of tracks. He figured a mother and cubs. From the tracks, the mother was teaching the cubs how to kill.

Kaiah and I went with him the next morning to see if he was right. Before we were within a half-mile, we knew he had her. We could hear her fighting the trap. She was big – sixty pounds or so. Coyotes don't get much bigger than that. She doubled her frenzy when we appeared only to step into another one of the traps. Granddad had set them in a circle, the larger traps fanning out around the smaller baited ones. I heard the clap as it closed with a sound like the time I fell out of the tree. I heard her scream.

The second trap was on a forefoot, the first on a hind-foot. She lay between them, stretched way out now. Still, she struggled, thrusting about, teeth bared, furious and fearsome. Granddad watched a while, talking to her some, talking so low I couldn't hear, saying things I have just lately come to understand. After what seemed a long, long time, he started to reach for his rifle, but Kaiah stopped him. She pulled the Bowie knife she always carried from its sheath. It has a bone handle and a long, heavy, ugly, 9" blade sharpened on both sides.

Kaiah barked the tree off an Aspen sapling and peeled off most of the meat until she could bend, then break it with her foot, cutting off a piece four or five feet long. She laid it over the coyote's neck as it struggled, stretched out as it was, and walked up the branch, her weight pinning the coyote to the ground until she had a foot on either side of the struggling beast. I still remember the look in the coyote's eyes as Kaiah took off the top of its head. It is something that has stayed with me for a long time. Whenever I think of death, I see those eyes.

Two years later, they sent me into the woods alone. I was 12 years old, and it was time for my Vision Quest, the Native American test of manhood and rite of passage. There is no 911 in the high country. There are no fire departments, police, first responders, Meals on Wheels, and few neighbors within riding distance. You are on your own.

This was a test of independence, self-sufficiency, and self-discovery. I could always come home, but it would be a disgrace if I came down from the mountain too soon. As I left, Kaiah said they had been preparing me for this all my life. It was time to find out who I was and who I was meant to be.

They gave me a Barlow knife before turning me loose. Lots of people have pocket knives. I know kids in some parts of some cities still carry switchblades, but this was something more. A Barlow is made of high-carbon steel with a bone handle and a high bolster. It is the knife coveted by every boy out West. It is something you keep in your pocket and always have with you, knowing it is functional with multiple uses while connecting you with thousands of explorers and pioneers throughout history. George Washington had a Barlow knife, as did Mark Twain, who wrote about them in Tom Sawyer and Huckleberry Finn.

Armed with my new knife and nothing else, I was ready to walk into the wilderness to see what I was made of and how long I could last. It was the last week in May.

Summer was coming on, but there was still snow on the mountaintops and a bite in the air. If the skies stayed clear, I knew the days would be comfortable enough, but the nights could easily drop below freezing. If a storm came in, all bets were off. Anything can happen in the mountains. I have seen two feet of snow come down in the middle of June.

I left with the dawn, following a good breakfast. I didn't know what or when I would eat again, so I packed it in – half a pound of bacon, four eggs, biscuits, and gravy. Then, I set off, walking toward the highest peak and the deepest part of the forest.

If you are lost in the mountains, the last thing you want is to wander around aimlessly, hoping you will stumble out. So, my first task was to establish a base of operation, somewhere I could feel safe and return to, as I searched the area and foraged for food.

The two essential requirements for a base camp are water and shelter. Water is most important. You will die of thirst a long time before you die of exposure or starvation. I walked up a stream flowing from the mountaintop, looking for a windbreak or an overhang somewhere near the water. It was slow going. The brush was thick, and the footing uncertain.

Halfway up the mountain, I found a stand of pines that looked like it might do. Three trees towered above the rest and blotted out the sun, creating something of a clearing between them with the shade of their branches. They looked like they could have been 100 years old. I put Barlow to work, clearing out low-hanging branches, shooters, and dry brush, gathering and stacking the branches for future use.

An old tree that had lost the battle for the sun provided most of my bounty. After I had a sizable woodpile, I went looking for a digging stick. A digging stick is a tradition as old as the tribes. It's a sturdy piece of wood about 3 feet long, sharpened on one end so that it can turn the soil.

I found what I wanted in a young aspen. I bent and hacked at it until it surrendered, then trimmed the branches and sharpened one end. I used the aspen to dig two holes, one at the base of the largest tree and the other two feet away from the first, facing the clearing.

Then I went down to the stream looking for stones in the riverbed. I found a good source just above my clearing. I made several trips back and forth. I was looking for long, flat stones. I placed them end-to-end in the first hole until I had a solid stone lining, then I piled wood on top of it and made a fire.

Making a fire is the first thing a boy in the mountains learns how to do. There are several methods. The easiest way, of course, is to carry matches, but matches don't travel well. Dad carried a pocket magnifying glass the size of a silver dollar that folded into a leather case. He used it to focus the sun's rays on dry grass and kindling when he wanted a campfire. In the high country, you can use a piece of clear ice the same way, but the river near me was nowhere near cold enough to form ice. I fell back on plan B – friction.

I made a fireboard out of a flat piece of dry cedar and

shaped a plow out of a piece of juniper. I cut a 6-inch groove into the fireboard and shaped the plow to fit, angling the head at 45 degrees. I moved the plow quickly on the groove in the fireboard until I had an ember I could drop into the dry grass I had gathered. Then, it was a simple question of feeding the fire with kindling and larger branches. When I had a good start, I began stacking wood in the second hole so I could transfer the fire when I was ready to call it a night.

The next chore was to start looking for food. I pried pine nuts out of sticky pinecones, gathered berries and wild onions from the riverbed as Kaiah had taught me, and set a snare on what looked to be a rabbit trail. Grandfather would have been proud of that. It was well-made and well-positioned. Whether it would yield a rabbit was another question.

One night in the wilderness was all that was required, but I wanted to prove something to myself as well as my family. I was determined to stay a full week – and I did. Most of my days were spent gathering food and fuel for my fire. When I wasn't doing one, I was doing the other. On the third day, I got lucky and found a rabbit in my snare. That gave me some much-needed protein and helped fill the hole in my stomach. Living on seeds and berries is a day job. You are never quite full.

That was the hardest part. I was constantly hungry and constantly cold. Each night, I transferred the fire from the stones and put down pine boughs over the hot rocks to make a bed. I pulled other, heavier branches over me to give me some protection from the night. But the heat from the stones always dissipated halfway through the night, and there was little comfort to be provided by my pine branch blankets, no matter how much I piled on them.

On the fourth night, hallucinations came and continued to come through that night and each subsequent night. Anglo scientists would probably say it was the result of sleep deprivation, hunger, and cold, but the people have a different understanding. The people believe these hallucinations reveal your true self and your spirit. They are sacred and specific to each person.

I saw ancient battles, fearsome creatures, raging rivers, and strange places I could not identify. No vision repeated, but the constant thread was one of violence. Someone or something was always coming after me, forcing me to defend myself. I always woke to a hard start with fists clenched. Today, when I dream, I still have the same kind of dreams.

Sometimes, it's not a dream.

On the sixth day of my Vision Quest, I awoke out of a particularly troubled sleep to the sound of huffing and puffing. I thought it was another dream, and it may have been. After all these years, I'm still not sure.

It seemed something big was moving nearby. I opened my eyes, peered through the thin morning light and the wisps of smoke from the remnants of my campfire and saw a large male grizzly. He was standing on the other side of the clearing, not more than twenty feet from me, hugging and shaking a tall pine tree. He clawed it, ripped off large pieces of bark, and then turned around to rub his back against the tree.

I don't know whether he saw me or not, but I felt his presence, and I was sure he felt mine. Bears' eyes are their weakest sense, but there was no way his nose would let him down. Not at that range. Even with the smoke drift telling me I was downwind. He had to know I was there.

You don't run from a grizzly. They can outrun you and the horse you came in on. You don't climb. Bears can climb anything you can. You don't scream and try to scare him off. They don't scare that easily. And the last thing you want to do is challenge him.

As I watched the bear, I found myself going to a different place. I was there, and I was somewhere else. It was the first time this had ever happened, but not the last. I know it now and welcome it as my body's response to imminent danger. The world slowed down. I saw myself floating above and beyond myself, detached, disconnected, calculating, and observing. Everything around me, every detail, came into sharper focus. Every moment, every movement became crystal clear. My heartbeat was slower, my eyes clearer, and my attention entirely focused on the threat I faced.

From a distance, somehow detached and removed, I watched, there and not there. In slow motion, I saw myself stand and stretch to my already considerable height, moving as silently and deliberately as possible. I opened the Barlow knife, my meager weapon, put it in my right hand and reached for the sky, trying to make myself seem as large as possible.

If he came for me, I decided I would go for the face, eyes, or nose, hoping a strike would discourage his attack. It wasn't much of a defense, but the only other option was to lie down, curl up in a ball, cover my head and neck, and kiss my ass goodbye.

The bear looked directly at me for several long moments as if he was trying to figure out what I was, what I was doing there, what I was trying to do. Then he shook his massive body, clearing the accumulated debris from his hide, dropped to all fours, and ambled away from the clearing.

When I told my story, Kaiah said it had immense significance. I had been visited by the spirit of Denali and was marked for great things. At birth, I had been named Theo James after my grandfather and father. After my Vision Quest, Kaiah would only call me "Bear," the name of my spirit animal.

As I grew, the name caught on. To the outside world, I am known as Theo or TJ, but to family, I will always be "Bear."

When I left Colorado to go to college, Kaiah gave me a bear claw on a rawhide necklace. She put it around my neck where it remains. It hangs from an eye ring set in a gold cap.

"You have the blood of great warriors in your veins," She said. "Remember who you are."

The Iceman

Sunday morning, May 23. The telephone forced me out of a deep sleep. It was a cruelly insistent sound, distant at first, then louder, closer, fiercely compelling like a police siren pulling me from my dreams into the harsh reality of the present.

My head throbbed. I waited, hoping the phone would stop. While I waited, I wished something unpleasant would happen to whoever would call me in the middle of the night. Then, I wished I had connected the home answering machine I got for Christmas. It was in the closet with several others given to me over the years by the people who keep leaving messages on my cell phone telling me to turn it on.

It had been a long, hard night, and I felt it: The wrath of the grape. My body was bloated and heavy. My mouth tasted like someone had stuffed it with a sweat sock. My mind swam with remnants of ghosts and troubled dreams chased by the persistent sound of the telephone.

When I couldn't stand it anymore, I reached for the phone.

"Can I speak with Leanne," Someone said.

Just what I needed. A wrong number.

"Just a minute," I replied.

I put my hand over the receiver, counted ten, and then responded.

"Who's calling?" I asked.

"Dwayne."

The clock on the nightstand said 3:10 - less than two hours before the time I had set the alarm to go off three hours before I had to head to the airport.

"Just a moment," I said.

I dropped the receiver 6 inches from my face.

"It's Dwayne," I said loudly to my empty bed.

After another ten-count, I brought the receiver back.

"She said to tell you she's busy. She'll have to call you back."

I returned the phone to its cradle and tried to get back to sleep. After tossing and turning for an hour, I gave up and headed for the shower. I consoled myself by trying to imagine the conversation my conversation with Dwayne would inspire.

It was some comfort, but not enough. I needed more than that single call could provide. It was too early. The night had been too long and too frustrating. Too many drinks. Too many people I didn't know. Too many people I didn't like. There were too many women I liked but did not like well enough to say the words they wanted to hear, words that promised what I could not promise.

It started with my reluctant promise to John. Weeks

ago, I told him I would attend his wife's party at what was already being called the "Macklin Mansion." It was time for their "Big Reveal." A day at the dentist would have been preferable.

Frankly, I must admit I find his wife, Pam, tedious and pretentious. She is not someone I would be around by choice. I suspect she feels the same way about me.

The Macklin mansion is in what realtors call a transitional area. Someday, it will be considered "gentrified," but at the moment, there are still a lot of questionable elements hanging around. After their marriage, Pam began looking for a home on The Hill that would match her social aspirations and advance John's career. She had married a staffer, but she felt there was no reason he had to stay one. With his looks, education, and intelligence, her name, contacts in the media, and her magazines' support, she was confident he had a bright political future of his own.

She surprised everyone by settling on an abandoned warehouse three blocks northeast of Union Station. The building had never been used for residential purposes, but it offered one feature that was particularly hard to come by on Capitol Hill – size. It was fifty feet wide and nearly four times as long, a solid, impenetrable brick building that dwarfed adjoining properties and dominated the block.

Pam refaced the front and gutted the interior. She removed large parts of the center ceiling, creating an atrium and a natural source of light, and rebuilt from the inside out around the light source she had created. From the outside, the three-story structure appeared largely unchanged, looking a lot like the warehouse it once was, but the inside was completely transformed.

The atrium, carved into the center of the building, divided the property while connecting the main house with a guesthouse created on the opposite end. Skylights were inset in the roof, and the residential quarters were bridged, illuminating a lap pool, hot tub, and gardens below. Large interior windows and sliding glass doors extended the sense of openness, providing an unobstructed interior view from either end.

The project had taken three months to design and a year to execute. She used the proceeds from the sale of her townhouse, sold his condo, and dipped into one of her trust funds to make up the difference. There was already more money tucked away in Merrill's wealth management program than she or her boys – Mark and Michael – would ever need.

This party was the unveiling, the first of many social events Pam hoped to host on The Hill. She was trying to make a statement, eager for people to see her and what she had done. She had made a mansion out of a warehouse. Just imagine what she could do with John – poor bastard.

So, skipping the party was not an option. John would never be forgiven if I didn't make an appearance, but no one said I had to be the first one there. I took my time getting ready and let my reluctance permeate my indecision on what to wear. It was the kind of party where people would dress up or dress down, whatever conveyed the impression they were trying to make.

After considering nearly everything in my closet, I

decided to wear one of the first things I had considered – one of my favorite outfits – a tailored black Brioni double-breasted jacket, white pin-point oxford shirt, a silver Drake Kingsman blended silk and linen tie, a pair of 501 jeans, and Lucchese boots. I am one of those people who was put on a horse before they could walk. I have always worn boots and jeans. The jeans have always been Levi's 501's – the original – but the boots weren't always Lucchese.

Lucchese boots are hand-made. Their comfort and fit are unrivaled. The more you wear them, the more comfortable they become. After my first pair, I became addicted. Now that's all I wear. I considered my options and chose a pair of tough black horn back caiman. They are heavily textured with deep ridges. They are among the most versatile pairs I own. You can dress them up or dress them down. They will take you anywhere you want to go. Plus, they have a steel shank and reinforced toe. Both come in handy from time to time.

By the time I was dressed, I had worked myself into a funk. I felt boxed in, obligated to do something I didn't want to do, but a promise is a promise. I knew I had to make an appearance, or John would pay for it. I told myself that at least it would physically and mentally put me in a different place. The party would be familiar territory, a political event for those who want to see and those who want to be seen. Once I was seen, John was off the hook, and there was no reason I had to hang around.

Cars lined the street around the Macklin mansion, filling the driveway and spilling out onto the side streets. Several dark cars with drivers hiding behind tinted windows waited patiently, double parked where they could see, ready at a moment's notice for whatever VIP might be looking to slip out and go on to the next event.

If you get a close look at a Member's schedule, you will see some of them are scheduled for half a dozen events a night every night. They show up, cash out, and go on, calculating with staff how much time to spend at each event, where they have to begin and where they must end, who to talk to and who to avoid for maximum benefit. An average Congressman must raise $15,000 a day to be competitive in their next race, and they know it. Getting re-elected is always top of mind.

The combination of the Macklin money and their media connections made this a priority event. When I walked in, it looked like most of The Hill's beautiful people had already arrived. They were clustered around half a dozen Members, strategically positioned to provide access, separation, and visibility. They were spread out in the Macklin's dining room, on the balcony overlooking the atrium, and near the bar.

It was true to form. Members rarely hang together at these events. It complicates the pitch and confuses donors. Besides, they see enough of each other on The Hill.

Scattered around on the perimeters of power were the worker bees, Capitol Hill staffers of every description, there for free food, free booze, and the nearness to glory. I recognized members of the press, staffers and former staffers, pages and cops, spear-catchers and spear-carriers, mopes and mud hens, opportunists, and true believers.

Pam was working the crowd. A red, form-fitting

sheath covered her small frame. She looked like a cardinal flitting around. John followed dutifully behind. He was dressed in a camel hair jacket over a tailored shirt with an open collar. Between the two of them, they probably had more on their backs than most staffers make in 6 months.

As far as I could tell, Les Tubin was my only friend there. Les is short and fat, with a face seemingly in a constant state of eruption. It no longer troubles him. He knows he is all but invisible to this crowd anyway – no one worth knowing, no one worth getting to know. That's the way it had always been for him going back to when we started on The Hill. It is as if he wasn't really there, like an unseen servant, a maid or a butler, or some other nameless cog in the giant wheel of government.

The only foothold Les had on power was his cousin's connection with the Sergeant-at-Arms. That was enough – just barely enough – to open the door, nothing more. Still, it had given him a chance to earn his education, doubling up and doing his homework on the night shift when the buildings were empty and no one else was there or wanted to be there – except cockroaches the size of tootsie rolls and rats as big as cats.

I like Les because he doesn't take himself too seriously or try to be anything he isn't. He had carved out a place by the bar. I worked my way through the crowd and joined him there. Within moments, almost as if she had been looking for me, Catherine Catlett appeared.

Cat has been with the hospital association for as long as we have known each other. It is no secret I find her attractive, but so do a lot of other people. It's part of the reason she is so successful at what she does. A lot of people look for a reason to make her happy and are more than happy to listen to her just to be seen in her company. She knows it and works it and isn't troubled by it.

"Theo," She said, after ordering a white wine, "Good to see you. It's been ages. I'd like to get together and catch up when you have the time."

It struck me as strange. We have never had trouble making time for each other – so what was this all about? I let it pass. If something was going on, I knew I'd find out in due time.

"I'm going to be traveling for a few days," I said. "Maybe we can get together when I return."

She gave me her best smile, maybe two kilowatts brighter than necessary, and raised her glass in a silent salute.

"Call me," She said and was off, joining the other lobbyists trying to meet and greet and earn their keep.

I went back to Les, but five minutes into our conversation, I found we had already said most of what we had to say to each other. I consoled myself with the thought that the booze was top quality and I wouldn't have to stay that long.

I was halfway through my first drink when Broadbent found us. He had a new girlfriend in tow. She was 18, if that, with big round eyes and a small round body that stretched the limits of her tube top and paint-on-pants. She looked like ten pounds of flour in a five-pound sack.

Her name was Brandi, she said, spelled with an "i" and dotted, no doubt, with a heart or, perhaps, a smiley face. She was an intern working at Commerce. It was fun, she said, but nowhere near as exciting as what we were doing. Her wide eyes and breathless voice made me wonder what Broadbent had told her we were doing. The reason he had told her whatever he had told her was never in doubt.

When Brandi turned to leave, something caught my eye. A swirl of blue. Dress of almost formal length, soft and clinging. Aniston-blonde. Bare back. Bare shoulders. Hair cascading in long, loose curls to her shoulders. It was a calculatedly careless look. Without any apparent effort, she commanded attention. When you work network news, you get used to it.

"Oh, my God," Tubin said, and then almost breathlessly, "She's coming over here."

The thought seemed to make him sweat.

She moved deliberately. When she got close enough, she held out her hand, palm down. I took it and held it. It was either that or kiss it. It was in the wrong position to shake. There wasn't time anyway. She kept coming.

Continuing the motion of extending her right hand, she brought her left hand to my shoulder, using its slight leverage to stand tippy-toe and fix me squarely with dark, mischievous eyes. I saw the fine lines of her fine face, straight nose, and a promising mouth coming close as she gave me a gentle little sister of a kiss.

"Hello, Theo," She said.

A small smile played on her lips. She was enjoying the moment.

I wasn't.

All I could think of was, "How the hell do I get out of

here?" There was no way. Too many eyes were on us, happily, most focused on her.

"Dee," I said. "Been a while."

"You know each other?" Tubin said.

It was a question that was not a question – more an expression of wonder.

"Only if you are being biblical," I said.

She was the last one, the last one to get close, the last one to try to carve her initials into my hide. I couldn't help noticing she hadn't changed much. She was still one of the better-looking women you see in broadcasting. Still slender. Her hair was a little longer and had a little more curl, down to and just past the light little birthmark I knew rested above her right shoulder blade. She had been taking good care of herself, and it showed.

"You look good," She said, shaking off my remark. "Maybe a little more worn. Maybe a little smaller than the last time I saw you."

"Clothes will do that."

She gave me her private laugh, the one that belies her demure look, the one closer to her true nature.

"Still the iceman," She said. "God, I was so afraid you had changed."

She stepped nearer, dropping her voice low enough to draw me in and shut others out.

"You could have called, you know. You could have answered my calls. You didn't have to be such a total bastard."

"If I weren't," I said, "Whatever would we have in common?"

The dark eyes emptied, then darkened. The smile was

gone. She turned sharply and walked away. It was not quite a drink in the face, but it had the same effect. Now, all the eyes were on me, most filled with wonder.

Pam shot daggers at me from across the room. I didn't envy John the evening ahead. I didn't think he would get much sleep or anything else in the wee hours after the guests were gone.

And I knew I wouldn't fare much better. I would be wrestling with the ghosts of girlfriends past far into the night. Sam had started it. Now Dee surfaced, resurrecting too many things I had tried too hard to forget, making me wonder why so many of the regrets I have in life have to do with women.

It made a Florida junket look better all the time. Time to get away. A boat and a break – anything to get me out of this toxic environment for a while.

I turned my back to the crowd and finished my drink before heading out. The night was heavy and humid. It seemed strangely appropriate. I had started the evening in a funk. My mood had only grown darker as the evening progressed, the clouds of my distemper building and bumping into each other, looking for release.

When I turned the corner onto Constitution Avenue, I saw Sam at my front door. I was three blocks away, but it looked like she was locked in a strong embrace or struggling to avoid one. As I got closer, it became clear she was trying to fight off a determined suitor. He was not someone I knew. From their interaction, I suspected he wasn't someone she knew all that well, either. He was about 6 feet tall, maybe 200 lbs. He was dressed in what could easily be called the Senate uniform – tan pants, a blue blazer and, of course, a red power tie.

She ducked and moved and pushed him away like a boxer, trying to avoid being locked in a clinch. He kept coming at her, trying to corner her, pin her against the door and press his case, grabbing her and pulling her close. She was wearing a simple sundress with a halter top, which put her at a disadvantage. She had to keep swatting his hands away as he tried to pull the halter down.

When I was a block away, I began picking up their conversation. By then, the world had taken on another dimension. Time slowed. My senses had grown more focused and acute. I heard the same words on a long-play loop, changing only in volume and emphasis. He told her to stop being so difficult, to be reasonable, and to let him come in 'just for a little while.' She said no, some other time, and asked him to leave. She was trying to keep her composure, but I could see the fear in her eyes as I started up the stairs.

As I put my left foot on the bottom stair, she found the strength to push him away, putting both hands on his chest and shoving him back with all her might. He backed up a step and stopped at the edge of the landing.

"Please leave," She said.

There was no mistaking her intent or her tone.

He replied by pushing her hands aside. He was trying to re-engage when I joined the conversation.

"What part of 'no' don't you understand?" I said.

He turned to look at me. His eyes were glassy and unfocused. He seemed to be on something – some drug, too much alcohol, or maybe just too much testosterone and the heat of the moment. Whatever it was had addled his brain enough so that he didn't recognize danger when he saw it. Or, maybe Forrest was right, "Stupid is as stupid does." Sometimes it's just that simple.

"What's it to you, asshole?" He said. He turned to face me, fists clenched at his side.

"I'll show you," I said and drove my right fist into his crotch.

I hit him hard. Hard enough to double him over in pain. He gasped and fell forward until his chest came to rest on my waiting left hand. I picked him up and held him above my head for a moment, then pivoted and threw him. I threw him as far as I could throw him. It was a two-hand shot put. Legs and torso fully engaged—all the power I could muster.

He tried to fly, hands fully extended before him like Superman. He almost made it. He cleared the stairs, his body landing hard on the bricks below. But the toe of one foot caught the side of the first stair. I was disappointed with that. I felt I could do better and was tempted to give it another try.

I was considering that when he rolled over and grabbed his shoulder. He looked up at me with shock and astonishment, holding his left shoulder with his right hand and his crotch with his left. His mouth dropped open, searching for words he couldn't find. The fog had cleared. Reality had set in. He couldn't see danger before, but he certainly recognized it now. Eyes wide, he crabbed into a sitting position, still holding his shoulder and crotch and scooting back.

"I have good news and bad news," I said. "The good news is you are still alive. The bad news is you are still alive…and now know how painful that can be. Remember that the next time a lady asks you to leave."

I came down two steps.

"Do you understand?"

He nodded his head and took one more step toward him.

"And don't even think of bleeding on my stairs or throwing up in my yard. If you do, I'll make you eat it. Now get up and go. Get out of my sight."

We watched him stumble and crawl away. He stopped long enough to throw up on a Mercedes halfway down the block and moved on. I think he decorated another car at the end of the block, but I couldn't be sure. He may have just been looking for somewhere to lean while he caught his breath.

"Sorry about that," Sam said. "He followed me home. I came this way because I didn't want to get cornered under the stairs trying to get into my apartment."

"No worries. That's why you have a key. You are welcome to come in this way any time you want."

She followed me in almost sheepishly. She was pale, her head down and dejected, clearly still shaken by the experience and perhaps my reaction to it.

"Sometimes I forget," She said, finally confirming the latter.

"Forget what?"

"You are so kind and gentle most of the time, like a big Panda bear. It's easy to forget you have another side… Oh, I see it occasionally when you are aggravated or angry. Your jaw muscles clench, and your eyes get really dark. You become quiet and intense. But it doesn't last long. And every now and then, I see you walking in the cafeteria or the hall by your office, and I can tell you have a mad on – not by anything you say or do, but by the path that kind of opens up around you. It's like you are shooting off sparks or something."

"So, I shouldn't be all that surprised…but I was. This is the first time I've seen "Bear." I know your family calls you that, but I never really understood it – until now."

"Sorry. I didn't mean to scare you."

"You didn't. I think it is kind of comforting in a way, kinda like filling in the picture I have of you. But I'll tell you one thing for sure. I'll bet that worm never crawls within two blocks of this place ever again."

"That would probably be the first smart decision he has ever made," I said.

I could feel the adrenaline releasing, my body settling as the storm passed, and my systems reset.

"Do you want a glass of wine, a cognac, or something?" I asked.

"No," She said at first and then had second thoughts. "Well, maybe a glass of wine."

Max, sensing something, had been holding back. Now, he came up to greet her. She kept her eyes down, focused on petting the dog, while I opened a bottle of Sauvignon Blanc. I poured her a glass and gave myself two fingers of Metaxa. It's not quite a brandy and not quite a cognac, but you can make a case it's better than both. I prefer the AEN Cask No 2 – Despina. It's made from the original blends in casks that have been under the protection of the Metaxa Master for five generations.

She took a sip of her wine while I settled on the other end of the sofa. Max jumped up between us and let his head rest on her lap.

"Why do I always attract men like that?" She said.

"You are always going to attract men," I said. "Always have. Always will. That's not your problem."

"What do you mean?"

"Your problem is that you are too easy."

"Easy?" She snapped back.

"Not like that." I threw up my hands, nearly spilling my drink in exasperation. "Sweet. Soft. A push-over. Laidback. Do you like any of those words better?"

"Hardly."

She shook her head defiantly.

"What I'm trying to say is you are nice to everybody. Too nice. You have to understand not everyone is worthy of your interest. You can't keep being nice to everyone who comes along because not everyone is like you. Cretins, like the worm who just crawled away, are only focused on one thing – themselves. They hear what they want to hear and take whatever they hear as an invitation. Give them an inch, and they are going to take two. Once they get started, they are going to keep coming unless you shut them down fast and hard."

"Like you did at the party tonight."

"Like I did tonight," I said, grimacing at the memory. "I would have preferred a less public place to do it, but that wasn't my choice – was it?"

"What do you mean?"

"It was a set-up."

"How so?"

"The best example is the guy who puts his wedding proposal up on the jumbotron at the stadium. Why would anyone do that? Why would you share such a personal and intimate experience with 40,000 strangers?"

"Maybe he just wants the world to know he loves her."

"That's the most charitable interpretation. The less charitable interpretation is that he wants to put her on the spot. Consciously or subconsciously, he thinks public pressure will make it more likely she will do what he wants. Whether she agrees to marry him or not, he knows she won't want to shoot him down in public and make a scene."

"Like you did tonight."

"Like I did tonight… Thanks for bringing that up again."

She smiled. Mischief worked there.

"You are enjoying yourself, aren't you," I said.

She brought her thumb and forefinger together.

"A little."

"That's alright. Go ahead. You deserve a break tonight."

She smiled more broadly.

"So long as you understand there was only one way for me to respond tonight without looking like a jerk," I said. "I wasn't prepared to do that. The bigger question to consider – when you are done smirking – is, where does that leave you? How are you going to respond the next time someone you don't want to be with puts a move on you? Unless you are willing to bite the bullet like I did and shut them down, the only alternative you have is to tell them what they want to hear and pretend they have a chance when they don't. Once you start down that road, you have to live with it. There is no way back."

She nodded her head in apparent understanding.

"I'll have to work on that. Meanwhile, there is one thing I have finally figured out. Never made much sense before."

"What's that?"

"Our relationship. I think I got lost in all the boy-girl stuff because that's the way I'm used to relating to men. You are not like that. You are more like the big brother I never had. Would you mind if I started calling you Bear?"

I smiled.

"Only if you promise to stop bringing cockroaches home."

She stood and gave me a hug before heading downstairs to her flat. Max stood when she stood, waited patiently at her feet, and then followed her.

Before going to bed, I confirmed my flight and printed a boarding pass. Meyer said the boat was in Naples, so the Naples airport would seem most convenient, but it's not. There are no direct flights from DC to Naples, and I have never been too big on flying somewhere to get somewhere else. I decided I would come in through Ft. Myers instead.

The Obverse

The flight wasn't bad—only the predictable aggravations. The lines were long. The screening was slow. Everyone was in a surly mood. Fortunately, peak season had passed. In the peak season, when you have to fight your way through the competing tides of seniors, families with kids on the way to Disney, students on spring break, and snowbirds, flying south can be miserable.

Even at its best, it's a long way from fun. It wasn't always this way. People used to look forward to flying. People even dressed up for the occasion. It's hard to believe now. Now, there are at least ten leisure suits, sweatpants and – God help us – yoga pants for every dress suit you see, and there seems to be some unwritten law that the more you weigh, the skimpier and tighter whatever you are wearing has to be. Maybe people are compensating by trying to strap it all in. I don't know, but it offends the eye.

My size complicates flying. Coach seats seem to be designed for shrimps and sardines. They are difficult to sit in for any period of time and seem to get smaller and tighter with every flight. I can't help thinking there must be rival teams of engineers and interior designers locked away somewhere working on this and trying to figure out how to cram in one more row of seats.

When I travel for the Senate, I put up with it. There is no need to do that when I'm traveling on my own dime. I booked first-class, so I had room to move and stretch my legs.

Meyer told me to meet him at a place called the Tin Inn in Naples. He said it was near the City Dock and part of Tin City. He said that like it was supposed to mean something to me. It didn't. I have been to Naples on several occasions through the years, but always in and out. I recall liking it more than Miami, but then I never cared for Miami all that much.

The road to Naples from the Ft. Myers International Airport was singularly unimpressive. I could have been anywhere in Florida. My Uber driver, an earnest, middle-aged Latino, tried to make the best of it by pointing out landmarks I couldn't see, most of which I didn't really care to see. From what he said, I missed a series of housing projects and community developments with golf courses. He said there were more golf courses in Naples than in any other community in the country. He said that it was a point of great civic pride. I took it as a sign of a population with more spare time and disposable income than they knew what to do with.

I responded to his travelogue by grunting a lot, not

wanting to encourage him, but apparently, that was encouragement enough. He launched into his Chamber of Commerce speech. Did I know Naples was one of the wealthiest communities in America? Yes, sir. Number 7 on the list. Did I know the tax rate and unemployment rate were among the lowest in the country? Almost 10 percent of the people who live in Naples are millionaires, he said, and a lot of them live on the water not far from where I was going. He said it would be worthwhile for me to go a little further down from Tin City and maybe take Gordon Drive to see the homes on Millionaires' Row.

I told him I had seen that area on an earlier visit and remembered it well. My tone must have conveyed how unimpressed I was. He got quiet after that. Maybe I offended him. I tried to make it up to him by doubling the tip when we arrived at our destination. That seemed to help. He gave me an earnest smile and gathered enough courage to suggest that if I wanted to take another look at Millionaires' Row before I left, I should give him a call. I didn't bother telling him how unlikely that was.

He had dropped me off at the entrance to a board-walk. A sign said we were at the City Dock. There was a big parking lot across the street that was half full. It was just after 2:00 PM on a fine Florida day. Cool and crisp with a breeze of the Bay. Not a cloud in the sky. Maybe it was a good sign. Hard not to like.

Eighty or ninety slips were laid out off the boardwalk in a pattern resembling a double "L" – one inset in the other. The first was straight ahead and went directly into the harbor for about 75 yards before turning sharply south toward open water. The second was set above the first and wrapped around a commercial area that included a hotel, a couple of restaurants, and slips for commercial charters. One large slip toward the end of the dock advertised sightseeing on the hour. A large pelican sat on the first piling near that sign, waiting for the boat's return.

The Tin Inn was at the end of the retail elbow, just before the charter slips. It was a small hotel with a restaurant out front – half a dozen open-air tables and another dozen or so undercover. I headed for the entrance, admiring the yachts along the way. Each one seemed bigger and more outrageous than the last.

I had a lot of company. People were coming and going, walking the boardwalk, enjoying the views of the harbor and the bay beyond. Clearly, it was a popular spot. Tourists or snowbirds. I couldn't tell which. The crowd was heaviest near the Tin Inn, where a sign advertised access to the Tin City. From the sign, Tin City appeared to be a waterside mall of sorts with shirts and hats, jewelry, trinkets, and all the other souvenirs people buy on vacation and never ever really want. It's a compulsion, I guess. I'm here. I have to buy something that proves I was here. I'll keep it until I get home and then wonder why – like a one-night stand you can't wait to forget.

Meyer was where he said he would be, sitting at the first table nearest the boardwalk. He was a short, round man with a kind, round face. He looked to be around 70. A bald head and wire glasses that copied the shape of his face gave him a professorial look. He wore a green polo shirt with a logo for Treviso Bay – the words wrapped around a PGA logo – embroidered on the pocket. Khaki shorts and a battered pair of tennis shoes completed his outfit. Mostly grey hair carpeted his arms and legs. He was drinking something fruity, something white with a strawberry stuck on the side. A Colada of some sort, I guessed.

He was facing me, looking down the boardwalk as I approached. He nodded his head in apparent recognition. I considered my seating options and dropped my bag on the seat across from him. Reluctantly, I took the seat next to him, sitting near his right arm, putting my back to the restaurant and an empty table behind us. I didn't bother telling him he had my seat. I have always preferred my back to the wall. Anything else makes me feel uncomfortable – perhaps for no greater reason than the reminder it serves that I am exposed to a situation and environment I can't completely control.

"You look just like him," Meyer said as I sat down, "only totally different."

He smiled at my puzzled reaction.

"It's like you are the obverse," He explained.

Who the hell is this guy? I wondered what he was getting at and what I was getting into. How did you know me? How well did he know me? He seemed to be suggesting he knew me well. How was that possible.?

Meyer, sensing my skepticism, went on to describe the man he said was my uncle. He said my uncle was different – tall, gangly, and loose-jointed, with short, sun-bleached hair. After a certain age, he said, every man is responsible for his face. My uncle's face was marked by the life he had lived, the battles he had fought, and the years of trying to impose his will on those who were inclined to go a different direction.

"He looked uncoordinated and moved kind of slow," Meyer said. "He was neither of those things, you understand, but that was the impression he gave people."

"And I am the obverse?"

"Yes," He said. "You have the eyes of a hunter – intense and coal black. You walk the way you look. Like a big cat. Maybe a leopard or a black panther."

What was he trying to say? Whatever it was, he was taking the long way around the park. Was he blowing smoke, or did he really know my uncle that well – if there really was an uncle – or was all that just an excuse for someone to get me in a defensive posture on unfamiliar territory under uncertain circumstances?

There was no reason I had to respond in kind, no reason to play games, no reason not to be who I am, no reason not to be direct.

"I've come a long way," I said. "I had an early start, and it's been a long day. What are you trying to say? Why are we here? If there is an estate in question, why aren't we meeting in some lawyer's office instead of sitting here drinking fruit punch and watching the tourists feed the ducks."

Meyer stops short, clearly taken aback. He took a deep breath and apologized.

"I'm sorry," He said. "Your uncle was my best friend. I miss him. I guess I didn't realize how much until I saw you. When I saw you coming up the boardwalk just now, my first thought was how much you act like him and how little you resemble him. I saw you coming, and even before I saw your face, I thought this guy was either expecting trouble or looking for it. You would never read that when looking at your uncle. Maybe once upon a time. Maybe I just got used to seeing an older and more subtle version of you."

Meyer gave me a quick smile at once, gentle and sad.

"So, the same, but different."

He paused, trying to pick his words.

"Let's put it this way," He said. "If he went to hell and came back, he'd look like you."

Dangerous Work

It took me a moment to process Meyer's comment. It was another strange observation.

"Do you think he went to hell?" I asked.

He shrugged his shoulders. His eyes watered, and he looked away.

"No…As I told you, he was my best friend." He dropped his head and took another sip of his fruity drink. "I don't know where he went. But wherever he went, I don't think I will see him again."

You have to trust your instincts. I still didn't know how I fit into the equation, but whatever else was going on, his loss and affection for my uncle were real.

A young waitress hustled out from inside. She was perky, short, and dark. Very animated. Very young. She wore a blue halter top and a short blue skirt. Both were patterned with little white sails in an apparent attempt to capture a nautical theme. The nametag pinned to her top said – "Darleene."

Darleene asked me what I wanted to drink. It was still early, so I settled for a lemonade. She took my order and scurried inside. She seemed to have only that one speed. I turned my attention back to Meyer.

"What makes you so sure?" I asked.

"As I told you on the phone," He said, "I haven't heard from him in six months."

His sadness was obvious.

"That's it?"

"Yes, and to answer your question," Meyer said. "I'm handling this the way he asked me to handle things should this situation ever arise,"

"Why would he think it might?"

"He often had to travel. I had standing orders whenever he left. He asked me to check on his home while he was gone, pay the bills, and make sure everything was in order. He left money where he knew I could find it and called me from time to time to get a report and let me know where he was and when he thought he might be back. There's been nothing in over six months. No contact. Nothing. If he were still alive, I would have heard from him by now."

"How can you be so sure? At his age, any number of things could have happened. He could have had an accident or gotten sick. He could be in a hospital or a convalescent center somewhere."

"Then they would have called."

"How would they know who to call?"

"He carried a note with my number in his wallet. It asked people to call me if necessary. His work was dangerous. I think he always felt his luck would run out at some point, and something or somebody would catch up with him. He always knew something could go wrong."

Darleene brought my lemonade. It came with a smile and a little Playboy bow – back straight, knees bent, slight forward tilt to show cleavage, just in case anyone was interested. She put my drink down next to me and asked if there was anything more she could do for us.

"You have to try the General Tso's cauliflower," Meyer said. "It's one of my favorites."

I nodded, and Darleene happily bounced away. I read some unspoken affection in the way she looked at Meyer. Maybe it was the cauliflower, but maybe there was something more than that going on between them. Clearly, she liked him.

"What do you mean his work was dangerous?"

"That requires a lengthy answer."

Meyer said he had known my uncle for more than forty years and that they had spent a lot of time together. He had started as a financial advisor based in Chicago. Since so many of his clients wintered in Florida, he used to go back and forth, staying in a boat he kept at a marina in Ft. Lauderdale during the winter and heading north in the spring.

"Your uncle had a boat in the same marina," He said. "That's where we met. I have always done pretty well for my clients. And you know how it is when things go well. Satisfied clients spread the word, and the business grows organically. I had a lot of satisfied customers, as many clients as I could handle, and a great reputation. Then I almost lost it all."

He dropped his eyes. Whatever it was and whenever it was, I could tell it still bothered him.

"No matter how good you are, you are going to make a mistake," He said. "And the better things are going, the more likely you are to make a mistake. You take on too much. You take shortcuts. You start to feel infallible."

"What happened?"

He shrugged his shoulders.

"Long story short, I got mouse trapped. A very smart guy came along and stole a big piece of my cheese. Oldest story in the book. He let me in on the ground floor —a surefire investment. I had to act fast. Too good to miss. The usual spiel. And I was too full of myself to check him out the way I should have. I gave him a big chunk of change. He was long gone before I found out I'd been had."

"What did you do?"

"What could I do?"

His hands went up, open and apart, in the gesture of helpless men everywhere.

"I knew if a word got out I had been scammed, my reputation would be shot. Going to the cops would be just as bad. The publicity would kill me. Then I remembered your uncle. We had met a couple of times at parties around the marina. He was living on a houseboat there and didn't seem to be doing much more than party and fish and chase the girls. That was my first real memory of him. It seemed like there were always a lot of girls around him.

"Sounds like a good life. How did he pay for all that?"

"Good question. Early on, it was unclear. Whenever

people asked what he did, he was vague and evasive. He said he was in the salvage business. He said he only worked when he wanted to or needed to. We knew he had served in the armed forces – one of those branches of the service where they teach you how to do a lot of stuff you won't learn anywhere else – and he said the one thing the military had done for him was to reinforce his need for independence. He said he would never take orders from anyone again. He had no interest in joining the rat race and didn't want to box himself in with a lot of arbitrary structure. He said life was too short to live for the weekends."

Meyer said my uncle's solution was to join those in the salvage business, searching for old gold, diving and picking the bones of old wrecks, some of the many treasure ships buried in the Keys. He was diving for hire, taking it job by job and taking a slice of what he came to call his retirement in between.

By the time they met, my uncle had taken it to a new level, combining recovery with a righteous sense of justice. Instead of lost ships, he started looking for lost souls. Righting wrongs. Stealing from thieves, helping people who have nowhere else to turn. He knew he could not change the world, but every now and then, you get a chance to change a piece of it.

I could understand that instinct. I have been there many times myself, but it was strange to hear it in another man's voice, stranger still to feel such a sudden and strong connection to someone I never knew.

"I take it you asked for his help?"

"I did. That's when he explained how he worked. He

said he only took on a project when he needed work and there was nowhere else for people to go. He was the court of last resort. He paid his expenses, gambled his time and money, and did whatever had to be done without bothering his clients with the details. He said I didn't have to worry about anything. It was all on him. If he succeeded, he said, he would keep half of whatever he recovered to finance the next stage of his retirement."

"Half? … Seems like a lot."

"Yes, but if you think about it, half of something is better than all of nothing."

He took another sip of his fruity drink. I wasn't sure why he bothered with the thing. I got the impression he didn't really enjoy it.

"Look at it from my perspective," He said, "the perspective of any one of his clients. The money was gone. I had no hope of recovery. I had nothing more to lose. The risks were his. If he could find a way to get some of my money back, we would both come out ahead."

"What happened?"

"I said "go," and he did. Within a week, he had found the shyster who clipped me and had the transaction reversed. I never knew how. All he would say is that sometimes you have to explain things to people in a way they can understand."

"And he wouldn't take anything. No real expenses, not that much work, he said. Knowing him as I do now, I think what he was really saying is that he knew it wasn't my money. It belonged to hardworking people who relied on me for their futures."

"I saw him do things like that fairly often through the

years. He had a hard shell and a soft heart. He liked tilting at windmills, slaying dragons, and rescuing damsels in distress. If he could make a couple of dollars in the process, so much the better."

"He could live on that?"

"Better than you might think. Every year, there are more people down here with more money than they know what to do with. Every year, an equal number of people try to steal what other people have earned. Word gets around."

"When your uncle saw something worth chasing, he did. He chased off a lot of vultures, but it came at a price. When you rattle someone's dish, you can't expect them to like it. A lot of people hold a grudge. A lot of people try to find a way to get even. A lot of people come looking for you or hire other people to come looking for you."

"I think that's the reason he kept his distance from you. That is probably the reason he never married. That and the fact that women tend to like predictable routines, the assurance their husband is going to come home at night, Sunday suppers, two kids, a 9-to-5 life, a house, a white picket fence, and the PTA. All the things that tie a man down to something called normal. And no one hiding in the bushes with a gun."

"Families make you hostage to fortune. Now and then, after a few drinks, he talked about all that and the collateral damage associated with his lifestyle. Too many people he had cared about had been lost along the way. Too many women he probably should have taken seriously had moved on."

Meyer said he knew my uncle felt increasingly alone

as he got older. He had isolated himself by his work and by his solitary nature. He lost interest in the beach people around the marina. They were a generation or two generations away. To them, he was a relic; to him, they were bores. He found the girls silly, superficial, self-absorbed, and vapid. The boys were unengaged, disinterested, and drifting.

And it was getting harder to do what he did. He realized he had lost more than half a step. He was not nearly as quick. More than that. Not nearly as sharp. He realized Father Time was catching up with him. There were too many close calls to carry on much longer.

Then, out of nowhere, he discovered he had a daughter, a daughter he didn't know from a woman he had once loved. One that got away. That reinvigorated him for a while, but two years later, the Grim Ripper driving a two-ton semi claimed the girl, blowing into her Kia at more than eighty miles an hour, pushing her across two lanes of traffic somewhere in Ohio before hitting a median, turning over, exploding, and making everything seem pointless.

She had been a beacon of light, a happy surprise with a connection to the future he didn't know he had until she walked into his life with a story and the memory of a long-forgotten love. It was a bitter irony – the girl, so recently found, so quickly gone. His path to the future was one of the casualties of that crash.

"I was here in Naples by then," Meyer said. "Many of my clients have retired in this area. It made sense for me to be here, too. Plus, I realized I was getting too old to live on a boat. There were too many chores. Treviso Bay is a lot more comfortable. You don't have to do anything there you don't want to do. Your uncle came over to visit a couple of times and stayed with me. I'm not sure he really wanted to be anywhere, but he liked it well enough to relocate here. He said he wanted to get away from Ft. Lauderdale and the people that remembered him well enough to keep looking for him there and the people he was ready to forget."

Meyer said my uncle sold everything he had in Ft. Lauderdale and came to Naples for a fresh start. He said he didn't know how long he would stay, but that's one of the advantages of living on a boat. You can easily pick up and be somewhere else. All you need is a hose connection, power outlet and fuel. It took him a while to settle in and get everything organized the way he wanted. That kept him busy, but only for so long. He became increasingly distant and grumpy.

"Then he latched on to you," Meyer said.

That caught me completely by surprise.

"How so?" I asked.

"Like a life preserver to a drowning man. You helped keep him afloat. I'll have to show you."

He raised his hand, caught Darleene's attention, and made a scribbling motion.

"You wanted to know why we are meeting here instead of some lawyer's office. I can't tell you. I'll have to show you."

"Why is that?"

"Because this is where your boat is," Meyer said.

He pointed to the second dock. All I could see was a line of yachts, each one seemingly larger than the next.

"If you made a hotel reservation, why don't you cancel

it while I pay the bill? There is no reason to stay in a hotel when you can stay on your boat."

He dropped some bills on the table. I saw Darleene pick up the ticket and bolt for the kitchen when I stepped away to make my call. She hurried back carrying a small bag. I was hoping to skip the cauliflower, but I guess there was no way around it now.

"That's Millionaire's Row over there," Meyer said, pointing toward the gulf.

I didn't have the heart to tell him I'd seen it before. No need to offend another resident.

"The Port Royal Yacht club is on this side. If you think there are some big boats here, cruise on down there sometime."

Meyer led the way back the way I had come and turned left at the entrance to the first dock. For a cowboy born in the high country, it was all a bit surreal. The yachts looked like they could have come off the set of the latest Bond movie. Pelicans and other water birds protested our intrusion and scattered as we came.

"Any boat requires a lot of maintenance; the older a boat is, the more maintenance it requires," Meyer said. "Your Uncle lived on a houseboat for years. He said it was getting to the point where it was too much for him. He sold the one he had when he decided to move over here and had another one custom-made. He wanted something a little faster and a little more comfortable for his retirement."

"It's kind of ironic. He had been taking his retirement in installments for years. He had retired so many times before he got old enough to retire that by the time the real thing arrived. He didn't know what to do with it. I think he realized this one might last a lot longer than some of the others and wanted to be prepared for that."

We were running out of boardwalk. I didn't see anything that looked like it could be my boat. I was wondering if we would have to turn around when he pointed to the end of the pier.

"That's it," He said.

I don't know what I expected, but certainly not what I saw. There were two boats in the last slip. One was a Day Cruiser, the 747 Mirage by Frauscher. It's what the boat boys call a "gentlemen's racer." It looked to be about 25' long, with a very deep V running to the stern, promising excellent stability. There was an expanse of teak from the windscreen to the bow and a bathing platform astern. "Little Doll" had been painted on her stern. She certainly looked like she would live up to her name.

"A houseboat can be cumbersome to move," Meyer said. "He used this as a run-about. It will take you pretty much wherever you want to go and get you back quickly. There is also a good-sized cabin, a kitchenette, and a couple of bunks for short cruises."

The houseboat looked more like the yachts next to it than any houseboat I had ever seen before. "Two Deuces" had been painted on her stern over the image of two cards – a deuce of hearts and a deuce of clubs. The second card was a little higher than the first.

"This was his second houseboat," Meyer explained. "The cards are there because he won the first one in a poker game. When you have luck like that, you live with it. He did for years. The first one was a conventional, barge-type houseboat. This one is ultra-modern – sleeker, 15' longer, and 5 knots faster. And as you can tell, there is nothing barge-like about it.

"He had it made to reflect his personal preferences. I pulled out the specs for your review. They are on the counter in the galley. One of the first things you will notice is that it is designed so you can live completely off the grid."

"I pay Jimmy from the Marine Shop to take care of it when he is gone. It takes Jimmy about 10 hours a week. I keep a log of his expenses. That's on the counter, as well. Everything should be in good order."

The Two Deuces was about the same size as my town-house – 2,800 square feet under cover and another 1,500 feet in balconies and terraces. There were four bedrooms, each with a private bath. The bed in the master suite was twice the size of any other bed I have seen. The shower was big enough to host a card game, and the tub was nearly 7' long. All the rooms had 9' ceilings. The galley was stainless steel with granite counters.

"Let me point out a few things before I leave you to explore on your own," Meyer said.

He put the carryout on the counter island in the center of the galley. I found a couple of forks while he split the bag open. There was no way I was going to eat all the cauliflower by myself. To my surprise, it wasn't half bad. I opened the fridge and found it well stocked. I didn't know who Jimmy was, but I couldn't help but wonder if he had traveled. Meyer pointed to a Corona, and I opened two.

"In that manila folder, you will find basic information

– mail, laundry, phone, TV channels, groceries, garbage disposal, shops in Tin City, Jimmy's contact information, the marina, and a reliable doctor."

"You will want to pay particular attention to the alarms. They are somewhat…" He paused for a moment, searching for the right word – "involved. A full description of all the systems is in the second folder. There is a safe built in over there under the cabinet nearest the fridge. The combination is your birthday. There is a second secure area with combination access under the yellow sofa in the bulkhead over there. That's where he kept the household accounts. The combination there is your mother's birthday. I have that combination as well, so you might want to change it. There is also a small storage compartment built into the frame of your bed."

"I told his attorney, Tom Cline, you were coming down and that he could expect a visit from you tomorrow. His number is in the first envelope you will see. I am your financial advisor – at least for the moment, subject to your direction. I have left a statement of accounts in the bulkhead, along with a list of my expenses."

"Earlier, you asked how much he knew about you. The best answer I can give you is on his laptop. It's kept on the nightstand by what is now your bed. If you open it, you will find a folder with your name. The password is your mother's maiden name."

"With that, I will leave you to settle in. Maybe we can get together tomorrow evening for dinner after you have had a chance to process all this. There are some excellent steaks in the freezer we can grill, or, if you prefer, I can bring over some of my world-famous chili."

"Let's grill the steaks. You have done a lot for me. Maybe I can take care of you a little bit."

"Fair enough."

"Thanks, Meyer. You are a good friend. Clearly, you loved him a lot."

"I did." He gave me a wistful smile. "I still do."

Whatever doubts I had about Meyer had dissipated. I still didn't fully understand my situation and the strange circumstances that brought me to Florida, but unless my instincts were way out of kilter, Meyer was for real. He clearly loved my uncle and was eager to do whatever he could to help him, even in death. The reactions of Darleene and everyone else I had seen interact with him confirmed that conclusion. He was comfortable and confident in his skin, the kind of a guy who could walk into a bar of strangers and come out a couple of hours later with half a dozen people who would swear they were his best friend. It's a rare quality. Much as I was tempted to question the situation I was in, the reality Meyer presented was hard to deny.

That didn't mean there wasn't something funny going on. That didn't mean someone hadn't found a way to lure me to Florida with an evil intent. It only meant that if that were the case, Meyer was not likely to be a part of it.

"What do you think happened to him?" I asked.

"Somebody set him up. He wasn't as good as he used to be, but he was still pretty damn good. No one with any sense would have gone straight at him."

"So, you are convinced he's dead."

"Yes. For all the reasons I told you earlier. But more than that… It's hard to put into words other than to say that when you love someone, they become a part of you. I feel like that part of me is gone. There's a hole where he used to be."

He dropped his head as I walked him to the door. Suddenly, he seemed a lot older. The day had taken a lot out of him. I put my arm on his shoulder.

"We'll find out what happened," I said. "If he met with foul play, I promise you, whoever is responsible will regret it."

He looked up with a small smile, reached out and rested his hand briefly on my back.

"Sounds like something he would say."

I watched him walk down the boardwalk, trudging back the way we had come, his shoulders slumped and head down. I walked to the bow of the boat and followed him to the parking lot across the street from the City Dock. The sun was starting to set. The sky was taking on rich golden colors on the horizon in welcoming anticipation.

Meyer got into a silver Lexus and took off on 12th Street, heading north. If I remembered my Naples geography, he would turn right on Tamiami Trail and head east past Lelo Resort to Treviso Bay. He was maybe ten minutes from home. As I watched him leave, I couldn't help thinking how lucky my uncle was. Meyer was probably as good a friend as a man would ever have.

Two Deuces

I took the folders over to the coffee table in front of the big, yellow sofa in the living room and went looking for a heavier drink. I found what I was looking for in a bar near a record player in the dining room. The record player was a happy surprise. They say vinyl is back. For my uncle, it apparently had never left.

Vinyl sales in the U.S. now far exceed CD sales. Serious listeners have found that manually playing a record can be an extremely satisfying and intimate experience — a feeling that hasn't changed in a century. It lends itself to being more engaged with the music and listening to albums in their entirety as opposed to skipping tracks. And many audiophiles will argue that you'll get a fuller sound from playing an album on vinyl versus digitally. People with good ears can hear instruments, tones, and other minute details in vinyl that sometimes get lost in compressed formats.

The player, a Fluance RT82, was built into a shelf near

the bar. It was a sleek machine with a solid, medium-density fiberboard plinth and a high-gloss Piano Black finish. It was modern, clean and inviting. I couldn't see the speakers so he must have had them built into the walls.

His record collection was neatly stacked on shelves built in below the player. The collection probably said a lot about him, but I wasn't sure what. At the very least, it said he was eclectic. He had everything from Gregorian chants to opera, country, pop, classics, and jazz. If there was an emphasis, it was there. He had every jazz album I'd ever heard and more. I played it safe and pulled Miles Davis *Kind of Blue* from the stack. Fifty years after its release, it still sells more than 5,000 copies a week, making it the best-selling jazz album of all time.

Before settling down to read and listen, I checked out the bar. It was just as interesting as the record collection and as carefully constructed. He had Plymouth Gin; Stoli Cristall; Golden Ring Vodka; Knob Creek Single Barrel Bourbon – the best Jim Beam has to offer; and Writers Tears Irish Whiskey, new to me but advertised as a triple distilled single malt whiskey. I poured a shot of Writer's Tears into a heavy crystal glass to see what it was like and found it to my liking. It was exquisitely smooth. I picked up flavors of almond, ginger, butterscotch, apple, and oak.

Quick conclusion. My uncle had good friends and excellent taste. I doubled the shot and took the glass with me as I walked the boat, buttoning it up, turning on lights, and closing the curtains. Back on the sofa, I started by reviewing the specs for the boat.

Meyer was right. My uncle had her designed so he could live completely off the grid. It was zero emission, carbon neutral, completely powered by solar panels and had a battery that conserved enough energy for nighttime use. There was a 4000-gallon freshwater tank and a wastewater tank of equal size. It could harvest rainwater as well.

There was a lot of glass – windows and doors all around – but not just any glass. It was the aluminon-silicate developed for the space program, the toughest glass known to man. He had it made with a smoky tint akin to that used in one-way mirrors, making it easier to see out and harder to see in.

There were floodlights on the corners, a 20' party top, and a security system out of star-wars. These days, everyone has security cameras wired to their phones so that they can detect home intrusions. This was something else. My uncle had installed a series of inconspicuous little security devices that would let him know when he returned if there was a stranger on board or if a stranger had been on board while he was gone.

That told me something else about him. He not only had good friends but also good taste. He was also a cautious man. Probably with good reason.

I punched in the security code and reset it so that it would feed to my phone, opened a panel in the port bulkhead outside the lounge and checked to see if the fail-safe bulbs were all glowing and everything was secure. It was designed so you could turn the systems off on entry and reactivate them once on board – the only way systems of this sort make any sense. I turned the intruder alarm on and off as a check and then went looking for gear storage.

A compartment in the bulkhead contained a couple of casting rods, some good spinners, a ten-pound test line, a big black tackle box full of plugs, spinning lures, leader material in various strengths, swivels, hooks, and an 18" fish bat – black aluminum with textured grip, a slight umbrella hook, and a small piece of cord running through the eyelet at the top.

At the bottom of the tray, under all the fishing lures, was a small 9mm with a staggered box magazine holding fourteen rounds. It was wrapped in a piece of oily flannel. I left the gun where it was and took the bat. For some people, caution is a habit. I am one of them. Clearly, my uncle was another.

After searching for 15 minutes, I found the first security box Meyer had mentioned. If I hadn't known it was there, I would never have found it. Only the slightest discoloration in the wood gave it away. When I pressed that spot, the catch released. The safe popped open when I entered my mother's birthday.

There was a stack of bills inside, banded in $5,000 and $10,000 bundles. I tallied $45,000 and changed. A notebook signed by Meyer explained the difference. He had put out nearly $5,000 to maintain the boat. Each expense was carefully recorded, explained, and initialed.

There was also a series of envelopes, one for each of the last 6 months, detailing transactions in the investment accounts Meyer was managing. He was doing well enough to dispel any thoughts of switching to another financial manager. I was staggered by the amount of money in those accounts.

I replaced what I had disturbed, fluffed the cushions on the sofa and turned out the lights in the living room. I took my drink with me and put it on the counter in the gallery while I opened the safe there. I found another $5,000 and a note instructing me to talk with Tom Cline, my uncle's lawyer, about the estate. I made sure I knew where the fire extinguishers were stored – another safety precaution – and headed for the master suite.

The third hidey-hole was built into the bed frame, positioned so I could tap it with my hand and open it quickly and quietly. The only thing in it was a Sig-Sauer MK25. I knew it as the weapon of choice for Navy Seals. It has several distinctive features: It carries one in the chamber ready to fire because it won't fire unless the trigger is pressed. It has a short reset trigger that allows rapid and accurate follow-up shots with less movement of the shooter's finger. It also has a high resistance to salt-water corrosion, which is one of the reasons Seals like it. There was a top-of-the-line suppressor in the compartment with it – the Griffin Revolution 9 – and three 15-round magazines of subsonic 9mm rounds designed to maximize the can's effectiveness.

More and more, my uncle was coming into focus. He was loyal to his friends, lived well, had good taste, seemed secure in himself and what he wanted, marched to his own beat, and ran against the tide. The weapons and the security system said he had made more than his share of enemies of the meat-eating variety and was cautious to the point of being paranoid – But what's the old saying:

Just because you're paranoid doesn't mean they aren't out to get you.

Knowing what I now knew about him, I was anxious to see what he knew about me. I found his laptop and put it on the bed for nighttime reading. Before getting to it, I unpacked my bag and headed for the shower. I felt a little lonely there, but the showerheads were wonderful – strong streams from every direction. Again, I had to give my uncle credit. He knew how to live. It made me even more determined to find out how he died.

The Family Connection

There were towels and oversized robes in the linen closet. All blue. All plush. The robe was a little tight across the back and short at the sleeve, but other than that, it fit well enough. I made myself another drink and took it into the bedroom to do my homework. I put the fish bat on the floor by what was now my bed and opened his computer.

There was only one folder on the desktop. It had my name on it. I opened it and found two files inside. One was labeled "Family." The other said, "Senate." I sorted by date created. The first file in the family folder went back a year and a half. The first file in the Senate folder was six months older. It looked to be a copy of the *60 Minutes* story on our clinical laboratory investigation.

From the number of files, he clearly followed everything I had done since that time. That helped explain Meyer's characterization of his interest in me. I have a top-secret crypto clearance. My security evaluation was nowhere near as thorough. Among other things, it said he must have had a lot of free time on his hands. Either that, or he had hired a very competent professional to do a background check on me.

The family file started with a black and white photograph of a bakery from *The Annapolis Gazette* taken on St. Patrick's Day. It was part of a feature on local businesses with Irish connections. The caption said: "Blasta Bakery, 131 Main Street." There were cutouts of shamrocks in the store window.

A number of other news reports followed, clearly taken from the archives of the same newspaper. They included a story on my mother's high school graduating class, identifying her as the valedictorian, an announcement of her engagement to my father, identifying him as an ensign in the Navy, and a wedding announcement two months later, saying the couple would honeymoon on their way to the family ranch in Colorado.

There was a photostat from Colorado's real estate records, identifying Grandpa's homestead claim, an aerial shot of the property, and tax records from the County Clerk for the last five years. The first reference to me came from *The Craig Crier*, which said I had won a merit scholarship and would be attending George Washington University.

My college records followed – fraternity, student activities, and student government. There were no athletic records because there were no athletics to speak of at GWU.

How did he find all this stuff? Again, I wondered. I was stuck with the same two options: Either he hired a professional, or he spent a lot of time online. Maybe it was as simple as that – an aging man looking for something productive to do, a man worrying about his posterity and looking for a way to connect with someone, even if it was a family he had chosen to ignore before.

The Senate files were straightforward. There was nothing difficult about obtaining that information. Everything the Senate does is public. A Lexus-Nexus run would pull up a bibliography in fifteen minutes. All you have to do is run it down. There were print, video, and social media files, appearances on various talk shows, and tapes of me filling in for the Chairman at press conferences, testifying at hearings, cross-examining witnesses, and the like.

C-SPAN records and broadcasts every non-classified Congressional hearing. He had a copy of every PSI hearing where I was involved, not only under Colgate but years before during my first run on The Hill.

He even had clips from *The Washingtonian's* social page with pictures of social events where captions said I had been "seen with" one or another TV anchor-woman or national correspondent at this or that event.

It was quite a collection. I went to sleep with the distinct impression that the person who knew me best was probably the relative I knew the least.

Why? I wondered. What was I missing? Was all this just the normal order of things, a natural progression, or a series of events orchestrated and organized to bring me to a specific place at a specific time, somewhere my movements could be monitored, somewhere I could be pinned down?

I tapped the compartment in my bed frame, took out the Sig, checked the load, and attached the silencer. I put it on the nightstand by my bed next to my phone. If I had any callers in the middle of the night, I wanted to be ready.

Life Questions Man

Monday morning, May 24. I showered and dressed, keeping it simple – a white t-shirt, jeans, and boots – and began to make a mental list of the things I wanted to accomplish. Working backward, I had promised Meyer dinner. I surveyed the galley to see what I had to work with.

As promised, I found steaks in the freezer – ribeyes three-quarters of an inch thick. I put them in the fridge to thaw. The cupboard contained all the spices and condiments I might want and a few I didn't recognize.

The only things I really needed were fresh vegetables. I was sure I could find some somewhere between Tin City and Cline's office. I called Uber and arranged a pick-up at the entrance where I had been dropped off the day before.

On the way out, I stopped by the Marine Store to look for Jimmy. I found him in the back, either assembling or taking apart an outboard motor. I couldn't tell which. He was a thin young man around twenty with earnest dark eyes and hands already showing the signs of hard work. He was trying to grow a beard without much success.

I introduced myself, thanked him, and gave him one of my uncle's hundred-dollar bills as a tip. He was reluctant to take it, saying he had already been paid. I liked him on sight and liked him even more for that. Besides, he said, my uncle had been very kind to him and had gone out of his way to help his girlfriend. That confirmed my impression of Meyer and told me something more about my uncle.

I told Jimmy this was his chance to return the favor and help me out. I know bupkis about boats, I said. I could handle the Little Doll, but if I tried to take the houseboat out, I would take part of the dock with me, and I had no idea how to take care of either one of them. I needed his help maintaining them while I figured things out, and I wouldn't feel comfortable letting him do that if he wouldn't let me compensate him the way I thought he deserved.

He smiled with that, dropped his head, and said he would be happy to help. Young people get a bad rap these days. There are more like Jimmy than we care to admit. I added him to the list of things I had inherited from my uncle. He was one of mine now.

Uber was waiting when I arrived at the entrance to the dock. The driver greeted me, double-checked my destination, and then asked if I knew that the area to the south of where we were was called Millionaires' Row. Fortunately, we were going in the opposite direction.

Cline's office was downtown in a trendy cluster of restaurants and shops created for the snowbirds. He was on the third floor of a corner building with an office that overlooked the street. The sign on the door said, "Slagle and Cline." There was no sign of Slagle – just a competent receptionist in a quiet waiting room and a door leading to Cline's office.

Cline came out and greeted me five minutes after his receptionist said I was there. He was a tall man, nearly my height, with classic features and short grey hair. He wore a dark, tailored suit that looked like money and a Halston tie with an abstract design.

Cline's office had an ornate desk, a couple of leather chairs and a small conference table. He asked me to take a seat at the table where some files had been laid out in anticipation of my arrival.

He said he was sorry to hear about my loss. I told him I appreciated his kind thoughts, but I had never met my uncle and wouldn't know him if I saw him. I asked him if he was sure he was lost, and he said that was his understanding from Meyer and that Meyer was handling things the way my uncle had instructed them both to proceed.

To my surprise, Cline said the estate was sizable. The boats were worth several million dollars on top of the other assets Meyer was managing. Those assets were being held in trust.

The trust was revocable if I chose to exercise that option, but there would be tax consequences. There would also be tax consequences if I decided to sell the boat. There would be tax consequences if I didn't maintain a residence in Florida at least 183 days a year.

You get the idea. Once I understood there would be tax consequences, he didn't have much more to say. He handed me a copy of my uncle's will and an envelope with a small key in it. Cline said it was a key to a safety deposit box in a branch of the Florida National Bank near Tin City. My uncle had left some things for me there.

It was hard to imagine what more there could be, but there was only one way to find out. The weather was cooperating. It was a bright and cool, another Chamber of Commerce day, and I hadn't exercised since I left Washington, so I decided to walk. It took 45 minutes at a brisk pace, but it felt good to stretch my legs.

It also gave me some time to process everything I had learned in the last couple of days and assess what it might mean for the way I live my life. The best thing about money is that it gives you choices; it opens possibilities that are not available to those without money. I had a lot more choices now than I had before, which said a lot because I knew I was already among the fortunate ones.

"Life questions, man,"

Viktor Frankl wrote.

"The question is always: What are you going to do about it?"

I couldn't begin to answer that fundamental question. I still had a lot of thinking to do. But one thing was increasingly certain. I was going to find out what happened to my uncle before I did anything else.

As I came to that resolution, I felt my pulse quicken, a heightened sense of awareness, and a little fire beginning to build in my gut. My step became a little lighter. The hunt was on.

THE FLORIDA NATIONAL BRANCH OFFICE WAS SMALL. A half dozen customers inside. A lot of cars lined up for the drive-through, taking money out of their ATMs, checking, savings and rainy-day accounts to feed the local economy.

I showed my key and asked for the manager at the door. The manager turned out to be the receptionist as well, a short Latino who took a break from directing traffic to take me back to a small room where they kept the safety deposit boxes. She smiled her best smile, closed the door, and left me alone.

The box was on the top level. I turned the key, pulled the box, and turned it over. A small photograph with a letter and a Purple Heart fell on the counter. The photograph was old, 4 x 5, sepia, and formal, with a woman holding a girl in a stiff "don't you dare move because this camera could never catch your movement" pose.

The woman had her hair tied back in a bun. She wore a long-sleeved, high-necked dress that almost touched the ground. Her hands wrapped around the girl in a way that told you this was her most precious possession. The girl wore a short dress with long stockings. She was smiling, but then she was always smiling.

"This is the only picture I have of your grandmother and your mother,"

The letter said.

"I wish I had more. Your mom was seven when this picture was taken. Our mom passed away 6 months later. I made up my mind to leave that same night. I lied about my age and joined the Navy. I always wished I could have taken your mother with me, but there was no way to do that. You were fortunate enough to have two great parents. Your mom and I had one great parent and one embarrassment."

"When my father, your grandfather, left to come to the United States, he left us behind. He told us that he would send for us once he was established. He never did. I was six. I watched my mother scrub floors and work as a housemaid for six years, trying to keep food on our table while she waited for him to send for her. Finally, someone we knew found him living in Annapolis and shamed him or threatened him into sending for us."

"Your mom was born the year after we arrived. I was twelve and already being asked to cover for the Old Man. He loved to drink more than he liked to work. He loved the bars more than he liked being at home. He would clean out

the till at the end of the night and go drinking, leaving me to clean up the shop and put things away."

"Sometimes, he wouldn't come home, and I had to open the bakery in the morning and prepare the shop for business. You are supposed to love your father. He made it very hard. It's hard to love someone you don't like."

"I stayed as long as I did because of your grandmother. She was a beautiful, wonderful woman. I wish you could have known her, but then you probably did in my sister, your mom."

"With my mother gone, I could see no reason to stay. I joined the Navy because I wanted to get as far away from him as fast as possible. Unfortunately, that also took me away from your mother."

"My biggest regret is that I know I left her alone to deal with things I couldn't handle. I can only imagine how hard it was for her, cleaning up after him, tagging along as he went to the bars, watching him drink and carry on. I took the easy way out."

"After I got out of the Navy, I found work in Florida, diving with the treasure hunters. We had enough success that I thought about going back for her, but a lot of time had passed. I didn't want to see my father, and I wasn't sure what I would say to my sister."

"Then my business took a turn. Something can easily become something else. I found there was more than one form of salvage when someone stole six months' worth of hard work and dangerous dives from my employer."

"He said if I could get it back, he would give me half of whatever I recovered. I did, and it worked. I found I liked the challenge and satisfaction that came from righting a wrong and began looking for other "salvage" projects. Word got around after a while, and people came looking for me."

"Often, the strong just roll over the weak, taking what they want unless someone stops them. Frankly, I enjoyed going after those who did, meeting out my own form of rough justice, preying on predators, but you can't rattle someone's dish and expect them to like you for it."

"That's one of the reasons I stayed away from you and your mom. It's not that I didn't want to see you or be with you both, but I couldn't stand the thought of putting you at risk."

"There were and probably are a lot of people who would come at you as a way of getting to me. So, I watched you from afar. I was proud of the man you turned out to be, the choices you have made, and the way you live your life."

"Meyer once said I had an overdeveloped sense of justice. I suspect you do, too. I would *have loved to have had a chance to talk with you about that."*

"Enjoy that gaudy houseboat I built. Play with the Little Doll, hug Meyer, and have a drink for me from time to time."

God Bless,
TM

I wiped away the tears that had started to form with the back of my hand and put the letter, photograph, and medal in my pocket. On the way out, I returned the key and told the manager my uncle had passed away and I wouldn't need the box anymore.

She expressed her regrets and said she remembered him and often wondered how someone so big could be so gentle. I took advantage of her local knowledge and told her I was on my way to Tin City and wondering if there was anywhere nearby where I could get some fresh vegetables. She said she had seen a stand between the highway and parking lot near the front entrance to Tin City on the weekends when she shopped. She didn't know for sure, but she thought it might be there on weekdays as well.

Fortunately, she was right. The owner said everything was straight from the farm and that he or some other member of the family was there every other day through the season.

When I got back to the Two Deuces, I laid everything out on the counters in the party top and lowered the awning to provide a little shade. The grill was on one end of the counter, and the sink and bar were on the other. I had decided to keep it simple. Steak, fresh corn, and a Greek farmer's salad – tomatoes, cukes, red onions, and feta cheese.

Before heading to the bedroom to shower and change, I put the steaks in a marinade. I took them out when Meyer arrived an hour later, dried them off, and gave them a dry rub with a Jamaican Jerk spice mix I'd found in one of the kitchen cabinets. I covered them with foil and let them rest. You have to give them at least half an hour.

Meyer had dressed up for the occasion, wearing a short-sleeved, green, collared shirt and long khaki pants. After he had examined my preparations and nodded his approval, I asked him to pick a wine while I finished up. He came back with a Pierre Morey Pommard, poured us each a glass, and asked me to tell him about my day.

Meanwhile, I made the salad and put a pot of water on it to boil. All I had to do was drop the corn in the hot water, ask him how he liked his steak, and put it on the grill. Predictably, he was a civilized man. He asked for medium rare. I like my steak, just this side of burned. When you grow up cooking on an open fire, you don't mind little char in your chew.

While the steaks sizzled, I told him about my decision and discussion with Jimmy. He said it was a good call. He trusted Jimmy without reservation, and it probably helped that his girlfriend was Darleene, our waitress from Tin City.

He said they were a good couple, very cute together, and wrapped in the wonder of first love. What Jimmy had said about my uncle didn't surprise him. He was that way with everyone, always happy to help whenever he could.

Next, I talked him through my tax problems. It was quickly clear he knew more about it than I did. But when I told him about the letter my uncle had left, he was in the dark. He listened intensely and said it answered a lot of questions for him and contained a lot of information he didn't know.

"He never talked about his father or your mother," He said, "but I sensed there were some issues there. Andre Maurois said, 'Without a family, man alone in the world tremble with the cold.' He felt that. We both did. Maybe that's why we were so close."

"When you get old, the world can be a sad and lonely place. The glue that holds humankind together is the desire to be here for one another to serve one another. He was finding it hard to make that connection on either end."

"He went through the motions. He had things to do but no will to do them. Increasingly, he hired out even the smallest chores, which was a big change for a man used to doing everything for himself."

"There was a growing sense of apathy. A desire to disassociate, to be uninvolved. He had lost the power of purpose. He found himself wrestling with the big "So What" question."

"He had lived with the delusion of total freedom of will and now questioned if there was such a thing. He wondered if he had made the right choices by taking the path less traveled, refusing to march down the same road as everyone else, or whether he had simply cut himself off from the herd and all the associations that make life rich and meaningful."

"These are the things that fill your head when you grow old and feel the big door closing. He had justified his existence with a spavined sense of mission, relieving the torment of others for his profit. Still, he never addressed the fundamental problems, the causation, and the greater inequities that affect most of us the way we do."

"We talked about that often, how most of us bitch about this or that and say someone should do something. You don't bitch. You do."

He emptied his glass. We had finished the bottle. I opened another and refilled his glass. He took a sip and looked up at me with shiny blue eyes, saying he knew something about being old and lonely.

"So, I guess the question is, knowing what you know now – What are you going to do about all this?"

The sun was inching its way over Millionaires' Row. The charters were all in, and you could hear the crews washing them down, comparing notes, cleaning up, and preparing for the next run. It was a beautiful night, and the harbor was busy with shoppers and diners.

Over Meyer's shoulder, I saw a man double park a dark sedan near the entrance to City Dock. That was no place to park, particularly when the public lot was across the street. He didn't seem to be waiting for a passenger or dropping someone off, so there was no apparent reason for him to do that.

He spent fifteen minutes there and seemed to be looking our way. Then his door opened, and he stepped out. He leaned against his car and stared intently in our direction. The hair went up on the back of my neck as I realized he was holding a pair of field glasses.

He watched us long enough to confirm the suspicions I had been harboring. I had been looking over my shoulder and waiting for him to make his appearance from the moment I arrived. The only question was whether he was one of my uncle's friends or one of mine. Either way, it was the kind of interest I welcomed. It confirmed my sense, my expectation, really, that someone was trying to set me up; someone was, in fact, coming after me.

That would have frightened most people. It made me smile. My senses began to tingle with that heightened sense of awareness that comes with knowing that battle will soon follow. He settled back in his car, flipped a U-turn, and headed out 12th Avenue. I watched him leave, knowing I would see him again. My thoughts flashed forward to that moment as I began to consider the various ways I could make him feel welcome.

Out of the corner of my eye, I saw Meyer staring at me. He had picked up something. I couldn't look directly at him as I answered the question he had asked. I told him I didn't know what I was going to do or what I wanted to do.

That was true for the most part. I was still working on it. I told him I would need his help sorting things out and thinking things through. He knew the law and finances far better than I did and I knew I would have to be schooled on the "tax consequences."

I didn't bother telling Meyer about the man with the field glasses. I still wasn't sure where he fit into all this.

All indicators were positive. He seemed to be a good guy and a good friend. On the other hand, he had made the call that triggered this series of events. Bottom line: You never know until you know. I'd find out soon enough.

"When was the last time you talked with my uncle?" I asked.

"About six months ago. We talked over the phone. I wanted to review his portfolio. He always listened, but he never had any real interest in that."

"Did he say he might be leaving for a while?"

"No."

"Did he tell you what he was working on?"

"He wasn't doing much. When his daughter died, I think he looked at what he had and decided there was no need to accumulate anything more. As you can probably tell by looking at this boat, he was running out of places to spend it."

"I went through his files last night. It borders on compulsion or – at the very least – someone desperately looking for something useful to do."

"There may be something to that. Money was always the McGuffin – the excuse to do something rather than the reason. It gave him some satisfaction for a long while, but he lost it somehow. He felt like he was just going through the motions."

"Do you think he might have been so bored he was drawn into something?"

"It's possible, but I think if it were something major, he would have told me about it. Aside from everything else, he was a realist. He knew he wasn't as quick or sharp as he used to be."

"So, you talked to him six months ago. When was the last time you saw him?"

"He invited me over to watch the C-Span recording of your pacemaker hearing. He was very proud of the way you handled that. He said, 'Who else could take a simple letter and turn it into a billion-dollar investigation.'"

"That's a billion dollars a year," I said with a smile. "They were stealing a billion dollars a year. And it would have continued if we hadn't put a stop to it."

Meyer smiled.

"It's probably obvious, but I think he saw a good deal of himself in you."

"We have a lot of things to sort out," I said, "but I hope you understand all that can wait. Our first priority is to find out what happened to him."

His pale blue eyes glistened when I gave him a hug as he left.

A Shadowy Figure

It was 3:05 AM. The sound of the buzzer mounted on the pier piling at the perimeter of my security system woke me up. Then, a small chime lit up the face of my phone, signaling an intruder was about to step over the chain and come down the gangplank.

As he stepped on the mat on the aft deck, another small chime confirmed his intrusion. The security camera caught a shadowy figure walking quietly and carefully toward the cabin. He appeared to be holding a gun, low on his right side.

I picked up the fish bat I had placed against the wall by my bed and prepared to meet him. The curtain liners were drawn, making it much darker inside than out. That's where the design of a one-way glass kicks in. The darker it is inside, the more reflective it is outside. I could see him, but he couldn't see me.

I stood by the bedroom door and waited. The best lock in the world won't slow a professional down too much. All you can really hope for is a security system that will alert the cops and give you enough time to prepare a welcome. I had plenty of that.

My now familiar response to danger kicked in. Everything slowed down. Time expanded. Every moment brought a greater sense of clarity. I was detached, there and not there, objective and removed, somewhere above, watching myself, watching my intruder, watching everything around us move in slow motion.

I decided to take the battle to him. He was halfway to the door, walking carefully now, crouched low, and trying to peer inside. From somewhere above, I saw myself walk back to the main cabin and disable the alarm. I reached across the door, unlocked it, and cracked it open. I didn't want him to make a mess of my lock or my front door. From the way he moved, I sensed he would.

A professional would have approached more quickly and more confidently. A professional wouldn't be standing out there on my deck, sniffing the air. A professional wouldn't be inching along, holding a gun for the world to see. I didn't know who he was, but by now, I knew that whoever he was, he wasn't on the A-team.

That didn't mean he wasn't dangerous, but my bigger concern was that he might get discouraged and leave. I didn't want that. I wanted to know who he was, and I wasn't dressed to chase him down the dock. I settled back, pressed against the wall next to the door, and waited. It took him five more minutes to reach me. It felt like forever.

When he saw the door was open, he stopped dead and tried to evaluate the situation. He stared inside and then slowly slid the door open. He poked the gun through the opening, aiming it in the general direction of the bedroom. I followed his arm and waited for his head to emerge. The moment it crossed the threshold, I brought Billy down with what I hoped was just enough force.

I had six or seven inches on him, and he was crouching a bit. That made it an easy strike. I found the base of his skull with a satisfying thump. He fell forward like the empty sack he was. I kicked the gun away and hauled him through the door. He was limp. I wondered if I'd hit him too hard. Not that I cared if he died. I just didn't want him to die too soon. He had something to say, and I wanted to hear it.

I felt for and found a pulse before I went looking for the filament tape I had seen in the bulkhead and trussed him up. I ran the tape under one elbow, pulled the other one over and tied them together, wrapped four times; then I passed it around his ankles four times. I found a large, green garbage bag in the galley and pulled it over his head. I ran enough tape around his waist to keep the garbage bag in place before going back to the kitchen to find the supplies I needed to clean up his mess. He had bled some, but not a lot. Still, it would be a permanent stain if I didn't pick it up fast.

Twenty minutes had passed. It was now 3:25 AM. It's not a nice time for a visit, but a good time for a boat ride. I got dressed and dropped him on the sun deck of the Little Doll. Half an hour later, I was anchored in the mangroves south of Naples, watching the morning wake. The waters were quiet, still as glass. The sun was just beginning to peak over the horizon when he started to stir.

His smallest movement irritated me. It spoiled the moment and rudely disturbed the perfect peace like someone loudly passing gas in the middle of a dinner party. It forced me to focus on him and consider the ugliness that pollutes the world.

I tried to ignore him – a squirming lump covered by a trash bag – by focusing on the Everglades coming to life. It reminded me of the high country in every sense but one. The topography could not be more different.

The overriding sensation both provide is one of solitude, serenity, and the inner peace that comes with being surrounded by nature so undisturbed you get the sense it has always been so.

Out of nowhere, a flock of small white birds descended on us, filling the mangroves with their cries and requests. I couldn't tell if our feathery friends were welcoming us or telling us to leave, curious or looking for a handout.

I would have preferred to sit there and enjoy the moment, maybe drop a line in the water and pretend I was fishing, anything other than dealing with my intruder. But then, if I didn't have to deal with him, I probably wouldn't have been there to enjoy the moment. I would have been sacked out in the oversized bed on the Two Deuces, wondering where to begin and what to do with my day.

I had emptied my intruder's pockets when I dropped him on the Little Doll. There wasn't much – a wallet, phone, car keys, and a gun. I placed everything on the console so they would be visible when I removed the garbage bag. I wanted him to know where we were and what I was doing.

He blinked his eyes as they adjusted to the light, then went wide-eyed in fright. He mumbled something incoherent, but then it is hard to speak clearly when your mouth is taped shut.

His face was pale and gaunt. He had the thin, wiry body of a creature that had to hustle to live off the land. Some kind of a swamp rat. His driver's license said he was Louis Martin, 38, out of Ft. Myer, 5' 10" and 140 lbs.

I took a moment to memorize his home address and then dropped his license into the water. I looked at him as I did. I wanted him to see my total disregard for him and his possessions. Credit cards followed, going overboard after examination, one by one. The information was consistent.

I watched him watch his identity disappear. There was nothing else in the wallet, just a couple hundred dollars in cash – fresh, new 20-dollar bills. I put the cash in my pocket, dropped the wallet in the water, and then pulled him into a sitting position.

I had placed him on the Little Doll's expansive sundeck. His hands and legs were still bound, making it hard for him to stay upright. While he watched, I picked up the piece of rope I'd brought from the Two Deuces. I watched him watch as I made a noose, something every boy growing up out west learns to do by the age of ten.

He flinched when I dropped the noose over his head. Rather than pull it up, I tightened the loop around his neck and then ran the rope down to his waist. I circled it and made a half hitch before passing it through the end of the drift anchor and continuing down to wrap and repeat the knot at his feet.

When I was done, I tightened the noose enough to get his attention and jerked the tape off his mouth. I leaned back, holding the end of the rope, and let him sit there for a while, absorbing the situation. I didn't say a word. I pulled my necklace out from under my T-shirt and held it in my hand. I remembered Kaiah's words as I closed my fist and felt the claw dig into my palm.

"Remember who you are," She had said.

He stared at me like I was from another planet, and then, finally, he spoke.

"What are you going to do with me?"

I let the necklace drop, watched it settle on my shirt, and then looked up at him with dead eyes. I wanted him to know he was of no more interest to me than the pond scum gathering on the surface around the mangroves.

"I don't know…Probably the same thing you were going to do with me."

He shook his head in a frantic denial.

"Hey, man," He said. "I wasn't going to do anything. I was just watching the boat."

The sound of his voice was an indictment of our educational system. It offended the ear. I gave a little tug on the rope. It startled him, and he instinctively pulled back. He would have fallen off the boat if I hadn't steadied him.

"Don't be in such a hurry," I said.

I tugged the rope once more.

"You just watched the boat?"

"That's all. I swear."

"Why would you do that?"

"They want to know who's there."

"How long have you been watching?"

"Maybe a couple of times a week."

"I didn't ask how often. I asked how long."

"Maybe a couple of months."

His head dropped. His eyes wandered. He was trying to be evasive and wasn't very good at it. I reached over and tightened the nose.

"Maybe more?"

"Maybe…But not just me," He rushed to say. "Another guy was watching. He was full-time for a couple of months. They took him off when nothing happened. After that, they asked me to drive by every now and then and check things out."

"Who is 'they?'"

"What do you mean?"

I pulled on the rope a little harder.

"You know what I mean. Who do you work for?"

"SafeCo," He said in a near whisper.

"What is SafeCo?"

"A security protection firm. We provide security for a lot of stores in the Naples mall and offices around town."

"What's your role?"

"Just a driver," He said quickly. "I'm nothing. A delivery boy."

"Who do you report to?"

"Ray Scartizina."

"Who does Scartizina report to?"

He wiggled some, trying to maintain his balance.

"I don't know. People kind of come and go."

“How many?”

“I don’t know. Maybe half a dozen. I’m not in the office that much. I see different people.”

“Why are they interested in my uncle?”

“I don’t know, man…I keep telling you. I don’t know anything. All I do is make my rounds. Sometimes, I check the boat. That’s all I do.”

“Is that what you were doing when you tried to break into my home?”

“I saw you on deck with that other guy. I didn’t know who you were. I didn’t know who he was. I hadn’t seen anyone before. I came back to see if you were still there. I knew they would want to know.”

“You saw us on your way home after work. That was about 8:30,” I said. “Then you came back in the middle of the night – six hours later – with a gun.”

He shrugged and inadvertently tightened the noose. It was under his chin now. He flinched as it cut into his throat.

“You’ve got to understand...Mostly, I’m just riding around in the car all day, delivering stuff, picking up stuff, and sometimes picking people up and driving them around. They never take me seriously. I’m an errand boy. That’s all I do. I knew this was important to them. I thought this was my chance to prove I am somebody.”

“With a gun?”

“I was being careful. They said you could be dangerous.”

“Who could be dangerous?”

“Whoever was on the boat.”

“Well, you got that right.”

I pulled the rope tight. He shook his head like a mare trying to throw the noose.

"Were you looking for my uncle, or were you looking for me?"

"I was just looking. I told you…I don't know why they wanted to know who was on the boat."

"You don't lie well… I'm sure it's not for the lack of practice. Fortunately for you, you won't have to lie much longer."

He saw my eyes and knew I wasn't buying his routine. He started shaking. The pitch of his voice changed.

"I was just looking, man. I keep telling you I was just looking. You can't kill me for that."

"I can't? Why not?"

I jerked the rope, pulling it tighter still.

"What do you expect me to do? Call the cops? Let them take you in, charge you, and turn you loose? You'd be back on the street before I left the parking lot, and I would be looking over my shoulder, waiting for you to come around and try again. Maybe next time you'd bring some friends, maybe even someone competent."

I picked up the anchor, holding it in my palms and feeling its weight. I did a small, slow curl. It was heavy. Not too heavy – but heavy enough.

"Last chance. Where is my uncle?"

"I don't know," He pleaded.

I looked through him, brought the anchor up to my chest, and held it there.

"I think I might have seen him once," He hastily

added. “I don’t know. Maybe 6 months ago. He was a big mean-looking son-of-bitch.”

Was. Sometimes, a single word is all you need to hear.

I smiled at him.

“So am I.”

I shot the anchor over his right shoulder. It reached the end of the rope before it fell into the water. As it did, I bent down and swept his feet, accelerating the momentum provided by the lead weight and pulling him overboard.

His body settled into the water quickly, going down in one piece. I watched the water until the air bubbles were gone. The water was quiet, and there was no visible sign of what had happened – above or below the water.

SafeCo

There is a top ten list for everything these days, including where to dump bodies. The Everglades is fourth on that list. It comes in just behind the East River, but one could easily question this ranking. Bodies dropped in the East River in the fall show up in bunches in the spring for what locals grimly call "The Spring Harvest." Most of them show up near Bay Bridge and South Street Seaport.

There are about 2,000 square miles of tropical and subtropical environments in the Everglades. The isolation and size of this area provide ample opportunity to stash a body with little chance the body will ever be discovered. Many more have gone to meet their maker there than we will probably ever know – a lot more, a man with civic pride would probably argue, than in the East River. I was counting on that.

Just in case, I disposed of the rest of his things. His gun was a Glock 17 semi-automatic. One of over 5 million in use worldwide. The one that shoots 9mm Parabellum NATO rounds. It's pretty high-end for an errand boy. I admired it for a moment, weighing it in my hand, muscle memory taking me back to other places and other times. Reluctantly, I broke it down and dropped the pieces in the water. I hated to do it. It was a beautiful piece. I had no such second thoughts about my intruder.

He was a predator. You always separate the predator from the herd as soon as possible. The longer you wait, the more damage they will do. That's probably what he had in mind when he came looking for me.

I turned his cell phone on to see if he had been missed. The phone was locked. No recent messages were in view. I would have kept the phone to see who popped up, but that would provide too many other challenges and hazards. Every high school geek knows how to track a cell phone these days. Now that I knew people were looking for me, I wasn't about to make it easy for them. I removed the batteries and tossed them.

I pulled up the boat anchor, picked up a fishing rod, and started half-heartedly fishing my way back to the dock, enjoying the boat and the water. The verdict was still out on the Two Deuces, but I knew I was keeping the Little Doll. It was a sweet ride. Nothing like the powerboats we used when we fished in Alaska.

For seven years, Alaska was a summer tradition. We would fly into Ketchikan and then take a float plane across the Bay to Bear Island. In the morning, we would head out to deep water in little two-person skiffs.

This reminded me of that, the serenity most of all, the obvious and abundant wildlife, feeling at one with nature, the quiet expanse of water – only there you could bust a kidney in rough water every time a wave would slap the skiff down.

The Little Doll took everything in stride, cutting through what waves there were like they didn't exist. I found a likely spot halfway back and caught a couple of Jack without much effort, gutted and cleaned one, and released the other. I put the fish I had cleaned in the garbage bag and dropped the bag in the well.

I was back on the Two Deuces by the time the sun cleared the horizon. The Saturday morning charters were just heading out, the fishing boats sprinting south toward the islands and the Gulf, the tourist boats chugging down along Port Royal to swing around and come back up the coast, giving the tourists a close-up view of the houses on Millionaires' Row.

I washed down the Little Doll, put the tackle away, and threw the fish in the fridge. Then I turned my attention to the Two Deuces, making sure I had removed any signs of the intruder.

There was still a little pink discoloration on the carpet near the door where he fell. It took some effort to remove, but not that much. The number of cleaning supplies on board suggested this might not be the first time something or someone on the boat had required industrial cleaning.

After a shower and a change of clothes, I went looking for my visitor's car. I found it in the public lot across from The City Dock. I hit the key fob, and it popped up on the front row, lights blinking their welcome. It was the dark sedan I had seen the night before. A Camry, four or five years old. Some manufactured shade of blue.

I walked up to it, ignored the ticket on the windshield, and got in like I owned it. I fired it up and took 8th Street, heading north toward the Trail and onto Naples International Airport. I was looking for auxiliary parking and found what I wanted on the North side, a mile from Enterprise.

There were only a half dozen cars in the lot. I parked in the corner furthest from the entrance, looked around to see if there were any observers, and began my search of the car's contents.

The glove box had nothing of interest other than the registration and car manual. It was registered to Martin at the address on his driver's license. There were a couple of parking tickets in the console. Both were given near the Naples Mall, which was strange since you'd think there would be ample parking at the mall. Lots of litter. Signs of a man who lived in his car. Fast food wrappers, napkins, straw wrappers and the like. Chipotle seemed to be a favorite.

The only things of real interest were on the backseat. There was a beat-up pair of field glasses behind the driver's seat covered by a plastic bag from Staples. The bag contained a $5.56 receipt for 300 self-sealing currency straps in denominations of 1,000, 2,000, 5,000, and 10,000 dollars.

There was only one strap present – a broken strap for $1,000. I found the money – minus the $200 that had been in his wallet – in the trunk. He had tucked it under the spare tire. There was a large black canvas bag there as well. It was nearly empty, containing only two smaller pouch-size canvas bags. Each was filled with 20 small white pills.

I wiped the car clean with an oily rag I found in the trunk, put the keys on the console, left the pills on the floor of the passenger seat, took the money, locked the car, pulled the ticket off the windshield, and walked away. Just another guy heading for the airport – except I stopped at Enterprise.

Any thought of a quick in and out of Naples was long gone. I knew now I would be there long enough to need a car. Given the situation, the choice of vehicles was easy. I picked a Camry in the same dark, manufactured shade of blue as the one I had just ditched and went shopping. I left the parking ticket in the trash can at Enterprise. I didn't want anything in my intruder's car, tying it to my location.

I needed some clothes, groceries, and a few other things. The Naples Mall seemed the obvious choice. Like everything in Florida, the mall is spread out. There were three shopping sections with fast food and convenience shops scattered around the perimeter. Martin bought me some Florida clothes and a few provisions. Then I went looking for a marine outlet. I found one on the north end of the mall. Now that I was a boat owner, I decided I needed to take an interest in such things.

I picked up a 50-pound river anchor to replace the one I dropped in the Everglades, two lengths of rope in two weights, and some cleaning supplies to replace the ones I had used. I also picked up a painter's drop cloth. The trash bag had worked well enough, but something told me I might need something more substantial in the future.

Back on the Two Deuces, after putting my packages away I put a call in to my office. I asked for Christoff.

"Do me a favor," I said. "I'm in Florida checking out a personal matter, and something strange has popped up."

"What can I do?"

"Run a security firm in Naples called SafeCo. Corporate and public. D&B. FTC. LexisNexis. Officers and activities. I want to know who is involved and everything they do, including what kind of toilet paper they use. The only name I have is Ray Scartizina. I don't know where he fits in – owner, operator, or employee. Run an individual scan on him. Check with Hugh Jones at the Bureau. See if he has a file. Any known associates. You know the drill."

"Sounds like the beginning of something."

"Could be. I'll know better when I see what you come up with."

"I'll get on it," He said, and I knew he would.

It had been an early morning, and I didn't feel much like cooking. I went over to the Tin Inn to pick up some carryout. I'm not normally big on carryout, but I couldn't think of anywhere I would rather eat than on the deck of my houseboat. With any luck, I would get back in time to catch the sunset.

Darleene came running when I got to the Tin Inn, almost as if she had been looking for me. She took my order – crab cakes, a baked potato and God help me, some more cauliflower – and then hurried back.

She said Jimmy had told her about our conversation, and she wanted me to know she appreciated what I said. He was a good guy, she said, much better than Donnie, her last boyfriend. Donnie was dumb, mean, lazy, and not like Jimmy at all. Jimmy was the sweetest thing, and she hoped he would ask her to marry in a year or so.

She didn't know for sure, but she knew for sure he was saving up for something, and she hoped it was a ring. A thing like what I did for Jimmy made her think of my uncle, she said. He was like that, always nice to everyone, the kind of guy everyone went to for advice because he was so easy to talk to. He would always try to find a way to help, like the one time Donnie had beat her a little too much, hit her hard, blacked her eye and cracked a rib so that she had to go to the hospital and was hurting so bad she couldn't go to work. When my uncle found out about it, he got a really cold, hard look like she had never seen before.

She didn't know what happened, but Donnie didn't come around or bother her anymore after that, she said, and the one time he saw her, he almost ran the other way. That's when she started going with Jimmy and couldn't believe how nice a guy he was and how well he treated her.

"So, thanks, Mister," She said. "You're just like your uncle. He was always doing stuff like that and helping people who needed help, like the time he drove Mr. Johnson, who has the vegetable stand out front, all the way to Ft. Myers to see his daughter cause his truck broke down. She only had just a couple of hours on the way to Iraq where she was in the Army, or the way he treated Jimmy almost like a son, or the way he tried to help Ms. Mitchell."

"What did he do for Ms. Mitchell?"

"I don't really know everything about that. I know she had some medical problems. Connie could tell you better. I just know she can't do for herself now like she used to. She used to take care of everyone else, but now she can't take care of herself."

"She was a schoolteacher until she retired. She would bring a lot of us from the neighborhood home with her after school, and some would just come on their own because there was no one at home, and they just needed someplace safe to go until their moms or dads came home from work. There would be ten or fifteen of us there almost every night. She helped us with our homework, gave us books to read and cookies to eat, listened to us and asked us what we wanted to be."

"We called her Momma Madeline because she did things for us, but sometimes our mommas couldn't do things for us. We all became kind of close, sort of like a family, because we were always together and the way she was with us, and how she taught us how important it was to take care of each other."

"That's why when Connie – she's my best girlfriend – said Momma Madeline was confused by the doctors and needed help, I thought of your uncle."

"Did she talk with him, or did you?"

"She did. I introduced her and told him some about Momma Madeline, but Connie did most of the talking."

"When was this?"

"Oh, I don't know. A while back…Let me think. It was just before I took up with Jimmy. That was a year ago last Christmas."

"Will you see if Connie will talk with me about all this?"

"Sure. No problem. She sees Momma Madeline almost every day. I go by every once in a while, but it gets harder with my work and the way she is now. Don't make no difference to Connie, though."

That night, I double-checked the alarms. My intruder might have been missed and might not. They might have thought he had taken the money and skipped. They might have thought he was avoiding their calls. They might have thought he was working up his nerve. Or they might be the cautious types and decide to send someone or a team of someones to come and check. I wasn't taking any chances. I knew there was more to come.

I pulled the Sig out of its cubbyhole, broke it down, put it back together, and checked the action. Then, I attached the suppressor, inserted a full clip, and jacked one into the chamber. I put the gun on my nightstand next to my phone.

With the way the security system was now programmed, any breach would trigger an alarm and light up my phone. The gun would be right there where I could see it and within easy reach. I would be ready to welcome intruders within five seconds. Such precautions were now necessary. I knew they were coming. I just didn't know when. And I didn't know how. I didn't know who or how many. And I didn't know why.

In the morning, I would go looking for Madeline Mitchell. She might be able to answer some of my questions.

Young Diogenes

Madeline Mitchell kick-started the pacemaker investigation. All it took was a letter.

It's a good example of the way things are supposed to work in Washington, but rarely do, the way you see it in the movies and hardly ever see it in real life. It's also as good an example as any of why Colgate hired me. No one else would have handled it the way I did.

Most Congressional offices have clerks who screen the thousands of letters and emails they receive and put them in buckets for easy response. Most offices would have dropped Madeline's letter into the "benefit of your views" bucket, dismissing her as a cranky, addled LOP (Little Old Person) and put her letter in a pile to be answered by a computer, one of a number of robo-letters prepared in advance to cover common requests and concerns.

"Dear Ms. Mitchell,"

The letter would read,

> *"I have received your letter of December 7 and want to thank you for giving me the benefit of your views on this important matter."*

In most cases, the Senator or Congressman never sees his constituent's letter or, for that matter, his response since an autopen signs the letters.

Colgate has a different instinct. It comes from the corporate world, where the bottom line teaches the importance of listening to customers and taking their complaints seriously. You can get away with ignoring your constituents, but ignoring your customers is always costly and often fatal.

Smart executives keep their ears to the ground and respond quickly and completely. They take every complaint seriously because they know there are thousands of people who share a concern for everyone who expresses it.

That kind of responsiveness has largely been lost in politics, which now operates with the functional understanding that while all men are created equal, some people are more equal to others. The system has increasingly become top-down and money-driven rather than bottom-up.

Constituents' concerns have been lost to ideology and indifference. What I do or don't do is less important than what I want you to believe because my re-election is more important than satisfying your needs. That's why so many things supported by the vast majority of Americans never make it into law. Money trumps constituent concerns every time.

Perhaps in large part because he has all the money he will ever need, Colgate comes at it from the opposite direction. He is one of those rare people who has the looks, talent, and resources to do literally anything he wants. He chose politics because it allows him to address big problems – the problems we all face – and answer the most persistent question in life: "What are you going to do about it?"

He came looking for me because he knows where he wants to go and what he wants to do, and he knows he will have to work with the best to get there. That's where I come in. That's not a boast. It's an objective fact measured by the way such things are measured on The Hill – dollars saved, criminal prosecutions, and, most important of all, press. It is no accident that I hold the record for the number of cameras at a staff-generated event on The Hill.

Yes, they do keep track of such things. That's the one thing every Member cares about. Rule of thumb. At any Congressional hearing, you can count on at least one Member for every camera present. I've seen staff members assigned to the Committee hightail it for the office when they realize they have misjudged an event. The last thing you want as a junior staffer is the unpleasant task of explaining to your boss why he missed a chance to get some free airtime.

There is no secret to my success. You just have to be willing to put in the work and be a little creative. First, you mop up and review all the papers that are out there.

You need to know everything that has been said or written about whatever you are investigating. The Library of Congress is an excellent resource. They have 170 million books and a copy of everything in print on any and every subject you can think of – journals, magazines, newspapers, digital files, social media, you name it. A Senator, or you in his name, can access all of it with a simple request.

The second step comes from the first. A paper review raises questions and helps identify people you need to talk with, people who can extend your knowledge, answer what questions you have, and suggest more. The good news is that if you work for the Senate, no one is out of bounds, no one is off limits, no one is going to say "no" to you. There's no one you can't reach. If you want to talk with the head of an agency, a corporate executive, or the editor of the New England Journal of Medicine, you do.

Unfortunately, most Congressional investigations stop there – if they get that far. Most Committees are content to know what's on the record and what people think of what other people think. They call a hearing, invite people with contrasting views – weighted toward people who share the position they want to advance – and call it a day.

Their end is my beginning. I want to extend what's on paper. I want to know more than anyone else knows. I want first-hand knowledge and direct evidence. If there is criminal activity, I want to see the bad guys up close, close enough to hear and smell them, close enough to kick them in the balls when the time comes. I want to see them in action – if possible. Then, I want to find a way to dramatize the problem so that other people can see what I have seen, understand it the way I do it, and feel obligated to do something about it.

When Madeline Mitchell's letter came in, it ignited this process. In a shaky, looping cursive that showed her age and perhaps her eyesight, she wrote:

"You may not be the one to handle this problem; if not, you will know who to give it to."

Her letter said she was 83 years old and had just had surgery to replace her pacemaker. She wanted to know why she had to have this surgery. Her pacemaker seemed to be working fine, she said. And she didn't know how it could be defective because when they put it in, they told her it had a lifetime guarantee.

So, why did she have to go to the hospital again? Why did she have to have another operation? Why was Medicare being charged for another pacemaker and the replacement of the device if it was guaranteed? How many hundreds of these things were called in all over the country, she wondered, how many other seniors were involved, and how many thousands of dollars had it cost Medicare?

"When a car under warranty is called in, there is no expense to the customer,"

She concluded.

"Why should Medicare pay for this?"

It was a strong letter from a tough old bird who was nobody's fool. She wasn't going to let anyone take advantage of her without making a fuss. Writing the Committee was just part of the fuss she wanted to make. It didn't take me long to decide to help her. She was asking questions that deserved answers.

When I came to work for PSI, I felt like they had handed me a giant spotlight. They basically told me I could shine that light on anyone or anything the Senate and the public should know about. That's why I enjoyed it. I took delight in exposing the bad guys, shining the light on the leeches that feed on the taxpayer and taking advantage of poor and older people like Madeline.

In law school, Doc English used to challenge my instincts. He said I had an overdeveloped sense of justice. "Young Diogenes," he called me.

Doc was an old Philadelphia trial lawyer. He knew the way it was. What he said wasn't meant to be a compliment.

"If you're looking for justice," Doc would say, "Get yourself a lantern and go look somewhere else because you won't find it here."

Whatever else you could say about Doc, he was right about that. After 40 years in the bear pit, he knew the law was just a spider web constructed to catch insects and small creatures. Bigger, greedier animals just break through – often without even slowing down.

PSI is my lantern. No matter how big they are, no

matter how bad they are, there is nowhere they can hide when I turn the light of the Senate on them – particularly when I can multiply the effect of the Senate's spotlight by inspiring, refracting and connecting with the thousands of other lights the media provides, showering the landscape with light until the sharpies and wise guys and bottom feeders and indifferent bureaucrats have nowhere to hide and stand naked and exposed for what they are.

I had no reason to think Madeline Mitchell was not telling the truth, but I had to be sure. I had to start by checking her out. Was she some kook – one of the tin-hat people – or was she who she said she was? Did she, in fact, have two operations and receive two pacemakers in two years? If so, where, why, who ordered it, and who paid for it?

I called Frank Kontas, the Senate's liaison to the Inspector General at DHS. I asked him to pull Madeline's Medicare records and send me a copy. That took a week. About par for the course. The bureaucracy is not known for the speed of its response – even for a Senate request.

When Madeline's file finally came in, I was surprised by how thin it was. It was the record of someone who didn't particularly like going to the doctor.

Some seniors go to the emergency room with a hang-nail and call their doctor every time they sneeze. It's almost a social occasion for them – someone to talk to, someone who will listen to their problems.

Others tend to avoid the doctor like the plague – unless they have the plague – and only go to the hospital when someone compels them to go. Madeline was clearly one of the latter, but she was telling the truth.

She had, in fact, been hospitalized twice and received two pacemakers in two years. Medicare paid $12,000 for each of the two devices. There were additional hospital expenses – $25,000 – and physician charges totaling $17,000. There was no explanation for either procedure other than the initial diagnosis.

Meanwhile, I received a response to my request from The Library of Congress – a printout six inches thick. I marked the index, told them what I wanted to see, and sent it back. While I waited for hard copies of these articles, I asked the Federal Trade Commission, the Veterans Administration, the Securities and Exchange Commission, and the Food and Drug Administration to search their records as well.

It took three months to gather and go through all the papers they produced – medical journals, industry periodicals, newspaper reports, technical papers, professional journals, and corporate reports – and another couple of weeks to identify all the people I wanted to interview. It becomes a rolling list. Everyone you talk to suggests someone else.

Along the way, I learned the little old lady had put her finger on a big problem. Six companies were controlling 95 percent of the industry. They were billing the government for $2 billion a year and had operated largely without professional review for 20 years, drifting into some bad habits and corrupt practices. Some of the things they were doing were truly outrageous.

To make sure my backside was covered as the investigation advanced, I found out where the companies' headquarters and satellite offices were located and cross-indexed them with records from the Federal Election Commission. I wanted to see who they had given money to and how many political contributions they had made directly or through their subsidiaries. I found donations to half of Congress.

There was no surprise there. All the big corporations do it. They may have a favorite, but they all cover their bets. They can't afford to be wrong and be shut out without access to a member with a memory and a grudge. This is the fundamental rule for lobbyists in Washington: Money is like manure. You have to spread it around.

Three members of PSI were heavily involved with multiple contributions and personal ties. Their connections were strong enough that I knew I would have to seal them off. I couldn't afford to be ambushed and have the credibility of the Committee undercut. I had learned that lesson the hard way. When personal interests are threatened, sometimes truth and justice do not apply. I made the Member in question regret it, but it took a couple of years.

When it came down to the wire, and we did the math, adding up all the scams, we concluded half of the $2 billion Medicare paid for pacemakers and pacemaker procedures every year was being wasted or stolen. Pacemakers that cost $500 to $600 to make were being sold to hospitals for $4,000 to $5,000. Hospitals increased the cost by 50 to 150 percent and passed the total on to Medicare.

That fat profit margin and the lack of scrutiny created a lucrative business and inspired a lot of creative marketing – kickbacks, consulting fees, and other illegal arrangements – all passed on to the taxpayer. Pacemaker salespeople were publicly bragging about pulling in a million dollars a year. The companies they worked for were showing double-digit growth.

Much of this waste was the government's fault. Medicare had not kept up with the advances of science. Pacemaker procedures had evolved from open-heart surgery 25 to 30 years ago to a quick outpatient procedure that could be done nearly anywhere by nearly anyone.

Medicare had never adjusted its payment schedule to reflect this fact. They were still paying doctors and hospitals at the same rate for what was no longer the same procedure.

Doctors shared the blame. The greedy ones were doing as many pacemaker procedures as possible, encouraged by everything from direct cash to stock options in the manufacturing company, payments for clinical evaluations, vacations in the Caribbean, fishing excursions in Alaska and the Gulf of Mexico, gambling junkets, and premium rewards like gold-plated shotguns, Rolex watches, jewelry, and all kinds of pacemaker accessories. It was a fat, greedy circle.

The Sting

After six months, I felt like we knew what the story was, and I had a good idea of how I wanted to make the case. I was going to get into the business.

I called in some favors and arranged to pose as the purchasing agent for a hospital in the Bronx and then a geriatric center in San Francisco. I needed one sting to validate the other. I wanted to show we were dealing with a national problem and bank the kind of evidence that could make that case while carving out local angles tasty and specific enough to interest multiple media markets.

I called the local number for each of the pacemaker firms and invited them to come in and make their pitch. My friends in New York made it easy for me. They gave me one of the offices in the psychiatric ward. There was a one-way glass already in place and an adjacent room for my cameraman to set up, film, and watch.

First up in New York was a representative from the industry leader. They were the oldest and most established company in the business. Their salesman was very New York, with a round face, lots of nose, big ears, and a sharkskin suit. He was well-groomed and well-fed. He set the tone for what would follow.

I told him I was the hospital's new purchasing agent and wanted to get the lay of the land.

"The first thing you should know is that the industry is totally unconcerned about price," He said, "Couldn't care less. Medicare reimburses everything, and they just don't care. God bless them. I love it."

One by one, his competitors paraded in after him, each offering their version of the best deal. There was no conversation about the devices or the benefit of their product versus another. It was all about the numbers and what they could do for me. Some were greedier than others, but they were all playing the same game. No exceptions.

The only wrinkle came late in the day. After a few minutes of conversation, the saleswoman representing GerriCare came around the desk and tried to sit on my lap. She was dark and dramatic, very animated, and apparently determined to do whatever she had to do to make the sale.

She said her firm was the last to enter this line of business. They made other geriatric products and had just branched out into pacemakers a few years before. They were the Avis of the industry. They had to try harder.

"Let me tell you a little bit about the way we work," She said. "We won't charge you for the paperwork or to train someone how to set up monitoring for the clinic because, obviously, no doctor is going to sit by the telephone all day and monitor patients."

"How long does that take - -"

"Five minutes. Not even 5 minutes."

"How much can I bill for that?"

"You bill $200. It's unbelievable. You can make one-quarter of a million dollars a year with a clerk just doing this --"

"For how many patients?"

"Around 400. I know a group here in Brooklyn that has 400 pacemaker patients – 400 that they are following. They take in well over one-quarter of a million dollars – just with monitoring."

"Sounds easy."

"It's very easy. A nurse can do 16 an hour very easily. And you're not paying anything…I mean stamps."

"Stamps?"

"You have to pay stamps, right? Because you are mailing your bills in. That's basically it."

In San Francisco, Mary Louise, a good friend, met me at the door of the geriatric center. She ran to me and handed me her keys.

"You are in charge," She said. "I'm going on vacation."

I tried not to run the place into the ground while she was gone. We set up in her office, put a microphone in a potted plant near her desk, and built a camera position by replacing a window with a one-way glass.

The same six companies were called. The same creatures appeared. If anything, they were a little more obvious, a little bolder. It was California, after all.

"Programmers, we provide free of charge. If you need one, two, or three, we will provide those for you," One salesman offered.

He wore a tan suit to go with his tan complexion, a gold watch and a pair of Gucci shoes. The devices he was offering in such abundance sell for $2500 a piece and are used to adjust the operating parameters of a pacemaker.

"Do you have a basic system analyzer?" He continued.

"No."

"It costs $3500. If we do business, we can get you one. All our equipment is offered totally free of charge."

He placed a half dozen pieces of electronic equipment between us on the desk and began to itemize.

"We wouldn't charge you for transmitters."

Transmitters are used to monitor the pacemaker's performance. They sell for about $250.

"That's one per person, right?"

"We'll give you dozens. We'll send dozens."

"What about a receiver?"

Receivers catch the transmitter's signals. They sell for $3000.

"You can have five or six receivers – whatever you want."

The next man came from GerriCare. Like his sister in New York, he seemed inclined to try harder. He was a dark man with a $200 haircut and a $1,000 suit.

"How does it work?" I asked.

"Are you a cardiologist?"

"No."

"Doesn't matter."

"We can send you to Florida and train you to put in pacemakers yourself."

"How long does it take?"

"Fifteen minutes if everything goes well."

"I mean the training."

"Oh, that. Three or four days. A little longer if you want to go fishing with us while you are there. You can bill it as a professional seminar."

"How difficult is it?"

"The training?"

"The procedure."

"It's relatively easy. Fifteen minutes, and you can bill between $4,000 and $5,100. Do you have a basic system analyzer?"

"No."

"It costs $3500. If we do business, we can get you one. I'll also go into the operating room with you. I'll scrub up, and I'll go in with you. I'll do all the measurements. I can help coax you along in placing the leads."

As he was leaving, he tried to close.

"Any pacemaker salesman will do anything for you," He said. "Face it, prices aren't that different. What it comes down to is service. We do anything you can think of, and if you can think of it but we aren't doing it, we'll start."

"What we want is for your doctors to use our pacemaker as much as possible. We pride ourselves on follow-up. With our no-hassle warranty, if you replace a competitor's product with ours, we give you a $500 credit."

That capped it. I hadn't seen that much concentrated greed in a while.

When I gave the keys back to Mary Louise, I was confident I could make my case. I came home and prepared to go to a hearing. I wrote a report summarizing the Committee's findings and sent it on to the Government Printing Office for publication.

I sent Colgate an executive summary as part of my status report. He responded with a personal note.

"This is going to be fun, T.J. Thanks!"

Then I started working the press. I contacted a friend who is a producer from *60 Minutes* and gave him an exclusive for a story previewing the hearing's findings the Sunday night before the Monday hearing. I told him he could use some of our hidden camera footage. He loved it.

With *60 Minutes* on board, I called another friend with *The New York Times*, walked him through the investigation over lunch and promised him the lead with an advance copy of the report if he agreed to embargo it until Monday morning.

It's all about building momentum. I knew the print media would follow the *Times'* lead and the broadcast media would follow *60 Minutes*.

With the media on track, I began working with the Committee. I chopped off pieces and specific angles of the story to parse out to sympathetic Members. It's not enough for them to say they were there, listening to the hearing. They need something specific to sell to the hometown press, a local angle or something that would advance the story even a little, something they could own.

With the friends in line, I sat down for a "come to Jesus" discussion with the three members of the Committee who could be problematic. I told them each, one by one, that I know one of these companies is based in your state and that they have contributed to your campaign. You may even have some personal relationships with their executives, so if you want to take a bullet for them, I'll understand. However, you need to understand what you are getting into if you do.

Here's part of a surveillance tape we shot, I said. It will air Sunday night on *60 Minutes*. Here is a copy of the Committee's report. The *Times* is going to lead with it Monday morning.

You know me, and you know what this hearing is going to be like. We will have saturation press. Every newspaper. Every TV station. Colgate is not going to pull any punches. These guys may or may not be your friends, but they have broken the law. A copy of the Committee's files has already been sent to the FBI. Criminal charges will almost surely follow.

If you feel strongly enough about this, you might have to justify that as well. The bottom line, I think, is that if you show up and defend them, it's not going to do them any good, and it will undoubtedly do you some harm. So, if you feel like you want to be somewhere else Monday morning, we will understand.

The exit line is important. You have to give them a way out. You have to give them a way to save face because your worst enemy on this issue is likely to be your best friend on the next. It's not personal. It's politics. Somewhere down the line, you will need them.

When you look them in the eye and see their reaction to the story, you can tell which ones are going to duck and run and which ones are willing to fight it and go down in flames. There aren't a lot of heroes, but you want to mark the ones who think they are, watch them, and perhaps investigate them down the line. There is something wrong with anyone willing to defend blatant corruption.

The final act is to focus on the Chairman's role and make sure he gets the credit he deserves. He is the one that handed you the spotlight. He is the one providing the resources. He is the one they will go after when it's over with PACs and soft money and phony, partisan stories.

I set him up by calling Madeline Mitchell and asking her to come to Washington to read her letter and start the hearing. She symbolized all the people affected and made the story real. Then, I gave Colgate an opening statement that summarized everything we had found and let him conclude by playing an edited version of the surveillance tapes.

The testimony of industry witnesses, medical professionals and representatives of the corporations involved followed, but the story was in the tapes, and everyone knew it. Everything else was a footnote.

Colgate handled it like the thoroughbred he is. The press loved the story, and they loved him. M.J. was standing near the exit into the Committee's antechamber. I saw her nod, a slight bow of the head, like the tipping of your hat when you are not wearing a hat.

As the final scene played out, Jerry Chambers, CEO of GerriCare, worked his way through the press and asked for a few moments of my time. He was around 60, thin, with the sharp, bony face of a marathon runner. In Hollywood, he could have been typecast as an undertaker. His clothes were probably worth more than the average person's car.

In his testimony, Chambers had tried valiantly to offer a defense, saying his company was just doing what everyone else was doing, but he knew no one was buying it. All the companies were complicit, but GerriCare was by far the most aggressive.

Chambers told me he wanted to know what came next. I was puzzled at first. I told him the investigation was over. We had made our recommendations to the Department and turned over our files to the FBI.

I saw his eyes flinch. They were pale and slightly discolored with tinges of yellow around the iris. He stared at me with the patient passivity of an old gator. He never blinked. Even though he didn't show it, I knew I had disturbed his equanimity. I wanted to extend it as much as possible.

If you are looking for advice, I told him, I would say you need a fall guy because the FBI is almost certainly going to nail someone for this, and then I would hire the best PR agent you can find. Blame it on the toxic nature of the industry. Perhaps you came to the party late and just did what you had to do to catch up and compete. Now you know better, you are determined to turn things around and help lead the reform.

"Try it," I said. "It might even work. History shows people will buy almost anything."

To my surprise, Chambers said he wasn't concerned about the pacemaker industry. That damage was done. His stock had already lost half its value and would probably fall further. He was concerned about the rest of his product line. He was concerned about the survival of his company.

I didn't try to make him feel better. In fact, I wanted him to sweat. I had no doubt the rest of his company operated the same way his pacemaker division did. There was blood in the water now. We had made him vulnerable, and he had to be wondering who else would be coming after him. Is some DOJ officer looking to make a name for himself? The FBI? One of his competitors?

And the last thing I was going to do was let him off the hook. In the seven previous years, his firm had increased revenues by a hundredfold. You don't do that without playing games unless you are Bill Gates, and I didn't see any resemblance.

Chambers went home and cut his losses. In the months that followed, his stock fell to $10 from a high of $70. The company pleaded guilty to paying kickbacks of up to $170,000. The company's national sales manager took the bullet and entered a guilty plea. I'm sure there was a golden parachute waiting on the other side. Chambers held a press conference and said he had cleaned house and was turning the page.

Maybe he had. Maybe he had forgotten me. Maybe he hadn't.

And maybe someone else was coming for me. Chambers isn't the only one whose dish I have rattled. I can think of a number of other people who would like to nail my hide to the shed. Some have already tried. I knew there were others still lurking around in the shadows, hoping for a clear shot.

I knew now what had happened to my uncle. I still didn't know who, why or how, but the potential connection through Madeline was a valuable insight. I had to find out how strong that was. And how was he tied into all this? Who knew we were related when I didn't know we were related? I didn't have a clue, but I was going to find out.

GerriCare

Wednesday, May 25. The rain came. They said it was just a passing storm. I guess every storm is.

This one took its time, lingering over the bay most of the day – not a hard rain, but a steady grey rain, coming from the south, muting and marrying the colors of land and sea. It suited my mood.

I stayed buttoned up in the Two Deuce, working on the computer and getting acquainted with all the bells and whistles on my uncle's playpen. It was hard to find fault with her other than a growing sense that her name really didn't work for me.

Meyer said the name was inspired by a poker game that had earned my uncle his first houseboat. It was hard for me to associate with that distant event. It may have had meaning at some point, but it didn't register with me.

If I kept her, and that seemed to be a more complicated decision than I initially thought, I decided I would have to rechristen her – the Big Girl maybe or better still, the Big Doll. The more I rolled it around in my mind, the more it seemed to fit.

However, named, she was a little much for me, but I could see and appreciate the thought that went into building her. It was a waterman's wet dream – "If I ever buy or build another boat, I'll make sure there is plenty of room to move, room to entertain, places to meditate, ways to let the world in, ways to shut the world out."

I wanted the latter on this dreary day, time to separate from the herd and find a quiet space to think. I pulled the heavy curtains and shut myself off from the dock and all signs of civilization. I left the curtains on the south side open so I could see and feel the rain descending.

I felt out of place and out of sync. I attacked my discomfort with an hour and a half of exercise, working off the furniture and the floor in the lounge. I finished by seeing how long I could hold a plank, switching arms, holding my core steady until the perspiration flowed and my arms started to wobble.

When I was pleasantly exhausted, I took a bottle of water with me and went swimming in the bathtub. It was decadent, but it felt good to be able to stretch out in the hot water. Most tubs scrunch me up like a kid muscling a Coke can. Part of me is always bent over or sticking out. This was a new and pleasant experience.

After a simple salad, I stretched out on the big bed with the laptops – his and mine. I wanted to go snooping on his computer to see what else I could find.

There wasn't much. No Gmail. No Facebook. I searched documents and came up blank. There was a folder for the boat – builder's specs and service records – and another folder for the security system. Recent items took me back to my folders.

There was only one item that I didn't recall seeing. It was in a folder attached to his pacemaker file. I opened it and found a link to three articles. I clicked on the first one. It opened to one of those "local angle" stories I always tried to stimulate in conjunction with a hearing.

This one focused on Jerry Chambers and GerriCare. The author was Lorraine Charles, a reporter with the *Miami Sun.* It was straight hearing coverage with a sidebar on Madeline Mitchell. It was a nice piece, accurate and fairly written, though a sliver of admiration for Ms. Mitchell came through.

The second article, dated a week later, reported fallout from the hearing. It suggested GerriCare was struggling to stay afloat. An unidentified source said Chambers had barely escaped a vote of no confidence and was desperately looking for a way to shore up the company and hold on.

The third article, dated about the time my uncle was said to have disappeared, focused on Chambers' personal problems and his lifestyle now said to be in jeopardy. Joe Morgan's name was added to Charles' byline.

A source speculated Chamber's home on the 3100 block of Gordon Drive, one of the jewels on Millionaires' Row, would soon be on the market. Real estate agents were said to be licking their chops. There was a photo of the sprawling property with a credit to Morgan.

The home was said to be located just above the Governor's mansion and valued at $45 million. Chambers was quoted as saying the rumors were false. He was not having financial difficulties, and he had no intention of selling his home.

I switched to my laptop and ran a search on Lorraine Charles. A number of more recent articles popped up – at least one, sometimes two a week. There were three more articles on Chambers.

The fourth article in that series profiled GerriCare's decision to broaden its portfolio and move from manufacturing products for seniors – pacemakers, intraocular lenses, and equipment used in hip and joint repair – to direct service. Chambers said the company was vertically integrating and rebranding everything as GerriCare, a comprehensive service company.

The fifth article was a puff piece, reporting on a charitable event Chambers hosted at his home to benefit Eldercare. Governor Divos was the guest of honor. Twelve hundred people were in attendance at $20,000 a couple. Top benefactors – limited to 10 couples at $50,000 a couple – were invited to conclude the evening with an overnight cruise with their host and the Governor.

Two photographs with Morgan's credit was attached. One showed the midnight march of the select – still dressed in their formal attire – to the limos that would shuttle them the short distance to Port Royal. In the second photo, the beaming host stood next to the Governor on the deck of his yacht, waving to the crowd that had been left behind.

The last story reported a remarkable turnaround for GerriCare, with 1st quarter numbers far exceeding expectations. The stock was working its way back up to its prehearing high. Analysts were bullish on the company and its prospects.

A photo search yielded a lot of people named Lorraine Charles. She might have been one of them, but there was no way to know. A search with the name of her newspaper attached drew a blank. Given how prolific she was, that said something. She was more interested in covering the story than being the story.

There was a Twitter account associated with the paper, but no Facebook or LinkedIn. Nothing personal.

Maybe it's understandable. Some members of the press deserve combat pay these days. There are too many haters. Too many people don't want to hear anything that disturbs preconceived notions, nothing that challenges them to think. It is better and easier to shout it down as Fake News and threaten anyone with a message that rattles their thought cage.

I checked my inbox and found a report from Christoff. First installment, he said. More to come. SafeCo was a small Florida firm with big plans. Their website promised "Serious Security."

There were three principals – Ray Scartizina, Willard Wolfe, and Diego Foster – who all advertised as former Special Ops. There is no list of clients. No reviews. No public comments on social media.

D&B reported significant income–income disproportion to a firm of their size. The Department of Defense confirmed the service of the three principles but refused to provide details. Their records were sealed.

There was something big under the cover, something either really good or something really bad – so bad no one wanted to talk about it. Christoff said he was just getting started. More to come.

I closed the file and put in a call to M.J. It was near the end of the day. Colgate was gone, so there was no reason for her to stay late, but she is the kind of person who checks her messages religiously. I left a message asking her to see if Colgate had time to make a call. I wanted to see that DOD file.

While I had my computer up, I went to my hearing folders and opened Madeline Mitchell's file. I found her address and phone number. Most coastal cities are built out of the water, like a layer cake. The icing is always along the coast. The layers get sketchier and poorer as you move inland.

Mitchell was in East Naples in Naples Park. It looked like an established area where you would expect to find transitional people and life-long residents holding on against the development tide moving in from the west.

It was just after seven. I debated about whether I should call her or wait until the morning. I finally decided it wasn't that late. To my surprise, she answered on the second ring. The phone must have been near her.

Yes, she remembered me, she said, after a little prodding. The fact that I had to remind her where we met three times suggested she didn't remember me all that well. She said she would be pleased to see me in the morning. Maybe sometime around ten before the medical people arrived.

The rains were slowing down, but I could still hear that most relaxing sound of raindrops striking the roof and windows. Small waves moved against The Big Doll – as I was starting to call her – rocking her gently to sleep. I shut down and put the computer aside.

The alarms were set. The Sig was still by my bed. I picked up the latest Thomas Friedman and settled in for the night. It's always nice to learn something, and Friedman never fails.

The Hunt Is On

Thursday, May 26, 6:30 AM. Colgate woke me up. I knew who it was before I answered the call. Not many people have my cell number. Not many of them would risk using it that time of the morning.

"T.J.?"

I smiled. He is one of the few people that prefers using that handle. Not that he has anything against calling me by my given name. I think he does it for the same reason Mary Jane is always M.J. It suggests a greater level of familiarity and confidence.

"Yes, Sir."

"Are you OK?"

"I am, but what I thought was nothing is maybe turning into something. Maybe it was a hangover from our last investigation. Maybe something else. I don't know."

"M.J. gave me your request. Your instincts are probably right. I spoke with the Pentagon this morning. It was not pleasant. After hearing what they had to say, I can understand their reluctance to go public."

"You are dealing with some nasty people, T.J. Be careful. Christoff will forward their files to you this morning. If you don't have them by noon, call me."

"Yes, Sir. Thank you."

I smiled again. When Colgate said he had an unpleasant conversation with the Pentagon, I didn't have to imagine how that went. He is not the kind of person you want to say "no" to.

If you are so inclined, he disabuses you of that notion in a hurry. It's what I expected. You don't bring out the big gun unless you are prepared to fire it. It doesn't hurt that he is a member of the Armed Services. I was eager to see what was in those files.

Once I'm up, I'm up. There was no going back to sleep. The alternative was to put on some sweats and get some exercise.

I locked up, set my security system, and started a light jog. I was immediately glad I did. It was a spectacular morning, scrubbed by the rain. Everything looked shiny and new.

I took 7th Street South until 14th Street South and then on to Gordon Drive, trying to stay as close to the water as possible so I could watch the sun coming up over the Bay. Traffic was light. I picked up the rhythm and set a comfortable pace.

Years ago, I shared a barracks at Ft. Bragg, home of the 101st Airborne, with Kenny Moore. They ran our tails off. Kenny, a marathon runner out of Oregon, taught me how to keep up.

He said the key to distance running is more mental than physical. He said his secret was to save things to think about. Once he was out and running at the pace he wanted, he turned his mind to the topic he had stored and let the physical machine run on automatic.

So, when I found the right rhythm, I locked in and thought about my uncle, wondering why he had entered my life after so many years, wondering what happened to him and what I could do about it.

I thought about his relationship with Meyer and had to wonder if there was anyone that close in my life. Sam came fleetingly to mind, and then the mind moved on. It wasn't that kind of relationship.

I wondered what was in the file Colgate had pried away from the DOD. When they bury something that deep, it has to be something particularly embarrassing or particularly ugly – something that "would not bring credit" to the service, as they are inclined to say.

Without intent or conscious thought, I found myself at The Port Royal Club. The size of the boats in the harbor should have gotten my attention long before it did. I slowed to a jog and admired these big boy toys, checking them out one by one.

There was no one around. These were sunshine sailors, not working boats. They had no reason to go out until their hangovers wore off.

It wasn't hard to find what I was looking for: the largest yacht in the harbor positioned at the end of the dock closest to the Club. It was at least 280' with a helipad. Two dancing stick figures, one with a cane, had been drawn on the steel hull with a caption that probably doubled for the name of the boat – "GerriAntics."

I jogged to the end of the dock, turned around and jogged back, picking up my pace along the way—one more thing to think about.

After a shower and a hearty breakfast – a four-egg frittata with bell peppers and feta cheese – I headed over to East Naples. I took the Tamiami Trail to Rattlesnake, then on to Collier and looped back around.

Naples Park was east of the airport in a mixed-use area. There were some run-down streets with dilapidated housing, some renewal streets showing signs of redevelopment, and some well-kept older houses.

Madeline was in one of the latter, a rancher in the middle of the block with a small, surprisingly well-kept yard. There was a rocker on one end of a small porch. I could almost see her sitting there back in the day before TV drove everyone indoors, watching the neighborhood and keeping an eye out for the kids.

The house was beige with blue storm shutters and a blue door. There were no chips or flakes of paint. I knocked on the door and waited the ten minutes it took for her to answer.

I wasn't prepared for what I saw. The woman who had come to Washington was a pistol. Sharp as a tack. Lively. A small, grey-haired woman with dark eyes, fully engaged, relishing every moment of the experience, wanting to know everything that was going to happen.

The light had gone out in the eyes of the woman who met me at the door. She stared at me vacantly, trying to focus and remember who I was, uncertain why I was there. She held on to the edge of the door for support. There was a walker a step behind her.

"Are you from the clinic?"

"No, Ma'am. I'm from the Senate. We talked last night."

She had to search her memory. It seemed buried a long way back.

"That's right," She said, pointing a bony finger at me. "You are the man from Washington."

She shifted to her walker and invited me in. The place was neat as a pin, but every flat space was chock-a-block with pictures, plates, and glass figurines – the accumulated mementos of a lifetime.

There was a gas fireplace that looked like it hadn't been used in years. The mantel was filled with photographs—pictures of Madeline with children in groups of two, three, or more.

She sat in a recliner and invited me to sit down on the sofa next to her. It was grey with laced doilies covering the back where a head might rest. She said she didn't have long to talk because the people from the clinic were coming for her soon. She seemed very anxious about that. Her purse was on the coffee table near her, ready to grab and go.

Just a check-up, she said. The house seemed to bear that out. There was none of the medical clutter we have come to expect in a senior's house. No pill bottles. No devices. No antacids or other over-the-counter meds were visible.

They came for her once a week and brought her back home after she had seen the doctor, she said.

Her eyes kept leaving me, and she darted to the window like she was hoping they might appear, afraid they might not come or that she might miss them. She said she had enjoyed coming to Washington but didn't seem to remember much about it.

Dementia is cruel. Some people lose large swaths of their past, and there are people who remember everything but what they did yesterday. You rarely lose both at the same time. It can happen, but it's rare.

She couldn't help me with any specific information and seemed unsettled by my questions, struggling to find answers that escaped her, all the while checking the window. She didn't seem to remember my uncle. It would have helped if I had a photograph, but as far as I knew, none were available.

After a few more moments, I concluded there was nothing to be gained by pushing her, so I thanked her and took my leave. I wanted to get out of her house before her medical transport arrived.

My car was parked halfway down the street. I waited and watched. There wasn't much going on in her neighborhood. No real activities. No neighbors are coming or going. Those who worked were at work. Kids, if there were kids, were in school. There were no soccer nets, basketball hoops or other signs inviting play.

Most suburban homes have two cars in the driveway and one on the street because there is no room in the garage for a car – let alone two. The cars in sight were older and spread out. There was plenty of parking on both sides of the street, including in front of Madeline's house. If she had a car, it wasn't visible.

At 10:45, a car much like the one I was driving pulled up and double-parked. The driver got out and walked up to her front door. He was wearing a collared shirt with a colorful tropical print.

He was around six feet tall and weighed somewhere around 200 pounds. She came out with her walker. He helped her navigate the uneven pavement where the porch met the walkway and stayed at her side until she reached the car. He settled her into the passenger seat, closed her door, and stowed her walker in the back seat. The whole interaction suggested familiarity and routine.

He took off heading east. I started my car and followed them. He worked through the neighborhood for about 15 minutes until he found a sprawling shopping center just short of Collier.

Up north, they would have built it on a third of the space, stacking retail shops on top of retail shops with parking underneath. There were no multi-level units here. Everything was on ground level. There were three big chunks of retail spread out, flanked by parking lots with gas stations, bank branches, fast food and casual dining establishments scattered around the perimeter.

He went by the first cluster, anchored by a Publix, crossed a dividing street, and stopped before a storefront near the beginning of the second cluster. It was double billed as "GerriCare" and below that, in slightly smaller letters, "Centro Medico."

Joe Namath could have designed the window displays. If you believed the signs, there was no charge for the clinic's services. Everything was free with special deals for Medicare patients: Free Eyeglasses, Free Hearing, Free Prescriptions, Free Transportation, and No Co-Pays. The same signs were repeated in Spanish in the second window.

There were six reserved parking spaces in front of the clinic. Madeline's driver pulled into the first one, helped her out of the car, and escorted her in. I drove on by, circled around and found a place where I could watch the storefront. The clinic was busier than I expected. Lots of walk-ins and foot traffic. Something I didn't expect to see in Florida.

At 11:30, a senior van pulled up and parked, taking up two of the remaining parking spaces. The side door opened, a ramp came down, and the driver came around to help unload half a dozen seniors – mostly women, but two men, one with a cane.

The driver helped the man with a cane into the clinic, taking his arm and opening the door. The others gingerly made their way on ancient hips and tender feet. They were the survivors. The walking wounded.

As they unloaded, an orange Nissan 370Z backed out of space two rows down and turned onto the access road. It seemed out of place amid all the sedans and SUVs. I hadn't seen the driver coming or going.

My first thought was that it reflected someone's sad and sorry attempt to hold on to their youth, but I couldn't figure out how anyone of a significant age could get in the cockpit of that car without breaking a hip.

Ten minutes later, I saw its long, low hood coming back. The driver was a woman, and she didn't seem to be all that old. She was chewing on a French fry as she turned to park in the space she had just vacated.

I followed Madeline's car when she came out. Her visit had taken all of 35 minutes. Rather than go back the way he came, the driver continued up to the third retail cluster and slightly beyond and turned into the drive-through lane for a stand-alone drug store called Graul's Pharmacy.

I pulled up Google on my cell and found Graul's advertised itself as a locally owned, state-of-the-art, independent compounding pharmacy providing custom-made medication for a wide variety of practices. They were professional-grade and full-spectrum – whatever that means.

Fifteen minutes later, Madeline was on her way home, and I decided I needed to go shopping again. I let Warren buy me a few more Florida clothes: two pairs of khaki shorts, three golf shirts, two black and two white T-shirts and some deck shoes and then went looking for a camera.

I found Farrin Photography tucked away near the end of the shopping center next to a shoe shop. Farrin was a pleasant surprise. A woman who said she was Diane Farrin, so happy to meet me, was behind the counter.

The walls were covered with her prints – the kind of stuff every tourist hopes to shoot. There were brochures on the counter indicating she could teach you how to do it and posters advertising Old Naples Photo Tours, Everglades excursions, and customized photo safaris.

On the opposite wall, she had a number of cameras and stacks of camera equipment. She had a limited stock, but it had clearly been thought through so that she could respond to any level of interest.

The cameras were arranged by price from $50 for a

point-and-shoot Coolpix to high-end Canons and Nikons. I went to the end of the line and picked out a Nikon D5 DSLR. Farrin smiled her approval. I think I made her day.

I asked her about it without talking about my intended use. She said it would shoot 12 frames a second and could be adjusted to 4K UHD video recording at 30 FBSI. It was the camera she used.

She threw in all the cables, chargers, adapters, and accessories you would want for the bargain price of $3,999.95. I picked an outdoor safari lens – a Zoom Nikkor 70-300mm – to go with it. With tax and carrying cases, we were looking at five grand.

I handed her my Black America Express, the one backed by and billed to Colgate. It is a lot easier that way. If I had to go through channels, it would probably take 6 months. I could just see some paper pusher asking – "Why do you have that camera?"

The Black AmEx is given out by invitation only. Still, at least occasionally – once for sure – that invitation can be stimulated by the request of a backer who could buy American Express if he so chose.

As I came back to my car with my packages, I noticed the orange Nissan had repositioned. The driver seemed to be looking in my direction. It hadn't taken long for me to become a person of interest.

I settled back in my car and checked my phone. There were a couple of messages. Darleene said Carla had agreed to talk with me. She had tentatively arranged for dinner and left a number for a call back to confirm.

Christoff's message was short and quick, but then all his messages were short and quick.

"Call me," He said.

I confirmed with Darleene first and suggested that Tin Inn carry out The Big Doll, realizing as I did that this was the first time I had spoken her new name out loud. It came out naturally and seemed right. I made a mental note to ask Jimmy to do something about that.

Darleene didn't skip a beat. Maybe it seemed natural to her as well. She asked what I wanted for dinner. I said maybe some of that cauliflower and whatever else she would recommend. She knew the menu better than I did. I was going to invite Meyer to join us.

"The DOD file came in," Christoff said. "It's encrypted. I forwarded it to you at your Senate account. You won't have any trouble understanding why they are trying to keep it quiet. I also sent you a copy of the full D&B report on SafeCo. Read and respond when you can."

"I will. Meanwhile, see if there is anything recent you can pull up about our friends at Gerricare. Anything since the hearing. Interface them with SafeCo and see if you get any hits. And see what you can find at a clinic called GerriCare in Naples. Ask Kontas at the IG's office to pull their history – ownership, affiliated physicians and companies or other interests and any recent changes in activity or billing practices. Run a cross-check with Graul's Pharmacy. I'd particularly like to know if there is a formal connection and see if the pharmacy has a Medicare footprint. If they do, what are they billing?"

"Sounds like the hunt is on."

"It is," I said. "Maybe more than one.

All of Sudden He Was Gone

Thursday, May 27. The DOD report came with a letter of transmittal to Colgate from the head of the Army Special Operations Command. If I hadn't thought there was a problem before, I knew there was now.

The Commander made all the right noises, but he was trying too hard. He assured Colgate he had told subordinate leaders to work on their command cultures and address warning signs before they grew into incidents like the ones described in this report.

> "It is incumbent upon our leadership down to the team level to intensify our emphasis on values and character,"

He wrote.

> "Service is a privilege, and this privilege is grounded in a culture of accountability and profes-

sionalism that extends far beyond program compliance."

When they cover their asses that quickly and completely, you know it is bad – and it was. Scartizina, Wolfe, and Foster were, in fact, former Special Ops, but each one had a troubling history.

DOD's 5,300-page report summarized a year-long investigation of their service records. They had each been investigated previously for serious crimes and misconduct – including spouse abuse, assault, dereliction of duty, misuse of Federal property, and petty theft.

While they were individually problematic, in combination, they became toxic. They found each other in Iraq when they were assigned to the same unit. From the report, it was clear they validated and brought out the worst in each other, much like high school bullies. And it didn't take long.

The three of them were cited for excessive use of force after their first mission together. Other abuses were subsequently noted. Citations were issued, but the problems continued unabated.

Pure and simple, they were shooters, not soldiers. A good soldier knows when to shoot and how to shoot. More importantly, he knows when not to shoot. We will never know if Scartizina, Wolfe, and Foster were born the way they were and just looking for an outlet or if their blood lust developed out of the things they had seen and done, the things that they necessarily had to do, but somewhere, somehow, the human component – the spirit, the soul, compassion, empathy, and judgment – started breaking down.

Why they were doing what they were being asked to do got lost in the heat of what they were doing, the joy they found in pulling the trigger and blowing things up. It grew until it consumed them, culminating in a mission that all but wiped out a small village in Iraq.

Wolfe and Foster were enlisted men. Scartizina was their Staff Sergeant. He claimed they were pursuing insurgents who killed a member of their battalion with a roadside bomb in Al-Subhani, a neighborhood in Haditha. Still, no insurgents were found in the rubble – only women and children. Twenty-six women and ten children were killed.

Scartizina acknowledged in military court that he had given his men the order to "shoot first, ask questions later" after the roadside bomb explosion but denied shooting at women and children. He said the insurgents must have slipped away. He was given 90 days in prison along with a reduction in rank and pay.

Wolfe and Foster said they were just following orders and fired when told to fire. They said it was difficult to see who they were shooting at. They were just shooting back, but no weapons were found among the dead and – insanely – no wounded.

They received a reduction in rank and pay but no jail time. In other words, they got off easy – probably because the Army was more interested in protecting itself than punishing them. They should have been indicted for war crimes.

When they were released from the service a year later,

the trio joined ProTect, a private security firm for contractors working in Iraq and later Afghanistan. There were a series of civilian complaints in their file at ProTect, but nothing major until the final straw when they were cited for the unnecessary use of lethal force, resulting in the death of 17 people, including four children.

They were leading a security convoy for a contractor looking to make a deal when they ran into a traffic jam in Kabul. It probably started as nothing more than an accident snarling traffic, but the trio took it for an ambush, or maybe they just got impatient, fearful, and frustrated. They blasted their way through the traffic jam with grenades and machine guns, destroying two vehicles and damaging five more.

The casualties were all passengers. None were armed. No shots were fired at the convoy from the ground or any adjoining buildings. Scartizina, again the leader of the detail, defended their actions, saying, as he had before, that in situations like this, you have to shoot first and ask questions later.

No one was disciplined, but the stink was strong enough that ProTect withdrew the three shooters from the country. One would like to think they were trying to do the right thing, but it was more likely a business decision. The continued presence of these three mercenaries in the country put the contractor in a bad light. It made commerce difficult.

Read between the lines, and it is clear who they were or who they had become. Some people kill to feed their families, people who kill because they love to kill and get a sick thrill out of it, and people who just like blowing everything up, people who get a sick sense of power out of destroying things other people create.

I am a hunter, and I understand the hunter's purpose and ethics. I have hunted all my life. And, like most hunters, I have no use for killers, the killing bravely and well crap, and the only slightly more sophisticated versions of the Southern rednecks and New Jersey file clerks who swarm into the nearest mountains in the fall, fully decorated in the hunter costume by Wal-Mart, Bass, or Cabella with a three-day beard, 9-inch cigars, loaded with beer and carrying Uzis with banana clips ostensive to slay a wild turkey or a ferocious mule deer. Men, by and large, are in search of balls. You can tell them on the road by the cast iron set hanging from the bumper of the biggest truck they can afford. Nothing like advertising what you don't have.

Headshots of the three killers were included in their files. All were taken while they were still in the service. Three tough-looking marines in combat gear. I copied the photos on my desktop and sent them to print. I knew not where it went until I heard the sound of the printer booting up and a whir that reminded me I'd seen it in a cabinet near the safe in the galley.

The DOD's files were disturbing on a gut level. Every male member of my family has served. We honor those who went and never returned. We cherish and elevate all those who put their personal interests aside, leave family and friends, put their lives and futures on hold, and put them at risk to serve the country they love.

People like Scartizina, Foster and Wolfe dishonor them and all the others who wear or have worn the uniform. They hide behind the flag and spit in honor's eye. The more I processed it, the more I understood what I read was not something I was likely to be able to forget if and when we met.

It seemed like a good time to break out the Knob Creek. I poured a double shot. I take it neat. I've never seen the point of polluting fine distilled alcohol with water. It seems like something of a sacrilege.

I was on my second drink when Meyer arrived. He opted for Stolli. We took our drinks to the terrace on the bow, where we could watch for the girls and enjoy the sunset.

I brought him up to date while we waited. I told him about Madeline and her day. I couldn't explain the change in demeanor. I told him about SafeCo as well, but without mentioning my intruder. I focused on the history of their founders. I didn't know how they were connected to all this, but I wanted him to know there were some dangerous people involved.

He was a wonderful listener and probed gently with the right questions at the right time. Somehow, he made you feel like the most interesting person in the world. I found myself talking more than I normally would. Maybe it was the bourbon. Maybe it was the company.

"So, what are you holding back?" He said finally.

I took another sip of bourbon.

"What do you mean?"

He looked at me with his pale, unwavering eyes.

"You are more like your uncle than you know," He said. "There is something you're not telling me."

So, I told him about the intruder and where he was when I last saw him. He nodded his wise, round head.

"A lot like your uncle," He said.

Nothing more.

Meyer greeted Darleene and Carla like they were long-lost friends when they arrived. Darlene was carrying a couple of insulated bags. She unpacked in the galley. She was still bouncing around if anything more animated than before. I wondered if she always moved at this pace. She wore a long-sleeved blue shirt with the bottom tucked in and tied at the waist and a pair of shorts with a subtle blue pattern.

Carla looked to be a couple of years older. She was taller and thinner, with a prominent nose and dark brown eyes. She was a full-figure girl. She wore a simple summer dress that showed it to her advantage.

Darlene unpacked the food. I asked her if there was a chit I needed to sign, and she said there was no need. It was on my account. She said everyone in the harbor had a house account at the Tin Inn. Nice to know.

I made a good call when I left the dinner selection to Darlene. In addition to General Tso's cauliflower, we had blackened grouper, fingerling potatoes, and a side salad. Meyer took it upon himself to set the table – which was probably just as well since he was the only one who knew where everything was – and we sat down to eat and talk.

The women said they had known each other forever, thanks to Momma Madeline. There was genuine affection in their voices when they talked about her and each other. Carla had been there first, maybe a year before, coming home with Momma Madeline every night after school and staying until her mom got off work. Sometimes, she didn't want to go home because her mom was tired, wanted to rest and watch TV, and didn't have a lot of time for her, while Momma Madeline's place was always warm with plenty of good things to eat and lots of friends around.

When Darlene came, they were together almost every night after school. They became fast friends. The same was true of many of the other kids in Momma Madeline's care. They were like family. While some had moved and some had married, they had always found a way to keep in touch and stay close.

Carla said they all wanted me to know how much they appreciated everything I had done for Mama Madeline. It meant a great deal to her that I had brought her to Washington to tell her story and have so many important people pay attention to her. I asked how often she saw Madeline, and she said she saw her two to three times a week. She would like to see her more often, but it was hard with her schedule at Ave Maria, her boyfriend, and all. She wanted to be an accountant and hoped to marry as soon as she graduated.

I told her about my visit and how surprised I was by the changes I had seen. She said that all came on rather quickly. Momma Madeline was fine when she came back from Washington. They had a little party for her with the gang from the old days. Ten or eleven people were there.

"Your uncle brought the tape from the 60 Minutes show," She said, "We had some cake and watched it together."

"Darleene said you introduced my uncle to Madeline. Was he able to help her?"

Carla turned those dark brown eyes on me and looked at me without comprehension, and then she looked at the other two at the table.

"Doesn't he know?"

Meyer dropped his head.

"He told her to write you," Carla said. "He helped her write the letter because she wasn't sure what to say. Hell, I think he even mailed it for her."

That called for another drink. I tapped Knob Creek again.

"They became friends," Carla said. "I saw him over there a couple of times when I visited. I used to tease her about being sweet on him."

"When was the last time you saw him?" I asked.

She said it was sometime around the first of the year. He was concerned about Madeline's memory loss.

"We couldn't understand what was happening," She said, "and why it was going so quickly. She was confused a lot of the time. A lot of the time, she might not even know you. It was really strange. The other change was that she had never been one to go to the doctor that much before – we almost had to force her – but she started going all the time."

"The clinic made it easy for her once the new manager took over, or I don't know how she would have managed. They started coming to get her and all. But nothing they did seemed to help. It seemed like the more she went, the worse she got. Your uncle said someone should find out about that."

"Did anyone try?"

"I don't know. I had this one crazy notion. Bobby, that's my boyfriend, knows someone who works there. He is like a friend of his father's or something. He works there, watching the door and keeping people safe. There are some nut jobs in that neighborhood. He makes sure none of them cause problems."

"I was going to ask Bobby to ask him maybe if he would snoop around a little bit for us. From what Bobby says, he doesn't like the new manager or the doctors there very much; he doesn't like how they treat people."

"But then your uncle left, and I just kind of let it drop. What could I do on my own? Meanwhile, Momma Madeline keeps getting worse. They'd probably be looking at putting her in a home if there was someone to put her in a home."

"Do you think he would talk with me?"

"Who Bobby --"

"No. Bobby's friend. I'd like as much information as we can get about what's going on in that clinic."

Carla took my number and said she would ask. After dinner, the women wandered off together, arm and arm. Both young and in love, in that precious part of life before your dreams start to get crushed. All hope and promise. The loving husband. Good job. Maybe even one that provides health care. A house in one of those new developments up near Corkscrew – not too close to the water because that would be expensive, but shiny and new and room for the white picket fence and, God willing, a couple of kids someday, PTA, dance class and Little League. It works out that way – sometimes. I wished them luck.

I convinced Meyer to linger. I needed some company, and I sensed he did too.

"Were we ever that young?" He asked.

"I wasn't," I said.

He said, "I don't remember."

We took our after-dinner drinks out on the terrace where we started. I had found some Remy tucked away in the back of the liquor cabinet and poured us both just enough to top off the night.

"How much of that did you know?" I asked.

"Some. Not much. Some, I guessed."

He said he knew about the connection with Madeline because he had helped arrange it. He didn't know my uncle had passed her on to me, but he had guessed it. Partly because this was out of his league, not the kind of thing he did, and partly because he knew he had lost a step.

He couldn't help trying to help people, particularly people in distress, because that was his nature, but he had gotten a little too old to be climbing up on his horse and grabbing his lance to go off the windmill tilting. The windmills were getting bigger and quicker and starting to fight back.

There was sadness in him that told me his mind had gone to other times, to remember fights when they were both young and invincible. He missed my uncle, and it showed.

"When was the last time you saw him?" I asked.

"Right after the pacemaker hearing. He grilled a couple of steaks, we had a bottle of wine, and watched the recording he had made."

He looked up wistfully.

"He was very proud of you, you know. I think he saw a lot of himself in you."

"Did you talk with him after that?"

"Once. I called to give him an update on his portfolio. He didn't seem to care, but then he never seemed to care. It used to infuriate me. How can you give somebody all this money and not care what they do with it?"

"Maybe he trusted you."

He shrugged at the obvious answer, and I knew the source of his frustration. He wanted my uncle to know everything he had done for him and how well things were going.

"I didn't think to ask him what he was doing. He didn't say anything about leaving. I just turned around, and he was gone."

One of the most difficult lessons we have to learn is to live a life of limited regrets. The little ones will bother you forever. Why did I say that? Why didn't I take that class or go for that promotion? Why didn't I ever have the nerve to ask that pretty girl to have dinner?

While the little ones will trouble you, the big ones will weigh you down, heavy on your heart like a stone, diminishing your sense of self – everything you are and hope to be. Why wasn't I there when you needed me? Why didn't I try to tell you how much you mean to me and how important you are to me? Why didn't I tell you how much I love you? Why didn't I make sure I had a chance to say goodbye?

I hugged him as he left and suggested maybe we could

have dinner again tomorrow. I could use the company. The slight mist in his eyes told me he knew what I was doing. He also knew it was true.

The Next Story

Friday, May 28. I was up early. I wanted to be at the shopping center in time to watch the clinic open. Again, there wasn't a cloud in the sky. But it was already hot and humid. I wore boat shoes, shorts, and a blue golf shirt. You never know, someone might take me for a tourist.

I stopped by a bagel joint located in the service perimeter and picked up breakfast – a half dozen jalapeño bagels toasted with butter and a couple of Cokes. Then I circled the mall, looking for a place to park. I pretty much had my pick. Most of the action was near Publix. I parked further down in a space with a direct view of the clinic and a decent view of Graul's Pharmacy off to the right.

I was settled and in position by 6:45 AM; the Nikon was on the passenger seat with the date and time stamp on, the telephoto zoom set at the midrange – 150 mm.

At 7:00 AM, the door to the clinic was opened from

the inside. I hadn't thought to check out the back of the building. It was too late to do that now. There were probably at least a couple of spaces back there reserved for the owner and administrator.

I got the camera up in time to catch the movement of the door and fired off a burst with no real hope of catching anything. To my surprise, when I checked the images, I found a partial image of a grey-haired man. Not much, but something.

Staff started rolling in at 7:15 AM. First came a woman, middle-aged and thin. Then, two men came in within minutes of each other. Both young. Maybe right out of med school. Two women I took to be nurses came in at 7:45. One was heavy. The other was heavier. I don't know what it is about nursing, but weight seems to be an occupational hazard. Maybe it's the stress.

An older man mid-fifties arrived just before 8:00 AM. I took him to be the man Carla talked about. He was wearing a blue outfit of some kind, not a cop but a pretend cop like you see in malls and other commercial areas. You might as well give them a funny face with a crooked grin and a scarecrow hat. They serve the same purpose – and about as well. Last in was a Hispanic woman in her forties. She propped the door open to let the clinic air out.

Patients started arriving almost immediately in ones and twos, a cross-section of Florida's population. I photographed them coming and going, leaving the date and time stamp on so that I would have a chronological history. That's the only way they could ever be used as evidence of anything. The patients stayed an average of 40 to 45 minutes.

Mixed in with these was a second set – younger, all male, more mobile, alone. The younger ones were in and out of the clinic in half the time – 15 to 20 minutes. They went directly to the pharmacy from the clinic.

I set the camera on video and recorded their march, capturing their movement until they disappeared from view. Another 15 minutes later, they came out of the pharmacy, scattering in different directions, and some returned to their cars in the parking lot. The returning set didn't seem to be in any hurry to leave. They sat in their cars, waiting for something or someone.

The senior vans started to arrive at 10:00 AM. They parked in the reserved spaces up front and discharged their passengers. The vans arrived about every half hour after that, picking up as they delivered.

The drivers looked like cousins of my nighttime visitor. They didn't seem eager to render any assistance to their passengers. They kept their distance as though aging was contagious, and they didn't want to catch it. Karma is a bitch. Their time would come.

The orange Nissan arrived at 10:15 AM. She must have taken Alligator Alley. My camera followed her car into a space not far from where she had parked the day before. I zoomed in tight. She looked to be around thirty with dark blonde hair in a ponytail pulled back through a ball cap. She had her sunglasses perched on the brim of her hat.

After killing the car and settling in, she pulled a small, narrow steno pad out of her purse and started scribbling things down. I have seen pads like that before. They are made narrow so reporters can stow them in a purse or pocket.

I felt like my head was on a swivel most of the morning, watching the vans and patients come and go. There were seniors – some walk-ins, most brought in vans – younger individuals – a ragged-looking bunch of swamp rats – and the runners who worked for the clinic and facilitated the flow of patients.

Just before noon, it got more complicated. Two men in a gold Lexus with tinted windows arrived and double-parked in front of the deli next to the clinic. A man with no neck got out of the passenger's side.

What neck he might have had was buried in great slabs of muscle that formed his arms and chest. He was bald with a round face and small, piggy eyes. He had a beach ball for a middle and short, stubby leg. He wore a black tank top, cinched around the middle with a thick leather belt, and worn khaki shorts.

All in all, he had the look of a European strong man or a circus performer, the kind who liked to show off by bending iron bars with their teeth. He left the car door open and waddled into the deli.

I couldn't see the driver clearly because of the angle, the tint of the glass, and his body position. He was leaning toward the open door, talking with some of the clinic customers, the ones who had been to the drugstore and stayed around.

They came up one by one, had a short conversation and left. I had the Nikon on motor drive, held it steady, and let it run. When no neck came out, I zoomed in on his face for a close-up. He carried a bag and a drink tray. He passed the tray in and worked his way back into the car. I still couldn't get a good look at the driver, but I caught the license plate as they drove off.

The Nissan hadn't moved. I could see her head down and assumed she was making notes. It seemed like a good time to get acquainted. I stowed the camera out of sight and walked up. She was still scribbling in her notebook when I rapped on her window. I got a startled expression before the window came down.

She had the kind of face that is hard to categorize and hard to forget. The most obvious thing was that there was nothing obvious about her, nothing pretty or petty. There is nothing you could put your finger on to describe her look. No freckles. No dimples. No turned-up nose. None of the cute, superficial stuff.

She was just your ordinary, everyday beauty with strong, striking features and killer green eyes. I tried to remember where I had seen those eyes before. It took a moment. Then it came to me – the famous cover of a National Geographic years back. A haunting photograph of a young Afghan woman.

Up close, her hair was somewhere between light and dark blonde with amber streaks. It was pulled back through a Dolphins ball cap. A copy of the *Miami Sun* was on the seat next to her.

"Isn't this car a little conspicuous, Scoop?"

My comment sparked a fire in her eyes. She looked directly at me.

"Look who's talking. What are you – 6' 5" or 6' 6"?

"About that."

Her eyes flickered with appraisal and speculation.

"I've seen smaller trees."

"What are you trying to say?"

"You stand out among these LOPs like an oak in the mangroves."

"Nice turn of phrase. You must be a journalist."

"You must be a trained investigator."

She kept her gaze steady, challenging me.

"What are you waiting for – an invitation? Either get in or send up a flare telling them we are here."

When a boy meets a girl, something happens on a level we can't always track. If one or the other is interested, that fact is transmitted in the ether between them, and the other is immediately aware of it. If the receiver is interested, the signal bounces back to the sender, and the relationship progresses. I could tell she was interested. I couldn't tell whether that interest was personal or professional.

"Can I buy you lunch?"

She made an impatient gesture, nodding toward the passenger seat.

"Get in."

I walked around and crammed myself into her Nissan. I levered the front seat back as far as possible and still felt like a sardine. I started to introduce myself but didn't get very far.

"I'm –"

"I know who you are."

"And you are – "

She cut me off again.

"I know who I am, too."

Her tone was curt and abrupt. Maybe I had misread

the signs. She ignored me, as if to say I don't have time for this and continued watching the clinic. When she dropped her eyes to scribble something on her pad, I thought I saw an opening.

"Not a lot of people still use those."

"Not a lot of people can walk into a store and come out with a five-thousand-dollar camera," She shot back. She made a quarter turn toward me. "Hope you aren't billing the taxpayer for it."

"Sweetheart, the taxpayer should throw rose water on my backside and kiss it every Friday afternoon."

"Why? Because you saved them a billion dollars with your last investigation?"

I smiled. Someone had been paying attention.

"Well, you know what they say. A billion here and a billion there. Pretty soon, you are talking about real money."

She put her notebook down. I saw something resembling a smile starting to form.

"So, what do people call you? Lorraine or Lori?"

Her guard went back up.

"Neither...Unless they are looking for a fight."

She gave me another defiant, challenging look, and then her face softened.

"It's Lorraine Taylor Charles. It's a southern thing. My mother's maiden name was Taylor. That's what my friends call me…I guess you can, too."

"Does that mean we are friends?"

"You never know."

Her tone suggested anything is possible. She fired up the car and revved the engine. It was the casual, almost automatic response of one who loved the sound. She kept watching the clinic as she pulled out, whipping her car around and out of the parking lot to the perimeter road for McDonald's. She drove fast. No indecision.

"Hope you don't mind," She said. "McDonald's is kind of my go-to place when I'm on the road. It is fast, and it's cheap."

"I can tell by all the wrappers on the floor."

Again, there was a flash of fire in her green eyes.

"You can get out any time."

I ignored her tone, picked up an empty bag, and started consolidating trash.

"Stop that," She said. "I don't need you to clean up my mess."

I made a production of dropping the bag on the console between us and picking up the newspaper.

"Anything interesting," I said.

"Not much," She said and glanced my way. "But I'm working on something promising."

"What's that?"

We entered the drive-thru cue. There was a half dozen cars in front of us.

"You," She said.

She kept her eyes fixed ahead while I admired her strong profile. Finally, she turned to face me. Her look was frank and challenging.

"I think maybe you are my next story."

"What if I don't want to be?"

"What makes you think you have a choice? When a hot-shot Senate investigator shows up in Naples and starts prowling around, it's news."

"Prowling?"

She shrugged her shoulders.

"It's the way you move."

I saw that hint of a smile again. The temperature in the car went up about 10 degrees. It made me wonder what it would be like if she ever cut loose with a real smile and what I could do to make that happen.

"That's how I recognized you," She said. "I saw you shopping yesterday. I knew who you were immediately."

"How's that?"

"I have been following you. You could even say I have been living off you."

"Does this mean I'm entitled to a deduction?"

Her smile became something more, broader and more inviting, suggesting something more might come.

"Anything is possible."

She had shifted gears and increased the intensity while keeping her eyes on me, waiting for a reaction. A lesser man would have melted. I stayed strong, but I felt a jolt like when I tried to rewire a lamp and cut into the power cord.

"Sorry about the trash," She said. "You hit a nerve. It's like having someone come into your home before you have had a chance to clean up. I tell myself to clean up every time I come home, but I'm generally tired, and I don't want my mom to see all the fast-food wrappers in the trash. That's a lecture I can do without."

"No worries. Care to tell me why you are here and what you are working on?"

"Something or nothing," She said. "The only thing I

know for sure is that it is a bigger story now you are here."

"What if I don't want to be part of your story?"

"Part of it? You are it. I have been following your lead on this for six months."

I nodded.

"I've seen some of that."

I offered to buy as she inched forward, but she wouldn't have it. I was a potential source, she said. Being in debt to me was not an option. I suggested a compromise. Rather than fight over a couple of dollars and change, she could buy lunch, and I would take care of dinner. After all, we probably have a lot to talk about. She pinned me with those green eyes. They seemed to get a shade darker as she processed the possibilities.

"Did you see my last article?"

"Yes."

"Then you know why I'm here. I can't figure out where the money is coming from. Six months ago, Gerri-Care was on life support. No one thought they were going to make it. Chambers was holding on by his fingernails. Now they are flush. The company is building, diversifying, and branching out into new areas. They are showing double-digit growth. Something is fishy."

"That's a pretty specific term. Is that something you learned in journalism school?"

She rolled with it, giving me that dismissive look girls learn when they are seven. Silly boys.

"It's local color. It means game on. There are a lot of sharks in the water down here. And more than a few on land. We know 'em when we see 'em."

"Look," I said, "Whatever is going on here, we are on the same side. It makes sense to share information and work together. Your story is your story. I won't interfere with that, but there may be something you know that will help me decide how to proceed."

"If you write about me, you'll just make my job harder and maybe give them a chance to cover up. If we work together, I'll see to it that you get the lead. Whatever the story is, I'll see to it you get all the credit. I don't need it. If you have been following me, you know I've done this before."

"I know you have," She said, and after a moment. "Apologies again. It was just a bit of pique. I called you a few months ago when I started following up on Chambers. The receptionist brushed me off. She said you were busy and passed me off to a guy named Christoff. Now you show up out of the blue."

I gave her my most disarming smile.

"Sorry about that. You now have my complete attention. I will be your personal point of contact from now on."

We were about to order when my phone rang. I told her I would have what she had and took the call. It was Carla. She said her boyfriend had called the family friend who worked in the clinic, and he had agreed to talk with me. I told her to come by for dinner if she liked. Meyer was making some of his chili. I would just tell him to add a few more beans to the pot.

"You are invited," I said to Taylor and explained what was going on. "I will share everything I know on the condition that you do not use it without my permission. I'm just getting into this. I don't know where it will go."

"As you said, there may be something here. There may be nothing. I don't want to tip anyone off until I know what we are dealing with and how to handle it."

I could see her relax a little. I had made the first offer and put my trust in her. She handed me the drinks – two large cokes – stowed the McDonald's bag beneath her feet, and drove back to the parking lot. She found a spot close to my rental.

"Let's eat in your car," She said. "You will be a little more comfortable there."

When we settled in, she took a drink and handed me the bag. There were four double cheeseburgers and two large orders of fries.

"Do you always eat like this?'

"When I'm on the road," She said and shrugged.

It is an interesting combination – fast cars and fast food. Something about her shrug was almost apologetic, endearing, and childlike. I know I'm being bad, it said, but I just can't help it. It made me smile.

"Why aren't you in broadcasting?" I asked. "You have a look."

She said that's where she started. She went to the Northwestern School of Journalism and got a job with the local CBS affiliate in Chicago right out of school. Chasing ambulances. Police stories. Somebody on the street trying to add something to a story the people in the studio already knew.

She began reconsidering her profession when the network cut her production team. When she started, she said, she was part of a three-person crew – a cameraman, a soundman, and a correspondent.

They eliminated the soundman first and asked the cameraman to double up. Then they began asking her to do it all – interview and b-roll – eliminating her crew altogether, turning her interviews into glorified selfies. Worse, they began limiting her independence and the scope of her interviews.

"The producer would say, go interview this person or that person and get their reaction to this story. We need a 15-second byte. What the hell can you say in 15 seconds?" She slammed the side of her hand against the door in frustration. "How is that journalism? It is demeaning to me and my subject."

"It made me think about what I was doing, why I was doing it, and where it led. I looked around at the people who came before me and saw that the further up the ladder you get in broadcasting, the less you do."

"The next step up from correspondent is anchor – the on-air team. Do you know what the production crew calls the on-air team? The talent. It's meant to be sarcastic. Other people write the stories, produce the news and script it. All they do is sit there, read the news, and try to look earnest and appealing."

"Ask your friend, the one you gave the lead to in Chicago. She used to be a damn fine investigative reporter. Now, I only see her filling in as the substitute anchor on one of the network's weekend shows on the weekends. I didn't want that. And I didn't want to be one of those Twinks you see on Fox."

"Twinks?"

"Industry term. Short for 'Twinkies' with blond fluff on the outside. Cream filling inside. Talking bubble-heads. Turn on Fox – any Fox broadcast – and you will see what I mean."

"They are not all that bad. I have worked with some good ones."

"I bet you have."

Her tone was sarcastic. She picked up the wrappers, stuffed them in the bag they came in, and threw the bag in the back.

"What are you trying to say?"

"I've seen the women you run with."

"What makes you think I'm running *with* them?"

"What do you mean?"

"There are always at least two possibilities."

"Sure, doesn't look like you are running *from* them."

"My daddy used to say everything in life can be compared to dating or fishing ---"

"Who the hell was your father – Will Rodgers? What does that even begin to mean?"

"It means you can't catch tarpon in a trout stream. If you have been tracking me, who am I around? They are either journalists, staffers or lobbyists. Relationships with other staffers create all kinds of problems. Relationships with lobbyists must be avoided. Relationships with journalists can be mutually beneficial."

"Like that Patterson woman on CBS in Washington. It seemed like she was always your local network outlet. Whatever happened to her?"

"I discovered she could deduct birth control pills from her taxes as a business expense."

"That's it? That couldn't have come as that much of a surprise. You know some correspondents will do anything for a story."

"Not with me…I don't like being used. Maybe it's as simple as that."

She looked at me long and hard. I could see the wheels turn.

"Where does that leave you?"

"With Patterson? Nowhere."

"What about the rest of the women who are chasing you? I'm sure there must be a ton."

"Too many and not enough." I held her eyes. "One would be enough."

I could see her absorb and react to my intensity, bouncing it back. The connection we made when we met fired up and amplified to a deeper level. I felt it, and I knew she did, too.

"What about you?"

Her eyes dropped, uncertain how to take my question – general inquiry or specific interest. I could see her struggle to collect herself. She took the safe way out.

"Same, I guess. I had a steady guy in Chicago, but it can be a long way from "Right Now" to "Right." When my father became ill, I said it was a sign to come home, but it was maybe more of an excuse – an easy way out of a comfortable, predictable relationship with an OK guy and a prestigious job."

"I didn't want to do either of them anymore. I told everyone – hell, I even told myself – I had to help my mother take care of my father, and that's true, but if I am honest with myself, a good part of me just wanted to get out."

Her father had ALS, she said, which may be the cruelest of diseases, where a perfectly sound mind is forced to watch what was once a perfect body deteriorate and rebel against the smallest commands. It got to the point where everything had to be done for him 24-7. It was exhausting.

She started turning stories into the *Sun* at first just as a release, a way to let go and think about something else. Then she found she loved the work again; the chance print gave her to dig into a story and use her mind. And the money didn't hurt. Her family had never been well off, and there is nothing like a catastrophic illness to drain your bank account, however much you have.

She wrote about whatever interested her, but a lot of her stories were medically related. Health is a big issue here in Florida, she said. When people retire here, the big concern becomes how long I can keep it going. How many Golden Years are left? Her family's experience focused on that interest. That's why she stayed at Gerri-Care. Whenever she was between assignments, she tried to see what more she could dig up. She was doing it on spec. If she found something, the paper said they would run it, but they weren't going to pay for rumors and hunches.

"Ok. What do you know for a fact?"

"First, GerriCare was nearly bankrupt at the beginning of this year. Second, Chambers had to do some fancy footwork to hold on to his job. He told the Board he was going to expand the business. Third, he found some capital somewhere and started buying things. The Naples clinic, for sure and an urgent care center in Ft. Myer. There's probably more – but wait, you said stick to what I know…what else? Fourth, somehow, GerriCare seems to have turned things around. Stock prices are climbing – not dramatically, but steadily. The clinics could account for some of his turnaround, but not enough. All of which leads to the conclusion he is getting money from somewhere we can't see."

I showed her the video of the man in the Lexus and the exchange with his mopes. When he made the turn to leave the parking lot, I froze on his face. It was a profile. Three-quarters above a tinted window.

"Do you recognize this man?"

"No. Who is he?"

"I don't know, but we need to find out. He is probably part of the answer. We also need to find out what's going on inside the clinic. We should begin to get some idea tonight."

She raised an eyebrow.

"How do you feel about chili?"

I called Meyer and told him there would be five for dinner if that wouldn't be too much trouble. He seemed pleased.

"Prepare your guests for a special experience," He said. "I hate to brag, but my chili is the best on the planet."

"We'll see," I said, "But I should warn you in advance that one of our guests has a very discriminating pallet. She is partial to McDonald's."

I think Taylor was amused. I couldn't be sure. I was a little unsettled by how much I hoped that was true.

The pace of patients slowed as the day wore on. I called Christoff at 4:00 PM, just after the last van arrived.

"Hey, Chief," He said. "Glad you called. You'll never guess where your friends from SafeCo turned up."

"Surprise me."

"The society pages."

"Really?"

"Apparently, there was a big bash at Chamber's home in February. Governor Divos and a bunch of high rollers from all over the state were there."

"Do you have photos?"

"No. That's part of what makes it interesting. I found the connection with word search. SafeCo came up as a platinum donor. That's the $50,000 level. There are no photos of them there. So, they were there, and they were not there, if you know what I mean."

"My guess is that they provided security and wrote it off as an in-kind contribution. There are only two reasons I can think of why they would be listed – publicity and taxes. If they were there for publicity, we would have found photos of them with all the players."

"Good work. Thanks."

Christoff's words confirmed my suspicion. A fire started in a cold, dark place. Spontaneous combustion. While it banked and built, I told him, "There are a couple of other things you can run down for me."

I gave him the Lexus license plate number. I asked him to find out who the car was registered to, and I said I was going to forward a couple of images I wanted the

Bureau to run through facial recognition. Then I asked him to pull up anything he could find on GerriCare: ownership, changes in ownership, billing practices, changes in billing practices after the change in ownership, physicians, physician's history, utilization rates, prescription history – particularly controlled substances.

"Why didn't you just say you wanted me to give them an enema?"

"You know how delicate I am. Besides, there is a lady present."

I glanced her way. I generally have tight control of my emotions, but I must have shown something. Out of the corner of my eye, I became aware Taylor was staring at me, her eyebrows arched in concern.

"You going to tell me or not?" She said when I cleared the call.

"What do you mean?"

"You went from this big, jolly fellow to someone or something else in a matter of moments. The temperature in this car must have dropped twenty degrees. I got chills, and the hair on the back of my neck stood up. I never knew what that expression meant before, but I sure do now."

Note to self. This one could be dangerous. She reads you too well.

"Looks like we have friends in common," I said.

"Who?"

"I'll tell you after dinner."

We stayed with our stakeout until closing. The three shuttle buses we had seen came back one last time around 5:00 PM. The drivers checked in with the office and then drove the vans around back. Just before 6:00 PM, a dark Camry double-parked in front of the clinic. A slight young man went in and came back out almost immediately. He went from there to the drive-thru at the Pharmacy as staff made their way out of the clinic in ones and twos and found their cars.

When I saw the security guard come out, I knew it was time to move. I told Taylor to meet me at City Dock and took off. She took it as a challenge and beat me to the parking lot by ten minutes. When I arrived, she was leaning on the hood of her car with a triumphant smirk on her face.

It was the first time I'd gotten a good look at the length of her. It was worth enduring the smirk. She was taller than I thought, with the lean body of a dancer and that rarest of all physical attributes – truly wonderful legs. Faces can be altered. Noses can be fixed. Ears pinned back. Tummies tucked. Boobs can be enlarged, reduced, and reshaped. But no matter how good the man with a knife is, they haven't found a way to fake the reality of long, elegant, well-shaped legs. Her's were spectacular.

We crossed over and walked on to City Dock. She started to turn toward Tin City and stopped when she saw me walking straight ahead.

"Where are we going?" She said.

"My place."

I enjoyed her reaction as I led the way down the dock. By the time we arrived at the last slip, she had figured out we were looking for a boat, but I still don't think she was ready for The Big Doll. That name for my inheritance had stuck in my mind. I made another mental note to get Jimmy working on the paint and paperwork.

"Where did you get this?" She asked as she made her way up the gangplank.

"It was a gift from my uncle."

She stopped and canted her head to look up at me as if trying to decide if I was kidding or not.

"He must have loved you a lot."

"Actually, we never met."

By the time we were on board and I had cleared the security system, I could see the questions piling up. I invited her into the lounge, offered her a drink, and gave her a quick tour, as well as the short version of The Big Doll's story. She asked for a beer. I let her take her pick from the selection in the fridge. She picked a Corona Light and asked for a lime. I told her she would find the limes where she found the beer, and the knives were in the drawer by the stove, and she could probably take care of herself while I poured myself a shot of my new favorite scotch. Something called Writer's Tears.

She was still trying to figure out which role to play, the attractive young woman in a stranger's place or the hard-boiled reporter with a nose for news in a place that begs for explanation when Meyer arrived. I heard the small 'bong' of the ship's alarm when he hit the gangplank and hurried to help him. He was sweating profusely from having lugged a huge caldron of chili all the way from the car. He happily turned it over to me and went on to greet our guest. He seemed to have a way of just taking over, introducing himself to her, and immediately putting her at ease. By the time I returned from putting the chili on the counter, they were chatting away like old friends.

"You have a really wonderful look," I heard him say.

"I know I'm hard to pin down," She said. "My father was Dutch and three or four other things. My mother was Irish and a mix as well. I don't know what that makes me. A mongrel, I guess."

"It makes you lovely," He said.

Maybe when I'm his age, I will be able to get away with lines like that.

"You are a composite," I offered lamely.

"Actually, that's not far off," Meyer said indulgently. "What it really makes you is a rare and wonderful new species, my dear. It is one of our great contributions to the world – "The American" distilled from all the races of the world. The French are the French. The Italians are the Italians. You are us at our best."

I asked Meyer to tell her the story of the houseboat while I put his pot on the stove to simmer. He looked at me like I was about to commit a felony.

"Don't mess with my chili, son. No one is allowed to touch it until I serve it."

He turned to Taylor and took her in tow.

"Come along, my dear," He said and reeled her in.

Carla and her boyfriend's friend arrived at 6:45 PM. He was the man I'd seen at the clinic, mid-fifties, not quite 6' but sturdier and thicker than he had appeared. His face was flat and broad with slightly sunken features, kind of like the doctor had pressed on the bridge of his nose when he was being baked and pushed everything in and closer together. He had the look of someone not quite sure what he was getting into.

He did a double-take when he saw me come in from the deck where I had been watching the sunset over Millionaires Row, and then he started to back away. I held up my hand to put him at ease and handed him my Senate box top. Sometimes, the trappings of authority can help reassure people.

He took the badge and held it, looking at my identification carefully as I told him who I was and explained we wanted to talk with him for background as part of an official Congressional investigation. He would not be quoted. He would not be identified. He would not be asked to testify or do anything that would put his job or his family in jeopardy.

He said his name was James Grodon. He didn't know how much he could help, but he would try. He didn't like the owners and made no bones about it. He sat on my uncle's big yellow couch, holding on to the beer Carla brought him in both hands like it was a prop in a movie of some sort. My Senate ID was on the coffee table before him. He kept looking at it and back at me as though trying to understand what was going on and reconcile the images.

I told him we had been watching the clinic from the outside, and we were trying to understand what was going on inside. He said he had been there almost two years, and it operated a lot differently than the way it operated when he was hired. He had been hired by the Andersons and stayed on when they sold.

The Andersons were good people, he said. They

treated everyone with kindness and respect. The new owners took over in February. They brought in their own people but kept him because his job was trivial, and they thought a familiar face would be reassuring to the neighborhood. He didn't know how much longer he would stay. He had never met the new owners and didn't know who they were, but the medical director was a man named Martin, Dr. Karl Martin. A nasty man.

Martin told everyone to move the patients through as fast as possible. He said the secret to the clinic's success was volume, and he issued standing orders to make sure all the Medicare patients who came in saw every doctor in the clinic, no matter what their problem or complaint was.

It was mechanical, Grodon said, kind of like an assembly line. It used to be that a patient saw the doctor they came to see and left. Not anymore. Younger patients not on Medicare were treated differently. They didn't have to wait. Sometimes, they didn't even see a doctor. They were in and out. Sometimes, in less than ten minutes.

I asked him if he knew the people in the Lexus. He said "no," but he had been told to look for them. He was told to report every time they came anywhere near the clinic.

"Who are you supposed to report to – Martin?"

"No. There is a card in the office with a number on it. Some kind of security firm. I don't remember the name."

"SafeCo?"

He looked startled.

"Yes, I think that's the name," He said.

When Carla asked him to talk about Madeline, his face softened. She was from the neighborhood, he said. She had been coming there a long time – at least as long as he had been there. She seemed to be coming more often now. She was a sweet lady and always talked with him, but lately, she didn't seem to know who he was. They didn't have much time to talk anyway because they took her in the back as soon as she came in and treated her there. She always seemed to have more energy when she left.

He said she didn't have any family and always came in alone after the driver dropped her off. He paused there for a moment and said there was a man, a friend, who came in asking about her once. He said this man was big and tall and sort of looked like me. That's why he was surprised when he saw me. He thought I might have been the same man, but he knew now that couldn't be true.

"When was this?" I asked.

"It's been a while. Months. I can't remember exactly. I remember the visit because he made a lot of noise. He said he wanted to see Madeline's records. They refused. He said he had her power of attorney and wasn't leaving until they showed him her file. He was standing by the receptionist and arguing with the office manager. They were making so much noise they were disturbing the other patients. I was afraid they might ask me to go over there. I didn't want to do that because he was a big man. I didn't know what I could do with him. I was relieved when Dr. Martin came out and took him back."

"Did you see him leave?"

"No."

"Did he ever come back?"

"No."

Another chill. Another jolt. Another log on the fire. Sometimes, it can be hard to tell the difference between fire and ice, but something was banking, building, and burning at the base of my spine.

There were other questions, but none I realized he could answer. Meyer settled the matter. He said his chili was ready and invited us to gather for a memorable experience. He was heartbroken when James and Carla said they had family waiting and couldn't stay. He found some plastic containers in the cupboard and insisted they take some chili home to share. He would not be denied.

So, when Taylor started making noises about the long drive back to Miami, he wouldn't hear of it. You are coming back in the morning anyway, he said. Why not stay here? As you can see, there is plenty of room. And if you want a change of clothes, he said, there is a considerable collection in the guest bedroom left by visitors and my uncle's friends of the female persuasion. He was sure she could find something that would fit. I couldn't help wondering if he was trying to set me up.

But she stayed. And the chili was extraordinary.

The Three Words Every Woman Wants to Hear

The chili wasn't the only extraordinary thing. It was a long and special night.

May 28. Saturday morning. I sorted through my growing Florida wardrobe and pulled my boots out of the closet, along with jeans and a black T-shirt. The shirt wasn't designed to be a muscle shirt, but I knew it would probably work out that way. I didn't mind. This was one of those times when size can be an advantage.

I wanted to be as large and intimidating as possible today. With the lift Luchesse provides, I come in north of 6' 7", and I knew the T-shirt would accentuate the 20-inch differential between my chest and waist. I was confident most people seeing me coming would be inclined to get out of the way.

Taylor was rattling around in the galley. I laid my clothes out on the bed and grabbed a quick shower. I put my robe on when I came out and went looking for her. She looked like she had been cooking for hours. The sink was full of pots and pans, and there was enough food for an army on the counter – pancakes, French toast, orange juice, sausage, eggs, and what looked like a pound of bacon.

"Sorry. I got a little carried away," She said.

"I remember."

A blush started to form. She covered her face with her hands and turned away until she could summon the courage to face me.

"Well, it's your fault," She said defiantly. "You seduced me."

She was wearing a green blouse with a pinstripe. The blouse picked up the color of her eyes. They were much lighter than they were last night when she came in for the gentle little sister of a kiss that turned into something so much more.

"I seduced you!? I was minding my own business, working on my computer, when you came into my bedroom, not wearing all that much and carrying what you said were a couple of nightcaps."

"I was wearing not all that much because there isn't that much to wear. I don't think any of your uncle's transient girlfriends had a nightgown. There were enough other things in the closet to stock a thrift shop, but no nightwear. All I could find was that T-shirt. And that came down to my knees."

"I brought you a nightcap because I wanted to thank you for such a wonderful day, for letting me in, for not shutting me out, and for introducing me to that wonderful, sweet man…And I came in to ask you what you thought Chambers was doing. You promised you'd tell me."

"I started to tell you. That's when you seduced me."

She shook her head defiantly.

"That's when you seduced me."

"How's that? I seem to remember you kissed me."

"And what happened just before that?"

"What?"

"You said the three words every woman wants to hear."

"What's that?"

"You said I was right…You know no woman can resist that. And that was after luring me into your playpen, feeding me until I couldn't walk, giving me your guest room with a tub big enough to swim in, and not even beginning to make a pass at me."

"How could you do that to me? How's that supposed to make me feel? All that sexy, irresistible, cool indifference. You knew what you were doing. You were setting me up. And sure enough, I tumbled tail over teacup at the first little nudge just as you planned."

"Tail over teacup?"

She hesitated, then gave me a shy, half smile.

"That's all I've got at the moment."

I laughed.

"I'm normally not that easy, you know."

She smiled back.

"You? I haven't had sex in more than a year."

"I think you may have caught up last night."

She blushed again.

"I'm not knocking it, you understand. I just normally like to take it slow. I don't want to be just another notch on some random girl's bedpost."

"You'd be a hell of a big notch," She said. "More like a groove. And I'm anything but 'random.'"

She had come into my bedroom with her hair still damp from the shower. The T-shirt she wore could have been one of mine, but it wasn't. It didn't take long to discover there wasn't anything under it. She handed me my drink, came in for a little kiss and pulled back six inches. She looked at me with humid emerald eyes and put the drinks down.

She led, and I followed. I let her set the pace. She was quick to shed the shirt and pull my covers down for the glorious feeling of skin on skin. Her hands were busy. My hands followed the contours of her body and found her figure riper and fuller than I expected.

When she was ready, she made the connection and began to move with a slow, steady rhythm that built and gathered force and speed until I felt like I was connected to a blender. I stayed with her until it was over for her, held her a moment while she caught her breath, and then began again, holding her in place, moving together until we both found a heart-pounding release. We snuggled together and held on to each other until our systems recharged and began again – and so it went through the night as we took turns initiating the next round.

She consumed me. She enveloped me. She was one woman. She was all women. Timid and shy. Bold and brazen. Tentative and aggressive – cycling through moods and moments and depths of desires she had packed away with the dreams in her hope chest. I don't think either one of us got more than a couple of hours of sleep, snatched in the momentary rest periods between rounds.

"I take offense at being called 'random,'" She said. "There is nothing random about this. I have had a crush on you for a while now…I guess you could call it a sort of a fantasy crush."

"Really? I don't think I have ever been anyone's fantasy before. Nightmare maybe ---"

"Cut it out. I'm serious. And you know it. Don't make fun of me. Not now."

She said it began in Chicago during the Senate's investigation of clinical laboratories. It was the first time we used a one-way glass. After we set it up, we invited *60 Minutes* to come in to confirm and film what we found.

As the story aired, there was a lot of tape from the investigation floating around. The first time she saw me was in the background of the CBS footage given to her station. She said there was something about me and the way I moved that caught her eye. She asked her producer to find out who I was. She started following me when she found out I was connected to PSI.

"As I said yesterday, I have been kind of living off you ever since."

"What do you mean?"

She smiled, grabbed the lapels of my robe with both hands and came in for a kiss.

"It's one of nature's laws," She said.

She released her grip and pushed herself away to look up at me.

"Small creatures follow every great predator. We feast on what falls and remains."

"You're saying I make a mess."

She laughed.

"Yes and no. You are no nine-year-old trying to make a peanut and jelly sandwich. You are more like a jungle cat, my dear – a lion or leopard –"

"A Grizzly –"

"Yeah. Maybe…No, more a Great White…That's the better analogy. You can see most predators coming – even in the jungle. No one sees you coming. No one knows when you will strike next until you come blasting up from the deep, suddenly bursting into sight with overwhelming force and energy. You tear into your target and rip it apart. Lots of big chunks come flying out."

"It gives the rest of us something to feed on. That's one of the reasons I kept following you. Sure, part of it was my personal interest in you, but a lot of it was that I knew I could count on you to tee up a good story for me. I followed up on your clinical lab investigation with a story about the lab owner who was doing sink tests on the south side. When you took on the Governor – that took chutzpah, by the way ---"

"He asked for it," I said. "He said there was no fraud in Illinois. Can you imagine that? Talk about chutzpah!"

"He said we were fake news when everyone in the State knew he was in the bag. All his biggest contributors were crooks. He had enough mobsters around him to cast a revival of The Sopranos – "

"-- And thanks to you, they all wound up in jail."

"The U. S. Attorney had a lot to do with that. We just made it easy for him."

"And I followed up with a story about the public aid official who had his car bombed after he cooperated with you. When you exposed the diploma mills – I was here by that time – I did a story for *The Sun* on the anesthesiologist at Magill who never went to med school."

"You name it, and I have been right behind you. I have been following you for so long. I couldn't believe it when you tapped on my window yesterday. I almost wet my pants. I didn't know what to say to you or how to react."

"Hope I didn't disappoint."

She smiled. It was a broad and bawdy smile.

"The only complaint I have is that I may have trouble walking for a while."

I smiled back as we sat down to eat, marveling at what a difference a day can make. You spend years looking, and suddenly, when you are not looking, when you least expect it, there she is. Yesterday, she was just another pretty girl. Today, she was *the* girl.

When I was growing up, I endured a seemingly endless series of lectures from my parents advising me of the perils of mating casually. They began when I was ten and continued until the day I left home. My mother was convinced the road to happiness was full of peril.

"There are a lot of girls out there just looking to grab a guy, any guy," She would say. "Be careful. Make sure it's the right one."

"How will I know when I find the right one?" I asked.

"You'll just know," She would say.

I was always frustrated by her vagueness. No matter how much I coaxed, how many times I asked, she could never do any better.

There was nothing vague about my father's response.

"It's like a punch in the heart," He said. "Boom!"

He made his point by waving a forceful fist.

"After that, you will never be the same."

Dad was not a sentimental man, but he always choked up at this point.

"The first time I met your mother," He said, "was the last time I looked at another woman. I saw her and knew we were meant to be together. I was getting out of the Army soon, but I began to dread the day. I knew I couldn't leave her."

"From that first day, all I ever wanted was to be with her. Nothing's ever changed. It's still the same. I don't care where we are or what we are doing as long as we are together."

And so, they were for ninety-two days short of forty years.

"Mother lived on for not quite three years after my father passed away. In those days, she could often be found sitting on the front porch in the morning after tending to the roses he had planted for her. She would be looking out at the mountains she had come to love as she braided her hair, and if you listened closely, you could hear her murmur, "Where has he gone, and when will I be with him?"

When you have seen love like that, you know what's possible. When you have seen love like that, why would you settle for anything less?

I thought about last night and the unbelievable fineness of her the evening had revealed, a deceptive delicacy that said fragile where nothing fragile was. I looked at her now with new eyes. It was as though our intimacy had given me x-ray vision. I could see her life flowing visibly beneath the surface's sensitive soft satin in the pulse of her throat and little light blue lines and small pulsations visible below her fair skin.

Nowhere in her face or body was there a straight line, a perfect plane, a flat surface. Everything curved from somewhere to somewhere else. More than the strong curves and counter curves of their breast and buttocks, the sweeping curves of shoulder, back and belly, the long, finely molded curvature of her endless, elegant legs. Everywhere, hollows, swells, indentations, muscle and bone, circles within circles, melted and molded with the texture of satin. She was amber and gold and all the shades in between. She was perfect.

"You know, you never answered my question," She said, stepping back and leaning on the counter facing me. "What's going on?"

"I don't have all the answers. There is too much going on. The clinic looks like a combination of a Medicare Mill and a Pill Mill. We have seen them both before, but not together."

"It looks like they are churning patients, doing everything they can to solicit seniors and poor people, and billing the government for everything they have done or can think of doing in their patients' names."

"At the same time, they are pushing pills – hillbilly heroin and who knows what else. I found some samples in the possession of one of their mopes. I couldn't tell if he was buying or selling. From the look of it now, I think they are selling – and selling a lot."

"The last place we saw something like this was in

Appalachia. You may remember it. Eleven physicians were involved. The FBI found they had sold 17 million opioid pills. The tell was the street traffic around the clinic. We tracked the number of patients coming out and going in and walked it back. Looks like something similar is going on here."

"I'm not sure where the Lexus fits in. I'll make a call to a friend before we leave. Maybe he can help us figure that out. But for now, it looks like two tracks, maybe even two operations."

"My guess is that they are having the drivers pick up the prescriptions for their patients and either keeping them for resale or shorting the count. They are charging Medicare or Medicaid and reselling the same drugs on the street."

"That's a lot of cash but chump change in the scheme of things. It doesn't begin to give them the margins they need. The average retail for 60 OxyContin is around $200. On the street, a $6 pill will sell for $50 to $100. That's a lot, but it still wouldn't generate the revenue they need. So, there must be another angle."

"Maybe that's where the pharmacy fits in. It makes me wonder if they are making their own stuff. There is a limit to what they can get legally, and going legal leaves a lot of footprints. Maybe they are supplementing everything they can get legally by reselling what they can on the street and supplementing that with homemade junk – like opioids and fentanyl. All it would take is a pill press. The pharmacy would have one of those and know how to use it."

"What slows me down is that this is a complicated set

of activities to coordinate. Is it one scam or several? If it's one operation, it would take someone with a very specific skill set. Maybe that's where the medical director fits in. I was looking him up last night when you attacked me –"

"Really!? Are you going to give me that schtick again?"

Her face scrunched up in something that was supposed to look like indignation. I threw up my hands in mock defense.

"I'm not complaining. I'm just trying to answer the questions you seem so concerned about. Are you going to listen or not?"

She softened her face and came closer.

"So, tell me."

"There is a Dr. Karl Martin associated with an addiction treatment center in Ft. Meyer. That would seem to work – if it's the same man. If it is, what is his deal here – principal or hired gun? The Martin in Ft. Myer advertises himself as a pain doctor. That could be the third component."

"We have had trouble with drug treatment facilities before. What we have seen is something called "body brokering." It first popped up in nursing homes and adult care centers 20 years ago. They fill their beds and keep their census up by paying other providers to steer clients to them.

"This could be that or a new wrinkle. There is no need to pay for clients if you can refer them to yourself. If you go that way, you can use up the patient's benefits, treat and release when the insurance runs out. Then, you readmit, claiming the patient had a relapse. I have seen cases where the same client has been admitted to the same facility nine times."

She nodded.

"I wrote a story about a place like that last year."

"I know. I read it."

That made her smile.

"So, what you are saying is maybe it's all tied together," She said. "They are making addicts so they can treat people with an addiction and cycle them back. Maybe that's what Chambers meant when he said GerriCare was going to integrate vertically."

"Just being a manufacturer of medical products is a chancy way to recover. They might never make it – particularly if the Board is impatient. Everyone in that business knows the development process is slow and uncertain. Chambers probably decided he couldn't wait that long or take the risk. Even if they succeeded in developing a new product, it would be years before FDA approval and years more before they would know how the market would respond."

"Chambers was hanging on by his fingernails. He had to find a faster, surer way."

"Yup. All of these lead to your very smart question: Where did the money come from? GerriCare was about to go bankrupt. Where did he find the money to expand when common sense would say he had cut back?"

She smiled triumphantly.

"So, you are saying I was right?"

"Yes. At the risk of being accused of seducing you again…You were right."

"Not to worry," She said. "You won't ever have to seduce me again."

We had gotten very comfortable with each other. It's difficult enough in relationships of any duration but truly rare in one so new. It was a good feeling. No games. No pretense. No conditions.

"So, what's the answer?" She asked.

"Ockham's razor."

"Sorry?"

"The philosopher, William Ockham. He argued that in complicated situations, the simplest explanation is probably right because it requires fewer assumptions. "Razor" refers to the process of shaving away extraneous material and assumptions."

"We are seeing a lot of moving parts, but if you shave away all the extraneous stuff, the simple answer is that Chambers found a partner. Somebody who has a lot of money or needs to hide or invest quickly and quietly somewhere."

"That generally means illegal and, in this part of the world, probably means drugs."

"My gut tells me whoever runs the street here pays the guy in the Lexus. We should find out something about that this afternoon. Is it his operation or something more than that? We need to start by finding out how he ties in – friend or foe."

"The Governor's involvement is another open question. I don't know how deep he is in this, but he is more than a next-door neighbor who happened to be the guest of honor at Chamber's clambake. My guess is he is wired in up to his fat ass."

"You think?"

"That's the pattern. It's what makes it so hard to nail all the sanctimonious bastards at the top. They insulate themselves with pawns and politics. You can take the pawns because they are always visible and out front and generally not that bright, but the big guys are harder to reach because they cover whatever they do and never get their hands dirty."

"If some ambitious assistant USA or a DA makes a case against them, they delay, put on a PR offensive, attack the prosecution as politically motivated, intimidate witnesses and, if convicted, appeal and appeal to delay enforcement while they look for political muscle to help on the inside. You see it all the time."

"Jeffrey Epstein is a good example. Were he in my court, or better, the court of my ancestors, he would have been buried on an anthill with his face and pecker exposed and covered in honey. It would be a lot cheaper and a lot more effective. You can get a jar of honey for two bucks."

"What aren't you telling me?" She said.

I wondered how she knew there was more. Yesterday, I would have dodged her question. But that was yesterday.

"There is a personal element overlaying to all this. It complicates things. After the pacemaker hearing, Chambers invited me to come down here and take a boat ride with him. He said we could go fishing in the Gulf and straighten things out. It came with his crooked crocodile smile. I couldn't help thinking that if I went out on a boat with him, I wouldn't come back."

"He has been trying to figure out how to get at me ever since. That's hard to do in Washington. I have a lot of layers of cover there. My guess is he found out about my uncle through Madeline and hoped that would lure me down here."

"After what we heard last night, I'm convinced they killed him out of spite and petty revenge. They have been watching this boat for months. I'm not sure if they were trying to see who my uncle was working with or hoping I'd show up to see what happened to him."

"Either way, they made a half-assed attempt to get me the day I arrived. I'm sure they will try again. The next effort is likely to be more serious."

"What happened?"

"They missed. The gentleman in question is feeding the fish."

I could tell she wasn't satisfied with that, but she wasn't going to get much more at the moment. As they say in the army, she had no "need to know."

"So, what do we do now?"

"I don't know about the "we" dear, but I'm going to go down to the clinic and shake things up. It will take time for me to do my job, run down all the leads we have, and build a case – six months, maybe more. I'm not waiting for that."

"They killed my uncle. They tried to kill me. They have made it personal. I'm going to see to it that they pay for what they have done and live just long enough to regret it."

"I'm tired of being on defense. I'm tired of reacting.

I'm going to take it to them. If I apply enough pressure, someone will crack. Starting now."

I put my phone on the counter, dialed a number and turned the speaker on.

We are calling Hugh Jones," I said. "He is my contact at the FBI."

She came close and stood by me, her hip brushing my side. I was very aware of her presence as I waited for Jones to pick up. He answered on the fourth ring. It seemed longer, yet not long enough.

"I was wondering when you were going to call," He said. "What's up?"

"I'm in Naples. I came down here on a personal matter, but I have run into something strange. As my partner would say, there is something fishy going on."

"Your partner? That's new."

"Very."

I smiled at her and felt a responsive bump of her hip.

"What can I do to help?"

"I need to talk with Sam. Will you ask him to give me a call?"

"Sure, but it will cost you. That guy goes through more burners than Best Buy."

"Fortunately, you have a rich uncle."

"Yeah, but you are closer to him than I am. You are going to have to be the one to ask."

"I'll take it up with Colgate."

"Can you tell me what you are working on?"

"I'll know better after I talk with Sam. If it's what I think it is, you may have to staff up your Collier County office."

"I like being called your partner," Taylor said when I cleared the call.

"He is another one…a different kind of partner but a good one. I can do a lot of things: I can investigate. I can turn the spotlight on the bad guys. I can embarrass the CEO and piss off the board of directors."

"I can close loopholes that allow them to operate or write legislation that makes it more difficult for them to do what they are doing. I can increase penalties. But I can't prosecute. I can't lock them up. I need the FBI for that."

"Jones needs a political ally on The Hill to protect them from people that want to shut them down. There are always people who want to limit the FBI's activities. He needs someone on the inside to fight those battles when they come up. He needs someone to serve up the high-visibility cases that make the Bureau look good."

"We both need you and your brothers and sisters in the press to tell the story. If we do it right, everyone wins. That's how something as silly as the diploma mills can grow from a prank I did with my dog to an FBI sting that identified 50,000 professionals operating with phony credentials."

"When I did my story on the anesthesiologist at MacDill. He said he couldn't understand what all the fuss was about. He had been working at MacDill for two years with no complaints."

"Dead people rarely complain."

She turned her head to the side, letting her hair fall away and revealing a greater expanse of her neck, and came closer.

"Whatever happened to Max?

"He is still around. He is getting kind of full of himself, but he is still there. He was just invited to join the International Platform Speakers Association."

"I'd like to meet him."

"You will."

"What about Sam? Can I meet him?"

"No."

"Why not? Who is he?"

"He was a hitman until he made the hit list."

"You'll have to explain that."

So, I told her the story of Sam "The Snake" Siciliano.

"You remember the investigation we did on factoring firms?" I said.

She nodded.

"Factoring is just legalized loan sharking," I said. "There is always a stream of money flowing from the federal, state, and local governments to the private sector – defense contractors, building contractors, medical clinics, what have you – and there are always people trying to get as much of it as possible. Sometimes legally. Sometimes illegally."

"Factors try to insert themselves in the process by controlling the faucet. They bet on government inefficiency and try to increase government inefficiency. In Chicago, they were paying City workers to bury invoices and slow payments down."

"They tell the provider we know you've got $10,000 coming for your week's work. You know it will take at least 6 months for the government to pay you. Meantime, you've got bills to pay. You want to live. You can't afford to wait, so why not sell your receivables to me? You give me the right to collect the entire $10,000 you have coming, and I will give you $8,000 today. Cash."

"The factoring firm advances $8,000, collects $10,000, and keeps $2,000 or 20 percent for their trouble."

"So, it's like a payday loan," She said, "with 20 percent of the taxpayer's money winding up in the pockets of middlemen who do nothing."

"Yes, but more."

"How do you figure?"

"The faster factors are paid, the higher their rate of return is. Most of the bills handled by factoring firms are turned around in 30 days or less. They bribe people to get to the head of the line."

"The same people who slow payments to other people down pay people to speed their payments up. So, it is not a 20 percent annual rate; it's a 20 percent monthly rate. They are turning the money over 12 times a year."

"Sounds custom-made for the mob."

"It is. And it was. If you recall the case we made against the governor, the company he was tied into was run by Paul Ricca. Ricca has a rap sheet that is as long as your arm."

"He also happens to be the guy who put the contract out on Sam. Sam heard we were after Ricca and contacted the FBI. He said he would help us if we could guarantee his safety. He has been in protective custody ever since."

"Is he really a hitman?"

"Was. Hopefully, no longer is. He confirmed 19 hits as part of his protection agreement."

"I appreciate the explanation," She said. "Now, there is something I need to explain to you."

"What's that?"

"It's about what you said earlier…It's definitely "we." It's *my* story. I'm going with you."

The look on her face left no doubt about it. Her chin was out, and there was a fire in her eyes. After a moment, it softened a bit.

"But do we have to go right now?"

"What do you mean?"

"Well, you said I was right…"

"Oh –"

"—And we just had a huge meal. It might be good to get some exercise first."

"I guess that's right. Exercise is good."

"And you haven't dressed."

"That's true."

"Then come on…"

The Snake

The morning was gone by the time we got dressed. I was pulling on my boots when the cell rang.

"Do you know who this is?"

"I do."

The voice was unmistakable. As always, it took me back to the first time we talked and the only time I have seen him face to face.

It was more than two years ago. Hugh told me to take a cab to an unlikely place - the corner of Kendell and New York Avenue in Northwest DC. That's the warehouse district. There is a city parking lot on the North side of that intersection, surrounded by an eight-foot chain wire fence capped with razor wire. Dilapidated warehouses line the south side of the street. Kendell cuts through them - one way going south.

It's known to be a tough area. There is rarely anyone around, even at midday. At a quarter after nine in the evening, the little traffic that normally would be there was long gone.

The driver who dropped me off was nervous and concerned for me. He knew this wasn't a place a suit would normally go at night.

"I wait?" He said.

"No need," I said.

I knew Jones and company would be lurking around somewhere. I started walking into the darkness on Kendell, as instructed. There was no one in sight, but there was a black sedan at the second intersection. It fell in behind me and followed – a block back, lights off, moving slowly.

Three blocks later, I passed another black sedan. Like the first, it was parked at the corner of a crossing street. The lights were off, but the motor was idling. Shadows of two men were visible through the car's tinted windows.

Halfway down the next block, the first car pulled up; a back window came down, and a passenger said, "Get in and put this on."

The passenger handed me a black bag. I put it over my head and felt the car accelerate. I knew the second car was following as we worked our way through the warehouse district, changing directions frequently. Then I felt the town car go down a ramp, enter a garage and stop.

Someone opened the door, took my arm, and guided me to an elevator. When the hood was removed, I saw Hugh waiting. There were four other FBI agents present. They surrounded a well-dressed, older man.

His smile was amiable, his eyes opaque and unfocused behind thick, black-framed glasses. His body was so thin he almost appeared frail. He sat in an armchair placed on a Persian rug, watching "The Golden Girls."

He said then what he said now. "I understand you want to talk with me."

Taylor heard the phone ring and came in to listen. I wish she could have heard our first conversation. It would have made for a good story.

"People make a big deal about organized crime," He had said. "Organized crime is just big business. Just as often, big business is organized crime."

He cleaned his glasses with his handkerchief, replaced them, and looked at me.

"What's the difference?" He asked. He gave me a moment to think about it and then continued.

"The law? Who writes the laws? A punk from the projects gets locked up for stealing $1,000. It's a felony. Two to three years. Minimum. Three strikes, and it's 25. Mandatory."

"The executive who steals millions walks away with a severance package and bonus. A kid doing drugs has a hard time. The celebrity doing drugs gets community service and a TV show. The bank that can't meet its commitments to its customers gets bailed out. The customer who can't meet his commitments to the bank gets flushed."

"You think that's an accident? Think about it. Who decides what's legal?"

He gave me a thin smile and lit a cigarette before he continued.

"The law is just a spider web. It only catches little

creatures. Big ones just pass through. They are connected and protected."

He took one more puff and put the cigarette out, adding it to a half dozen just like it in the ashtray before him. Maybe he had read the warning label and decided it was time to quit.

"So, how do you build those relationships?" He said. "Simple. You find out what people need. You give them what they want. You help them out. You know? It's an investment. The longer they are around, the bigger they get, the better your investment pays off."

"Who knows, the alderman could become a state senator or mayor or even governor. And so on. One hand washes the other. You help them. They help you."

The feeling of that moment never escaped me. It was surreal. He came across as a kind uncle trying to teach me a lesson about life. It was hard to reconcile with his candid admission that he had killed 19 men.

He didn't brag about it, but he had no regrets either. Just business, he said. Nothing to do with our relationship. There is no reason for distrust. We had a common cause.

"The enemy of my enemy is my friend," He said. "Right now, you are about the best friend I have."

Since then, The Snake has proven to be a reliable source. He had also helped the Bureau make several high-level cases against members of the mob. In exchange – and at considerable expense to the taxpayer – the FBI had kept him alive.

He was in witness protection, with security so tight that no one knew where he was. He could have been next door or a thousand miles away. When anyone in law enforcement needed to talk, they would file a request and wait for a call, just as I had.

He treated burner phones like Kleenex – to be used once and thrown away. He couldn't afford to have a number someone could walk back.

I said, "Thanks for calling, Sam. How are they treating you?"

"No complaints. I've got a suite like the Ritz. I can't go out, but why go out? I have everything I want here."

"Good. I have a question for you. I am in Naples ---"

"I heard. I have been wondering what you were going to step in next."

I stopped short. Clearly, there was no need for a long explanation. Sam might be squirreled away in the mountains or at the beach somewhere with a half dozen feds babysitting him night and day, but his sources hadn't dried up.

"What have I stepped in this time?"

"A turf war," He said. "Just a good old-fashioned turf war."

I could almost see him smile.

"What can you tell me about it?"

"You already know most of it – the history. It's nothing new. The only difference is where, not what."

"The big money on the street used to be in grass. The old guard resisted for years. They didn't want to be involved in drugs of any kind. They felt it was too dangerous – not to the runners, but the family."

"It's dangerous because you have no control, and the family likes control. With drugs, you are always exposed because your distributors inevitably become users. That makes them unreliable and easy to turn."

"That's what the smart money said, but the big money shouted them down. While the old guard held back, everyone else and his brother got into the business and got rich enough to buy a mansion in South Beach."

"There were a lot of amateurs fighting for territory and competing for control – particularly in south Florida – unaffiliated gangs – Jamaicans, Columbians, Cubans, and rednecks – anyone and everyone looking to make a quick buck."

"Finally, it was too much. The families realized all the competition had made it easy for them. The networks were already established. The operators were small-time. They just came in, lopped off the top layer and told the troops they were under new management. Then, all they had to do was centralize operations and tie it all together."

"Over time, they expanded the product line and pushed it nationwide. It became a big business, but big businesses have big problems, such as controlling supply and distribution. That's difficult when you are dealing with an illegal product you have to import in great quantities."

"After 9/11, it got harder. The terrorist threat made the Feds get serious about the borders. They had to switch to domestic production. That takes more effort and more time. Then, along comes the opioids."

"They were a game changer because there was no production problem. Lots of people have access to or can provide access to an unlimited supply. So, if supply is not an issue – What does that leave? It comes down to distribution and control."

"That's what you are seeing. Two groups – the Latinos and the Europeans – are competing for the territory, trying to build their distribution networks. The Europeans have always controlled the streets in Naples, but the Latinos have been coming on strong. They have a lot of money to redirect. The Miami crowd is sitting back and watching. Why fight two when you can fight one? They will take on the winner."

"How is Chambers involved?"

"He's made his bed with the Latinos. They have money. He needs money."

"That helps, Sam. Thanks."

"No problem. By the way, I heard you have a new lady."

"I do."

"You should know the boys in Miami have been watching her. They say she is a good one. Smart. Straight up. They particularly like her Florida Man series. But you understand what this means – Right?"

I took a deep breath before responding.

"What's that?"

"If they know where she is, they know where you are. The family talks. Which means Ricca knows or will soon know where you are. It's a dangerous situation, Paisano. Be careful."

I looked up at Taylor as Sam clicked off. I wasn't sure if she had caught the significance of what Sam had just said, but I didn't want to open that can of worms if I didn't have to.

There would be a better time to tell her about Ricca and Scarpace – Ricca's pet gorilla. I knew they both would like nothing more than a clear shot at me.

I had to find a way to keep her out of it. With that thought came the realization that keeping Taylor out of harm's way was going to be a major concern from now on.

What do you do when you don't want to go there? I tend to deflect. I focused on the other thread.

"Florida Man?"

She shrugged.

"Syndicated stupidity. Any news story with the words "Florida Man" in the headline. They are endless. Whenever news is slow, I crank one out to pay the rent."

"It's made me the "Queen of Florida Man." To this month. "Florida Man Loses Lip Kissing Pet Alligator." The operative word there is "pet." And my last one – "Florida Man Shoots Himself for the Third Time."

"Three times? That's ambitious."

"Yup. Once in the thigh. He was playing a quick draw, and the gun didn't clear the holster. Once in the hand. He was bird hunting, and his shotgun was fired when he tried to adjust the choke. The last one was the best. He was balancing a beer can on the toe of his boot and decided to shoot it off."

"The toe or the can?"

"The can."

"I take it he missed."

"Not the toe…They found what was left of it."

"Could it be reattached?"

"Not really. It's hard to put the pieces together when

you can't find all the pieces. The toe had to be reconstructed."

"The upside is that his swamp buddies would probably still consider him a good hunting companion. As far as we know, he has never shot anyone but himself."

"As far as we know..."

"So, you heard what Sam said about Chambers and his friends. You sure you want to get in the middle of all that?"

"I already am," She said. Her jaw was set. "It's my story."

Go Ahead and Die

It was noon by the time we got to the shopping center. I had convinced Taylor to leave her car in the lot at City Dock. It was too easy to mark, and if there were any problems, I didn't want them to know where to go looking for her.

She was hungry again, so we stopped at McDonald's.

"Same as yesterday?" I asked.

"No," Came the reply. "I'll have a Big Mac. Two of them."

If I had any doubt before, I knew now that this was not a pass-the-parsley kind of girl. This was a lovely, healthy woman with a healthy appetite who wanted what she wanted when she wanted it and saw no reason to apologize for it.

She ate like a stevedore. I had no idea where she put it. I had made a rather thorough inspection earlier that morning and several times the night before. I half expected an anaconda bulge but found none. There were no pockets of fat or evidence of overindulgence of any kind marring her sleek loveliness. I concluded she must have the metabolism of a hummingbird.

I parked near the pharmacy so I could get a better idea of the activity there while monitoring the clinic from a distance. Most of the pharmacy's clients seem to come from the clinic, but not all of them. Some wandered in from the neighborhood. Those people seemed older and better fed.

All the seniors from the clinic went through the drive-up kiosk – including those in the senior vans. Their prescriptions were processed so quickly that they must have been ordered in advance.

My telephoto lens picked up the transactions. The driver pulled up and identified the passenger. He presented some form of identification – probably a driver's license or a Medicare card – received the prescription and pulled away. Total elapsed time. Maybe five minutes. The walk-up clients went inside. Most of them came back with their prescription in hand. Some came out and walked away empty-handed.

"That's curious," I said. "Their prescriptions must not be ready."

"What does that mean?"

"Graul's advertises itself as a compounding pharmacy. That means they make a lot of their own remedies. It could be benign. It could be generic. It could be homeopathic. Could be something else."

"You are not telling me everything again."

"Sorry. I do that when I'm not sure what I'm seeing."

"You can just say that, you know."

"All right," I said, "I am processing a lot of the things we talked about yesterday and this morning and trying to figure out how it all fits together.

"How many crimes are we looking at here? Is it one interrelated activity or a bunch of specific crimes? We need to figure that out before we decide how to handle it. There are a lot of players and moving parts."

"Start with what we are looking at here. Graul's is clearly dispensing controlled substances. So what? A lot of pharmacies do that. Some, including some of the big chains, have gotten in trouble for being too cavalier about it and not putting screens in place."

"'Just following doctor's orders is their out. It's not us; it's them.' It's not a get-out-of-jail-free card, but it may be enough to make it an acceptable risk – particularly when the margins are so high. In the four cases I know, everyone got off with a slap on the wrist – fines and probation."

"But what if it's more than that? What if they are taking something bad and making it worse? Like what? Like making their cocktails. Maybe mixing fentanyl with opioids or other designer drugs. Not only illegal. Potentially lethal."

"And how are they tied into Chambers and GerriCare – if they, in fact, are? Is there a formal relationship and/or an ownership link? Or are they on their own?"

"With me so far?" She nodded her head. "Ok, walk it back," I continued. "We know the runners are connected to the clinic. How are they connected – if they are – to the men in the Lexus?"

"Or are the people in the Lexus playing for the other

team? If so, how are they connected to Graul's? Do they have a direct link, or does it all go through GerriCare?"

"One way or another, they are pushing a lot of drugs out onto the streets. Is that what this is about? Or is it something more? If so, what?"

"It feels like an unholy alliance between a man who desperately needs money and some dirty old dogs learning new tricks. That would tie it all together, but why would Chambers take that big a risk? GerriCare has built its business manufacturing surgical products. They make pacemakers, of course, but they also make products used in hip and knee replacements and intraocular lenses for cataract surgery – the most popular Medicare procedure. They sell about 4 million a year. Why such a radical shift?"

"And how do I fit in? Is it personal or professional? Revenge or target of opportunity? If all we have is what we see, it could just as easily be handled by the FBI and the DOJ."

"What makes it a Senate concern? Is it really a national problem of that significance? We have gone after individual providers in the past, from time to time, but there has to be some compelling reason. Something more than a personal vendetta."

"That's a lot of questions," She said. "What are you going to do?"

"Try to get some answers. It's a big, tangled ball of yarn. If we are going to untangle it, we must start with the loose end."

"The personal piece."

I nodded.

"I'm going to go into that clinic and see what I can shake loose. If I apply enough pressure, someone will break. The fault line will lead us to the heart of this hot mess."

It was just after 3:00 PM. I drove around to the clinic and parked on the first row of the parking lot, as near the entrance as possible. I backed in so the clinic was in full view. When I switched off the engine, she put her hand on my arm.

"Can I do my job before you do yours?"

"What do you mean?"

"If I don't get something on the record before you go in, I sure as hell won't after. I want to interview some of the people leaving the clinic – not the seniors, but the ones walking to Graul's. Once you go in and shake things up, they are going to scatter like pigeons in the park."

She had a point. And I had promised to respect her story.

"Ok," I said reluctantly.

Skeptical as I was, I could tell she was even more determined. I could see it in her eyes and the jut of her chin. But I couldn't help adding a note of caution.

"Be careful. They are almost certainly on something."

We all do that. Projecting our concerns by telling people things we know they already know. We know it won't change anything, but we do it anyway.

Taylor left the car and took a position just above the deli, halfway between the clinic and the pharmacy. She looked small against the grey wall of the mall.

The first man out of the clinic brushed by her. She

tried to ask him a question. He ignored her. The second man spoke to her briefly, but he kept on walking.

She had to wait a few minutes for the next opportunity. She calculated her move and was about to step in front of him and block his progress when the Lexus appeared. As before, it parked in front of the deli. As before, the passenger left the door open and went inside.

Taylor redirected, approached the car, and started talking to the driver through the open car door. I couldn't tell if he responded, but he quickly got out. His passenger hurriedly returned.

The driver was a small man with slick-back, black hair. He wore pointy Italian shoes and a silver-tipped belt wrapped around and tucked down and through the loops on his tapered black pants, the silver tip pointing at his crotch. There were a lot of gold chains and pinky rings. He was a nobody trying too hard to look like somebody.

His passenger was bigger than I thought. His chest, legs, and arm muscles said he was someone who liked to lift weights. His protruding belly said he still liked to lift a fork.

They moved in and sandwiched Taylor between them. I was out of the car as they converged on her and pressed her against the wall. Slick grabbed her arm. She resisted, twisting to get free, until muscles grabbed her other arm.

Three long steps, and I was there. I told them to let go of her. They both turned at the sound of my voice, and Slick said something to Muscles.

Muscles released his grip and squared to face me, blocking my approach. He had close-cropped blonde hair on his head and no visible hair on his arms or body. It probably interfered with the shine of the oil on his muscles. His eyes were small, deep set in his fat face. Up close, he looked like the Michelin man with short arms and legs emerging from an inflated body. Slick had the sharp features of a ferret, shifting dark eyes, a big nose, and big ears.

Slick didn't seem to know who I was, but he knew he didn't want me around. He told Muscles to get rid of me. I was close enough this time to hear his command.

Muscles got the message and stepped in to stop me, shuffling his little feet forward like a boxer. When I got close enough, he let go of a roundhouse right that would have put me out if it had landed. I saw it coming from the time the thought crossed his dim little mind.

There was a lot of power in his punch, but the angle was all wrong. I was at least 8 inches taller. To land one on my chin, he had to wind up and bring it up from the ground. I waited until he was fully extended, ducked, and blocked the punch with my left forearm, lifting and pushing his right hand skyward. When he was fully extended, I stepped inside his punch and launched my own right hand.

For reasons unknown, my college roommate, Lou Roche, decided to take up boxing. Lou was the whitest white man you ever saw. He was a gentleman with a great sense of humor and the last person you would expect to see in the ring with a bunch of seasoned black and Latin Olympic contenders.

Maybe that's why he did it. Some of our friends said he was trying to prove something to himself. His brother was killed in combat. His parents had made it clear they would not allow him to serve. Whatever it was, he wanted it badly enough to persuade Pappy Gault to take him on and train him for the Golden Gloves.

At that time, Pappy was a legend in DC. His gym in the Northeast smelled like a jockstrap. It was basic, with no decor beyond the posters on the wall of the many successful fighters he had trained, including notably a young Sugar Ray Leonard. Inevitably, I got drafted into being Lou's sparring partner. Pappy said he had never seen a bigger body bag in his life.

One of the first things he explained was the gloves we wore in the ring. The bones in the human head are many times harder than the bones in your hands, he said. Boxers wear gloves to protect their hands, not their opponent's face or bodies. A fistfight like you see in your standard movie would put your hands in a cast for weeks.

The other thing he taught me was how to throw a punch. Poorly done, it is all hands and arms. Properly done, it involves the whole body. With Pappy in mind, I put everything into my punch, driving from my legs, engaging my core and shoulder muscles, and twisting my hand as it made an impact deep in Muscles' solar plexus.

I didn't just try to hit him. I tried to hit through him, driving my fist through the muscles below his rib cage, aiming for the spine on the other side. The blow was greeted by a mighty "OOMF" as the wind went out of him. He backed up, stumbled, and went to the ground. His hands went to his belly as he struggled for breath. He made little gagging sounds, turned, and threw up.

With Muscles on the ground, I turned to Taylor's other assailant only to see there was no need. She had pulled free and kicked him powerfully in the groin. He staggered back and doubled over.

I smiled at her.

"Judo, Taekwondo, karate?

She smiled back.

"Ballet."

I grabbed Slick by his fancy belt and pulled him up until he was at eye level. When you are fully grown, you don't expect another man to be able to do that for you. Psychologically, it does something to your sense of self – Maybe I'm not all grown up. Maybe I'm not so tough after all.

He weighed somewhere around 150 pounds. I held him up with my right hand and steadied him with my left, pressing a fist full of shirt against his chest. His face was six inches from my face. He was sweating with fear and pain. It didn't help that the way I held him was adding pressure to his already sore testicles.

"Do you see this woman?" I said. "Take a good look at her,"

His dark eyes shifted in her direction.

"Now, take a good look at me."

His eyes came back. I held him close. My eyes were fixed on his eyes with a hard, unrelenting stare. He smelled of too much cologne mixed with too much sweat.

"Do you ever want to see this face again?

I looked through him, releasing the menace I felt. I wanted to tear him apart, and I wanted him to know that. As I looked at him, a pungent smell was added to his cologne as he wet himself. He shook his head vigorously and tried to look away. I didn't let him. I pulled him closer and lifted him higher, increasing the pressure on his groin.

"If I ever see you anywhere close to this woman again," I said. "Same street. Same block. Same zip code. You will. I'll find you, and I promise you – you won't walk away."

I let that penetrate.

"Nod your head if you understand."

He nodded quickly.

"Good."

I extended my arms and pushed him away with enough force to bounce him off the wall. His neck snapped, and his head hit the wall with a satisfying crack. He slid down the wall and fell near his body man, who was now on his hands and knees, still struggling for breath but trying valiantly to get to his feet.

I saved him the trouble and kicked him in the head. I didn't try to put everything in it. There was no need to kill him. I just wanted to put him out for a while. I caught him under the chin with the top of my right boot and watched his head snap as he went to sleep.

"Jeez," Taylor said. "Remind me not to make you mad."

"You haven't begun to see it," I said. "But I'm getting there."

"What are you going to do now?"

"It's time to find out what happened to my uncle. Here are the keys to the car. Lock yourself in. Photograph anything that happens out here. Make sure the date and time stamp stay on. Photograph these guys and anything that happens to these guys – especially if somebody comes to help them. Photograph my entrance."

"If anything strange happens out here, call my cell. Let it ring once and hang up. I have it set to vibrate. I just want to know if I need to watch my backside. Stay in the car and don't try to do anything brave. You have to trust I can handle whatever may come at me in there."

Medicare and Medicaid clinics are not known for their décor. This one was sparser than most. Half a dozen seniors sat around a small waiting room on stacked chairs. Spare no expense there. They were the kind of chairs you find in a church basement.

Grodon was standing in the corner nearest the door. The walls were either a bland beige or a dirty white. Hard to tell. From the look of the place, dirty seemed most likely. The only decorations on the walls were copies of the posters I had seen taped to the windows. Lots of free stuff.

The reception was on the wall opposite to the entrance. A low desk guarded the doctors' offices and treatment rooms. There was a sign-in sheet on the desk and a disinterested receptionist behind it.

It was the middle-aged Hispanic woman I had seen yesterday. She was wearing an institutional blouse with a flower print and black pants. Her dark eyes came up as I entered. She stared. Not your usual customer. I could feel my presence fill the room. I could have touched the ceiling flatfooted if I tried. Everyone looked my way and followed my every move until I stood towering over the receptionist.

I handed her my card. It's a heavy linen stock. The

gold seal of the United States stamped in the left corner. My name and title – Theo James Alexander, Director, Permanent Subcommittee on Investigations, United States Senate, Washington, DC, 20510 – centered with a phone number, bottom left, and an email address bottom right.

She fingered the card thoughtfully. This was something she had never encountered before.

"I want to see one of your patient's files. Her name is Madeline Mitchell."

I pulled a letter out of my back pocket.

"This is a letter giving me her power of attorney."

The receptionist didn't know I had typed the letter myself that morning and printed it before leaving The Big Doll. She didn't need to.

"I can't do that she said."

"Then find someone who can," I said.

I pulled out my box top and flashed the badge. That was something else she did not need to know. No Senate staffer is authorized to carry a badge. The one I carry was made for me in Chicago by a very accommodating young man who provides all kinds of useful things for law enforcement types out of a small shop on the South side.

It may not be official, but it sure as hell looks official. And it helps. People have to think about a card or even a Senate ID. Most people have never seen one. Most people don't know what it means. Everyone understands a badge.

"And while you are at it," I said, "tell them I'm here as part of a federal investigation."

The receptionist pushed her chair away from her desk and scurried back through the hall into the inner sanctum.

A few moments later, she returned with the thin middle-aged woman I had seen yesterday. She had her hair pulled back in a bun. It made her pale face seem gaunter than it probably was. Her head was up, shoulders back, conveying the impression she thought she was in charge of something.

"Who are you?"

"Ms. Cantrell. I'm the office manager."

"As I told your receptionist, I want to see Madeline Mitchell's file."

I flashed the box top again.

"That won't be possible."

Her nose elevated in defiance.

"Why not?"

I moved close enough to tower over her.

She backed off a step but maintained her defiance.

"Our patient files are confidential."

Her resistance confirmed my suspicion. She was no innocent party. She was part of whatever was going on.

"Ms. Cantrell, I helped write the privacy laws. I know what they say. I have a power of attorney. I also have federal authority. I want to see that file, and I will not be leaving until I do."

She backed up another step, her face wavering. I pressed on.

"Have you met Maria Chavez – the U.S. Attorney for the Middle District of Florida?"

She shook her head. I pulled out my cell.

"I'll see if I can arrange it. I am going to call her office and ask her to send a couple of agents over here with a subpoena. And if they are going to go to that much trouble, we might as well subpoena you personally and everything here related to Madeline and her case."

"And just to make your day complete, I'm going to stand right here until they come. I'm sure all your patients will want to know who I am and why you are being investigated. And if they ask me, I'm going to tell them."

She backed up another step and put a hand up in surrender.

"Come with me."

She walked me down the hall past two treatment rooms with charts stacked up on racks near the door. The doors were closed. She pointed to a corner office.

"I'll get Dr. Martin."

The diplomas framed on the wall said Dr. Martin had gone to Florida State, medical and undergraduate, and had been certified in a number of subspecialties, including pain management. I stopped being impressed by such things when Max got his first degree. His ego wall would put Martin's to shame.

There were a couple of framed pictures and a few medical texts on a corner bookshelf, a filing cabinet behind the desk, a desk chair, one guest chair and the obligatory potted plant. There were no windows. The only source of light came from the overhead fluorescents.

I walked around the desk to get a closer look at the photographs. One was a vintage portrait of a couple. Parents probably. The other was a trophy shot. Dr. Martin is on a boat holding a rather large fish. Big toothy grin. He was ever so proud of himself. He was the grey-haired man I'd glimpsed yesterday morning.

Martin was quick to come in. He was about 5'10", maybe 170 pounds. Square tortoiseshell glasses. He came up to my shoulder. He was trying to give me the doctor's look with the lab coat and the stethoscope draped around his neck. I have been in enough clinics and urgent care centers to know that no one does that without premeditation. Mostly, it's some residents trying to impress the girls.

We were in his comfort zone. I needed to take that away from him. I turned my back to him and left him standing by the door. I went back to his desk, turned around, and sat on it, casually dangling one leg off the ground. I heard some papers crumple as I sat down. I didn't much care. It served my purpose. I wanted him to feel my complete disregard for him and his possessions.

"You know why I'm here," I said. "Where's Mitchell's file?"

He seemed unable to get beyond the physical impact of my size. Even in a reclining posture, I was still a head higher.

"You sure are a big one," He said. "Don't think I have ever had anyone in my office quite so big."

"Maybe one," I said. I let that sink in, then added, "Not quite so big, but close."

He tried to control his reaction as he realized the implications of what I said, but he was too slow. His eyes dropped, and his mouth tightened. Confirmation enough.

"Get the file."

If I wasn't threatening before, I knew I was now. My blood was up. I could feel the anger building in my body, looking for release. I stared at him, almost hoping he would give me an excuse to stand him on his head or separate his arms from his body. He read the signs and backed away.

"Ok, Ok," He said. "Have a seat."

He gestured toward the guest chair facing the desk. Either he wanted to get me off his desk, or he had something else in mind. My nature is such that when someone wants me to do one thing – particularly in a situation like this – I am likely to do something else.

When he left, I walked around and sat in his chair, taking command of his desk. There was nothing of significance on his desk – general correspondence and bills. The desk drawers were full of drug samples – the kind of thing drug companies hand out to doctors as freebies.

He was surprised and unhappy to see me sitting in his place when he returned. I could see him struggling with it. He wanted to get me out of his seat, but he didn't know how. Finally, he reached across the desk and handed me a thin file with Madeline's name on it.

It wasn't much to show for a person who was said to have been making weekly visits for months. As I opened it, Martin came around behind me, leaning over me with his left hand as though trying to explain the notations.

As Samantha Jean had pointed out, I am notorious for sitting with my back to the door. I don't like people behind me. As soon as I felt his weight on my shoulder, I pushed off the desk, using the full force of my arms and legs.

I heard his shock as the chair hit him in the sternum and the great gasping release of air as he hit the filing cabinet behind us. I was out of the chair and facing him in time to see his right hand coming out of the deep pocket of his lab coat, holding a hypodermic needle.

I brought my right forearm around and hit him hard at the base of the neck, pinning him there, and turned in the same motion to grasp his right arm with my left hand. He was holding the hypodermic needle with his thumb on the plunger.

He struggled for a moment, trying to complete the injection before I helped him out and forced the hand with the needle up to his neck. I was looking in his eyes as he administered the injection, my thumb on his thumb.

I saw the panic in his face as he realized what he had done. I pivoted on my right heel, turned him around me and sat him in his chair. His eyes were already starting to turn hazy.

As I watched him, I knew what happened to my uncle. The same thing would have happened to me if I had taken the guest chair.

"You know – and I think I know – what was in that needle," I said. "If I'm wrong, you might as well just go ahead and die and get it over with. If I'm right, you would probably like to have this right now."

I held up a box of naloxone I had taken from his sample drawer. He saw it and reached for it.

"No," I said. "Questions first. And you better be quick. My guess is you set the dose for my size. That won't give you much time. What did you do to my uncle?"

"Nothing."

"Last chance."

I held the bottle in front of his outstretched hand. His hand opened and closed.

"No. No. Nothing," He said. "I just sedated him."

His head was starting to sag as if it had suddenly gotten too heavy for his neck.

"Chambers couldn't understand why he was so concerned about a beat-up, old woman. SafeCo took him to the boat. They said they just wanted to ask him some questions. They told me he fell off. He got confused or was trying to resist or something. I don't know. I wasn't there."

His speech slurred and slowed down. The words were getting harder for him to find.

"One of the guys tried to say it was my fault. I know it wasn't. He said I gave him too much, and he wouldn't come around. But that's not true. I know my dosage. I think they got what they could and pushed him off the boat."

The confirmation should have provided some relief. It didn't.

"I hope you know your dosage," I said, "Because this isn't going to do you any good."

I threw the box into the trashcan by his desk. I stood by, waiting and watching. Another man might have called 911. Another man might have hollered for a nurse. Another man might have seen enough humanity in this rodent to give a damn about what happened to him. I waited until his breathing slowed and put my fingers on his neck to check his pulse. I picked up Madeline's file and walked out of his office as he died.

Instead of going out the way I came in, I went looking

for the back exit. It was at the end of the corridor, properly marked with the mandatory exit sign. When I opened the door, I found a meat wagon waiting. It was parked near Martin's Mercedes and backed up to the door. Two men dressed in white were sitting on the back bumper. They looked surprised to see me.

I gave them a reassuring smile.

"I think he is ready for you," I said.

Bear

I walked down the back side of the mall until I got to Publix and went in through their loading dock. When I was inside, I texted Taylor and asked her to bring the car around. I picked up some chips and a couple of Cokes on the way out. I didn't want to walk out empty-handed. When you use the facilities of a commercial establishment for whatever reason, even if it is just for shade, you owe them something.

Taylor's eyes were wide as I slid into the passenger side. I told her to drive.

"Where?" She asked.

"Just drive," I said.

I wanted to get out of there before the manure hit the propeller. I doubted the clinic would call the cops and wouldn't have been worried that much if they did, but Chamber's people had already shown they were capable of a lot less- -palatable things. I didn't know what else they might do, but I was certain they would feel the need to do something. I wanted to be somewhere I could think that through and prepare.

I told Taylor to find the Trail and head south. I knew she wanted to know what happened, but I only wanted to have to tell the story once. I called Meyer and asked if he could meet us somewhere other than the City Dock for a quick drink. It didn't take him long to figure out where and why.

"Come here," He said. "I'll leave your name at the gate. I'll meet you at Villa Rilassare. It's Treviso's activity center. It's on the right, about half a mile after you clear the gate. We can have drinks at the bar by the pool."

It was a good option. If they came after me – when they came after me – they wouldn't be looking for me there. And if they had followed, they would be stopped at the gate. I left a message for Carla, told her where we were, and asked her to join us if she could. I left her name at the gate as we entered.

Treviso Bay is a retirement community carved out of the Everglades. It is known for its Tuscan-style clubhouse, elegant homes, and a particularly challenging golf course.

"As you probably know, there are more golf courses per capita in Naples than anywhere in the country," Meyer explained, "But Treviso Bay is a cut above. It's the only TPC course on this coast. That's its unique factor."

"I don't play golf that much myself, but it is important to my clients. That's a lot of the reason they are here, and I'm here because they are here. It's a lot easier talking about investment options and portfolios in the clubhouse than trying to do it long-distance from Chicago."

He smiled almost apologetically.

"Plus, I've gotten too old for Chicago. The winters are brutal, the traffic is unbearable, and the population has become surly. Maybe because of the weather and the traffic, I don't know, but it seems everyone has a chip on their shoulders. Everyone is mad at everyone else."

It didn't take long to see why he liked this development. It was self-contained and peaceful. The grounds were immaculate. The homes were spread out around a series of small lakes and spaced nicely.

Villa Rilassare was the name of their salon and spa. It included a lagoon pool, a lush waterfall, cabanas, an expansive sundeck, fitness facilities, every recreational amenity you could imagine, and a casual restaurant called La Piscina.

There were several families around the pool, kids splashing and chasing balls. Half a dozen young adults were gathered around a diving board in the deep end. Meyer was waiting poolside by the bar when we arrived.

He was wearing blue shorts, sandals, and a light blue logo shirt. Mostly grey hair was trying to escape from his shirt and shorts and covered his legs. I couldn't help but think that if you could hold him down and shave him bare, there would be enough hair to make a fair-sized carpet.

He was drinking something fruity again. This one was a mango colada, he said, and he insisted we try one. From his look, he had a good head start. Maybe he knew what was coming. Maybe the market was down, or one of his big investments had gone sour.

We humored him, let him place the order for drinks and made small talk until they arrived. I let Taylor bring him up to date. She described our activities, observations, and tentative conclusions in detail with the orderly mind of a good reporter.

She kept looking at me, shy darting, side-wise glances as she talked, checking for my reaction or wondering, perhaps, if there was something I wanted to add. I let her talk until she ran out of things to say.

Meyer took it all in quietly. I could tell he was processing it, but his mood was subdued, not so much for what he heard, perhaps, as what he hadn't heard. I slid Madeline's file across the table and made the bridge. Taylor looked over his shoulder as he examined the half-dozen pages in the file.

"Doesn't make much sense," She said.

"It does when you understand what they are doing."

"They are running two sets of books," Meyer said.

"Right."

"They had to know you would figure that out," She said. "Why would they give you this folder?"

"Because they thought I wouldn't have a chance to read it."

I let that sink in.

"This is their private clinic file. Madeline's Medicare file would be two inches thick with the extensive forms, identifiers, and explanations required by law. They probably picked this one up because it was lighter and easier to handle, yet specific enough to hold my interest while they needled me."

Meyer sat motionless. I saw his jaw set. His big, sad eyes were looking into my soul.

"They figured if it worked once, it would work again," I said. "They even had an ambulance waiting at the back door so they could cart me away. They probably would have gotten away with it if it weren't for my uncle."

Taylor stopped with her drink in mid-air.

"What happened?"

"Martin put the file on the desk in front of me with his left hand and came around behind me with a needle in his right. He slipped and injected himself instead."

"Is he dead?" She asked.

"I certainly hope so."

I put a hand on Meyer's hairy arm. It was resting on the table between us.

I told him, "We had time for a little talk before he left us. I guessed right. I found a box of Naloxone on his desk while he was getting the file. It's the stuff first responders carry to counteract opioid overdoses. I let him see it after he injected himself. He wanted it badly enough to answer my questions."

"He told me all he did was sedate my uncle. He said SafeCo, Chambers' security firm, took him to the boat for questioning. It seems like a strange place to take him for that if what Martin said was true."

"What is undoubtedly true is that it ties it all back to Chambers. They probably gave him something to keep him alive while they questioned him. Martin said at some point, he resisted, lost his balance, and fell over."

"I doubt that" Meyer said. "He was a Navy seal. Seals don't drown unless they are unconscious. I think they got what they wanted or as much as they could and threw him overboard. I think they made sure he was in no condition to swim."

I could see tears starting to form in Meyer's soft, pale eyes. It was not loss but confirmation of loss. Nothing he didn't know. But that didn't make it any easier.

"So, what are you going to do about it?" He asked as soon as he could.

"You know what I'm going to do. Blood runs deep."

His eyes hardened.

"I want to help."

Casablanca

Carla arrived in time to give us a break. She was overdressed for the pool and looked like she might have come directly from class. Now that everyone was there, Meyer said he wanted to order dinner. He looked like he needed it. He recommended blackened salmon or the chicken Parmesan.

There was an uncomfortable silence after the waitress left. When Carla settled in, I felt obligated to tell her what we had found. I said it looked like they had taken their revenge on Madeline by injecting her with something or some combination of things designed to fog her mind.

I let her look at the file and explained its significance. Unless you know their internal codes, I said, there is no way of knowing exactly what they had done. The last notation was made on Monday. They gave her a shot identified with the clinic number and prescribed a month's supply of some medication identified only with a clinic code. My guess is that both were custom-made by Graul's according to the clinic's specifications.

I said I wanted to check Madeline's Medicare records to see if there was a parallel charge on the same date. That could be evidence of fraud, but it wasn't the most important thing. Carla said she understood, but I wasn't sure the reality had penetrated. So, I gave it to her more bluntly.

"They can't bill anyone for what's in this private file," I said. "No insurance company would give them a dime without more information – and probably not then – because they would argue Medicare should pay for whatever Madeline needs."

"They are using her as a 'prescription mule,' someone to get drugs they can give someone else to sell. I would guess they are doing the same thing to a lot of other people, stockpiling medications with street value."

"Is that why she changed so much?"

"There is no way to be sure, but it probably is. She was a feisty woman. She wouldn't have tolerated any of this if she knew what was going on. They probably gave her something early on that scrambled her brain."

"Whatever they have been giving her is enough to create dependency and induce dementia. It's probably permanent, but it's possible she will get better once she is off whatever they have her on. That's uncertain. What's certain is that she is going to have withdrawal symptoms of some kind for who knows how long."

"This means she is going to need you more than ever now. Someone is going to have to be with her as she comes down. Someone needs to explain to her what happened. Someone needs to help her find another doctor. Tell her that her old doctor is gone, and she needs to find someone she can trust. She may need home care or a private duty nurse. Somebody needs to help her sort all that out."

It was a lot to unload on her. Maybe too much. After all, she was still a kid working on growing up and starting her own life. Her face was stoic. I couldn't tell what she felt, so I asked.

"Do you think you can handle this? I know you love Madeline, but it's a lot to take on. No one expects you to stop living your life, but Madeline is going to stop living hers unless she gets some help. You told me she helped you a lot when you were young. You said she helped a lot of other kids, as well, and you were like family. Maybe it's time for some of those folks to pitch in and return the favor."

I read her wrong. There was no hesitancy. She was quick to nod her head.

"I'll get Darleene to help. We will round up the crew. They will all want to help. It's the least we can do. I'm a little embarrassed because I stopped going as much as I did. It got hard to talk with her. It was like she wasn't there half the time. I wasn't sure she was ever coming back. So, I kinda deserted her."

"Don't be so hard on yourself. We wouldn't have gotten this far without your help. But now is when she needs you the most. The next time you visit her, check her medicine cabinet. Put any prescriptions you find in a

Ziploc bag. Find a marker. Date and sign the bag. Treat it like evidence and put it somewhere safe. Don't let her take anything Martin prescribed for her."

After dinner arrived, almost as an afterthought, she said, "What you told me explains a lot."

"Like what?"

"James called. He saw you come into the clinic, but he didn't see you leave. He said things got hairy this afternoon. A lot of people waiting a long time. Some people got cranky and made a fuss. There wasn't much he could do. There wasn't anyone who could tell him what to do."

"Finally, a couple of tough-looking guys came and took charge. He hadn't seen them before. They had short hair and hard eyes. They sent everyone home. They pulled him aside and asked about you."

"What did he say?"

"The truth. He said he saw you come in and that you talked with Ms. Cantrell. He said she took you back to the treatment rooms, and that was the last he saw of you. Things were really getting busy so that you might have come back out. He didn't know."

"Anything else?"

"They told everyone Dr. Martin had gotten sick and they were going to close the clinic until they could find a replacement. They told James they would call him to come back when they needed him. He said he has seen enough. He is not going back. When they call, he is going to tell them he found another job."

It was near dusk when we broke up. The drinkers had

replaced the diners and divers. They were an older, more sedate set. Meyer seemed to know some of them. He acknowledged their greetings but did not attempt to interact. His eyes were glazed, and his step unsteady.

I offered to drive him home, but he wouldn't have it. There wasn't far to go, he said. So, I gave him a hug and watched him trudge off toward his car, walking straight, steadily and deliberately enough to tell me he was probably all right. Still, we waited long enough to see him drive off. He drove the way he had walked. He wasn't going to set any speed records, but he would get there.

We were ten, maybe fifteen minutes, away from City Dock when I told Taylor I didn't think she should stay the night. I got the reaction I expected. After a certain age, the circuits are pretty well wired.

You have to be aware of the distance between what is said and what is heard. Her experience said I should have known this was coming. Just another guy. Just one of those casual things. No promises. No strings.

I saw the hurt forming in her eyes and the cant of her head, but she tried to power through.

"Oh…sure…"

"Stop it," I said.

"I'm sorry…I didn't expect…there is no reason."

"Just stop it! That's not what this is about."

I put my hand on her long, slender neck and pulled her toward me just enough to get her full attention.

"Don't make me go Casablanca on you."

She looked at me without comprehension.

"Casablanca?"

"You know, my dear…'Where I have to go, you can't

follow. What I've got to do, you can't be any part of that one."

I smiled at her, looking deep into those killer green eyes, now a little moist where tears had tried to form.

"You have to understand," I said. "They will be coming after me now. And you need to know I want them to come after me. I just don't want you caught in the crossfire."

"So please, go home. Get some rest. Type up your notes. Start drafting your story. Take a break now and then and think humid thoughts about me and what we will do the next time we are together. Do whatever you have to do to keep busy."

"They attacked my family. Nobody does that. They poked the Bear. Now it's my turn. It won't be pretty, and it won't be over until I say it's over. Until then, I would appreciate it if you kept your pretty head down. I've gotten very fond of that head. I don't want anything to happen to it."

"Ok."

She gave me a small, tentative smile.

"So, you are Humphrey Bogart. Does that make me Ingrid Bergman?"

"Pretty much. You even look a little like her. Could be her sister."

"I like that. It's been a while since I've seen Casablanca. I'll have to pull it up while you are gone and play it a few times – maybe once or twice a day until I see you again."

"Sounds like a plan. Do that…What did you say to those clowns outside the clinic?"

"Not much. I just identified myself as a reporter and said I was working on a story about the clinic."

"All the more reason to make yourself scarce. They will be looking for you now. This might be a good time to visit your mother. Let her watch Casablanca with you."

"Will you call me? I'm not asking you to impress my mother, though I wouldn't mind getting her off my back. I just need to know you are safe."

"I will, and you can tell your mother you are off the market now, and the guy calling wants to meet her and is going to come visit when he gets back."

She let that settle and then gave me a broader smile. She wasn't happy, but her lip stopped quivering. I dropped her at her car in the parking lot and watched her wave and take off.

I checked for a tail or an unwelcome observer and came up blank. No one followed her. Then, I went on board and double-checked the alarm system on The Big Doll. Everything seemed in order.

I reset the alarm and prepared for the evening. I found the Sig and attached the silencer. I put it on the bed with the fish bat and 20' of rope. I made a loop on one end, thinking about my early days on the ranch, and poured myself a shot of Knob Creek while I undressed and dressed again.

I put on dark sweatpants, a black turtleneck with long sleeves and my new deck shoes. I pulled the bear claw out from under my shirt, let it hang where I could see it, and settled back on the sofa to watch and wait.

It was a beautiful night. The sunset over Millionaires' Row was spectacular, with ribbons of yellow and gold as the sun picked up strings of low-hanging clouds. The last of the charters came in with the setting sun. I could hear the chatter of the crew and happy passengers talking no doubt about the day, the weather, and the gifts of the sea.

Beyond them, I could hear the sounds of the harbor, the tourists working their way through Tin City, the diners, casual observers admiring the sunset and snapping innumerable selfies to show they were there, and the interminable sounds of birds flying, scrounging on scraps from the fishing boats and gifts from the tourists ignoring the signs saying don't feed the birds. Things quieted down around ten as the shops began to close.

Last to leave were the stragglers nursing their drinks at the tables outside the Tin Inn. I watched them go from on top of The Big Doll. I had closed the drapes with the sunset, turned off the lights and eased out the forward hatch.

It was one of the lessons of my youth. One of the first lessons I had learned, in fact. It was the lesson of Denali. When preparing for battle, take the high ground. Be where you can see them coming.

It was a warm summer night with a sliver of a moon rising over the Everglades. I wrapped myself in a dark blanket I brought up with me more for cover than warmth, and I settled down in the deep shadows formed by the solar panels. The Sig with a silencer, fish bat, and rope were at my feet.

As I settled in, I was reminded again how thoughtful and careful my uncle had been. Meyer said he had escaped numerous villains and had too many close calls to count. It was easy to see why. He had positioned The Big

Doll at the end of the dock at the slip closest to the Bay. It was next to impossible to approach unseen. There would be no reason for a visitor to casually wander that far down the dock, and any approach by sea would be seen just as easily.

There was nothing I could do about it now, but I couldn't help wishing I had been given a chance to get to know my mother's brother. He must have been a remarkable man.

Ambient noise disappeared after 1:00 AM. Then, there was just the sound of sea licking and lifting the boats at the dock and an occasional motorist passing by on 12th Street. There was very little movement of any kind, which made it easy for me to see him when he arrived.

He was driving a non-descript Ford sedan a couple of years old and so dull it would be lost in dishwater. He pulled into the parking lot just before 2:00 AM and sat there for a while, watching the harbor. Then, a swift, small shadow, half seen in the glow from the distant dock light, exited the car and came on the cat's feet, pausing at each and every sound. He kept low to the ground and hustled up the dock, looking left and right like a nervous bird.

He looked to be about 5' 10", maybe 160 pounds. He was dressed in something that looked like army surplus. He came directly to me. He didn't pretend to have any other interest.

Without hesitation, he stepped over the chain at the dock, hurried down the gangplank, and jumped on board The Big Doll. His tread was so light I hardly heard the sound even though I was right above him. He was holding something in front of him.

I could have shot a mosquito off his nose at that range, but I didn't want the mess. I decided to go another way. I picked up the rope, doubled back on the loop to make a lasso, swung it twice and let it fly. He was looking for a place to put his package when the lasso settled over his chest. I flicked my wrist and pulled it tight.

He dropped whatever he was holding in surprise and started fighting the rope, trying to shrug it off, but by then, it was too late as I pulled hard and fast. The rope settled around his neck.

His hands clawed at the noose as I pulled him up to his tiptoes and led him around to the starboard side. I wrapped the rope under and over the top rail and used his weight as a counterbalance as I slid down to his level, holding the rope tight. He came up as I went down.

The first thing I noticed as our heads passed was the way he wore his watch. It was backward, the face on the inside of his left hand. It is something you learn in Black Ops. You are told the last thing you need is a ray of light bouncing off the crystal face of your watch at the wrong time. People who forget that lesson are subjected to all kinds of physical and mental abuse until they learn it. It gets to be a habit.

It was too soon to know which one of SafeCo's partners I had hanging from the end of my rope, but it was soon enough to know it was somebody I had to take seriously. I tapped him on the head with the fish bat as my feet touched the ground and then released the tension on the rope. He crumbled at my feet.

As he fell, I followed through with my cowboy training and hog-tied him like a stray calf in a roping contest, feet and then hands. When I was sure he was secure, I took my time and did a more thorough job, wrapping the rope around his body, inside and out, until his arms and legs were pinned together. Then I went looking for the present he brought me.

It was C-4, a M112 demolition block. A rectangular block 2" wide by 1.5" deep and 11" long. It was wrapped in an olive color Mylar-film container with pressure-sensitive adhesive tape on one side.

There was a five-foot detonator chord assembled with detonating cord clips and topped with a booster. It's the configuration recommended by al-Qaeda in its training curriculum for operatives using explosives. It's what they used to sink the USS Cole.

C-4 is dirty white with the distinct smell of motor oil. It is soft and malleable. It can only be exploded by a shockwave from a detonator or blasting cap. Dropping it wouldn't do it – thank God – or we would both be long gone. The triggering device on his present was a Nokia cell phone. Again, standard practice.

The Nokia105 is the most popular device ISIS and their kin use for setting off explosives. They are super durable, dirt-cheap and have a long battery life. They don't have apps or a camera, but they sell for less than $30. There is no point in blowing up an iPhone or a Samsung Galaxy at 20 to 30 times the cost – particularly when it takes two phones to complete the process. One calls the other, which sends a signal to a circuit board and sparks the explosion.

With the help of the flashlight on my cell, I was able to disconnect the leads in a few moments. I dropped the package on the Little Doll's passenger seat and went looking for the other phone. It didn't take long. It was in his right pants pocket. His car keys were in his left pocket. There was nothing else, no wallet or any other form of identification.

The second phone was identical to the first. A number had already been keyed in and was ready to send. I put the phone on the seat, picked up the C-4 and taped the package to his chest. He was starting to stir when I used the last of the tape to close his mouth.

I got my first good look at him as I carried him to the Little Doll and put him on the sundeck. It was Foster – the one the files said had a history of beating up women. I wondered if he had drawn the short straw or if he was supposed to be their demolition expert. Either way, it wasn't going to matter much longer.

The sea was calm and quiet. Smooth as glass. I took the Little Doll out slowly, putting her into the channel heading towards Port Royal. It is a shade less than two miles. There was no one else on the water, but the sky was full of stars.

I called Meyer on the way and told him what happened.

"Do you still want to help?" I asked.

"Yes," He said.

His voice was weary and sad. I could tell he had been drinking, but there was no way to know how much.

The Gerri-Antics was where I last saw her. Her rear end was pointing toward me as I pulled up. I took it as an invitation and snuggled the Little Doll in close. I reattached the leads on the C-4, picked Foster up and held him in place as I looped the end of the rope around the anchor assembly twice, then pulled it back and wrapped it around him before tying it off.

He hung there like a reverse and ironic figurehead on an old sailing vessel. The figureheads of that time were placed prominently on the bows of these vessels, which contributed to the identity of the vessel itself. So, the statement of a crook and murderer hanging from the stern of this decadent vessel seemed more than a little appropriate.

The figurehead started to move, shuddering and shimming like a gaffed fish as I cast off. I waved, giving him the classic child's bye-bye gesture, clenching and releasing the figures of my left hand.

I called Meyer as soon as I was back in the channel.

"Call the number I gave you," I said, "in 5 minutes."

Then I called my girl. She answered immediately.

"Hey. Is everything alright?"

"Yes. Do you have a stringer in Naples?"

"Yes, Joe Morgan. He worked with me on the charity bash."

"Call him. Tell him to get a camera and get over to Port Royal. There's been an explosion on the dock."

"When did it happen?"

"Right about now."

As I hung up, the silence of the night was shattered by a massive explosion. It came with a sonic boom, a physical force sending shock waves rippling through the sea and air. I smiled as the first wave hit me and dropped

Foster's cell in the water. I hate to add to the pollution in the harbor, but there is one thing you can always rely on – the sea keeps its secrets.

A second explosion followed a few moments later as the fire found the yacht's fuel supply. By the time I tied up the Little Doll, flames filled the air, towering above and beyond Port Royal, billowing smoke across the Millionaires Mile, turning night into day.

I found the bar and poured myself two inches of Plymouth over ice. I'm not much for gin, but I knew my uncle was. I pulled up a chair on the southern deck and watched the fire burn. I heard the sirens and saw – even from a distance – firefighters try to quell the raging inferno. It was a losing battle.

I raised my glass in a silent salute to my uncle.

"This one's for you," I said, then I called Meyer.

"That was a most satisfactory sound," He said. "I heard it all the way over here. Maybe now I will be able to get some sleep."

He was right. It was a very satisfactory sound.

I called Taylor again as I watched Port Royal burn.

"So, here's the story," I said. "Hopefully, your friend Morgan will get some pictures to go with it. A boat called 'The Gerri Antics' exploded at Port Royal near Millionaires Row."

"The Gerri-Antics is registered in the Cayman Islands and owned by Jerry Chambers, President and CEO of GerriCare. She was custom-built by Trinity Yachts two years ago at a cost of $61 million."

"The cause of the explosion is not immediately clear, but rumor has it Chambers and his associates are involved in a conflict with gangsters. Drugs are said to be involved."

"You can say you have it on good authority that at least one person was on board."

"Jesus"

"Not hardly…Call me Bear."

Inviting Trouble

Sunday, May 28. The fire burned out by sunrise, but the air was heavy and filled with smoke. It was so dense you could almost taste it.

Taylor's story made the front page of the *Sun*. She had been smart enough to pull images of Chambers' February charity bash, providing context and contrast.

The Governor was standing next to Chambers in the before photo, waving to the crowd. The after photo showed a fireball that consumed the yacht, with flames billowing 30' into a dark blue sky.

The local papers were quick to pick it up and run with it. Inevitably, all the local TV stations followed suit, repeatedly running footage of the burning yacht with shots from every possible angle – air and sea. They would have put divers in the water and tried to shoot it from below if they could have figured out how to do that.

The talking heads in the studio expressed their opinions of what they saw and interviewed each other, speculating endlessly on the cause and cost. Port Royal was all over the news. The Chamber of Commerce must have been thrilled.

Taylor was the only correspondent reporting the loss of human life. Other news outlets said it was a possibility without attributing the source. Such is the nature of the news business. It's always a better story if you can pretend you are the only one who has it. There is no point in giving the competition credit. Readers and viewers might think they are as good, or perhaps even better than you are.

A local reporter interviewed a testy Chambers on the dock. The yacht was still blazing behind him. Another interviewed him an hour later in front of his multi-million-dollar home. He said the loss was devastating, but there was no truth to the rumors of a crewmember on board. By 9:00 AM, CNN had picked up the story. Fox followed. Fox was certain terrorists were involved. How else could you explain it?

As the morning progressed, the piranhas came out – most of them anonymously. No one gets that big that fast without making enemies, cutting a sharp corner, stiffing suppliers, and irritating the competition. Chambers was no exception. He was down – if not out. What better time to pile on and take a shot? And it came from every direction.

Soon, the various news outlets were reporting rumors suggesting there was more to the story. There had to be more, of course. Otherwise, they would have no reason to keep talking about it.

Some said Chambers was mobbed up and being taught

a lesson. It was not exactly the head of your favorite thoroughbred in bed with you, but he was close enough when you consider that boat to be his pride and joy.

Others said he was an innocent caught in the crossfire – a turf war between rival gangs. Or, maybe it was nothing more than the backfire from a deal too sharp.

Curiously, no one said they felt sorry for him. There was blood in the water. The predators were circling, looking to take as many bites as possible out of his all-too-sudden, all-too-vulnerable hide.

Police and first responders were no help. If anything, they added fuel to the fire. An explosion of that magnitude could not possibly have been an accident, they said. There was no evidence of any human remains, but they couldn't rule that out until forensic examinations were complete. They said the blast originated on the stern. Only minute particles of that part of the yacht had been found.

They said what was left of the boat would take weeks to resurrect and examine. They were still trying to determine the nature of the specific explosive used, but they were confident it was not a home-grown product or the work of an amateur. The size of the explosion and the amount of damage suggested professionals were involved.

I kept thinking about Meyer's reaction. He was, by nature, a gentle soul. While I understood where he was coming from, I had to disagree. My nature is less forgiving, more vengeful.

Turning the table on Chambers and destroying his boat when he had tried to destroy mine with me on it was gratifying but not nearly gratifying enough. Our debt was far from satisfied.

I called M. J. at 9:35 and asked for a few minutes with Colgate. She put me through directly.

"Are you alright, T.J.?'

"Yes, Sir. Things have gotten complicated. But I'm OK."

"Is that what I'm seeing on CNN?"

"Yes."

I didn't offer an explanation. If he wanted one, he would have asked for it. I would shoot him a memo later. That would give me a chance to pick my words and make sure I didn't tell him things he didn't need to know and preserve his deniability.

"I called to ask a favor."

"What do you need?"

"A ride. I am inviting some people to the ranch. I want to make sure I get there before they do. I was going to call General Aviation in Ft. Myers, but it seems like a lot to put on the AmEx without asking permission."

"Don't worry about that. I'll take care of it."

A Bombardier 700 was waiting when I got to Ft. Myers two hours later. It was the Global Express. I expected a rent-a-jet. This was the top-of-the-line – Colgate's personal plane. There were no markings on it other than his initials on the nose and a number on the tail.

Two men were waiting on the tarmac when I checked in. Both were around forty, fit and well groomed. If you worked for Colgate, you would expect nothing less. They said their names were Carson and Mills, pilot and co-pilot. Carson took the lead.

"Where to?"

"Steamboat Springs."

Carson said the Bombardier was one of the fastest business jets in service. It should cover the 1700 miles in about 3 hours and thirty-three minutes.

While they filed flight plans, I dialed a number stored in my cell. I had only called it once before – six months ago when I called Chambers to tell him his company was going to be mentioned in a Congressional hearing.

"Did you say mentioned," He responded, "or *mentioned*."

I said, *mentioned* and invited him to be present and respond. He accepted my invitation, but he didn't enjoy it.

He picked up my call with a gruff voice, "Yeah?"

Maybe his voice was affected by the smoke from the fire. Maybe it just expressed his mood. He was having a bad day. I tried to help.

"They say you are looking for one of your men," I said. "He shouldn't be too hard to find. He was seen all over town this morning."

"You son-of-a-bitch – "

"Yeah. I love you too, Jerry…That's three strikes. You want to call it?"

"We will call it when we catch up with you, you asshole. It's only a matter of time."

"I'll make it easy for you. I'll be at my ranch. By myself. No one else around. No witnesses. Feel free to visit…But if you do, you had better bring your A-team.

I'm tired of dancing with your mopes and those clowns in camo. It's tiresome and insulting."

Three hours and fifteen minutes later, we were taxiing into private aviation on Steamboat. Brad Ferguson, my foreman, was waiting with the Land Rover. He married Cheyenne, the youngest Baxter girl.

Brad had worked on the ranch for 15 years, taking on more responsibility as Dad grew older. It seemed natural for him to take over when Dad passed on. I certainly had no interest in doing it. By then, I was pretty well locked into the East.

The Yampa Valley Regional Airport is 22 miles from Steamboat. There isn't much traffic on the ground or in the air this time of year. During the season, The Boat can quadruple in size.

Come summer, you are looking at maybe 12,000 full-time residents. Still, though our place, The White River Valley Ranch, was only 40 miles away, I knew it would take at least another hour and a half to get there.

The roads – to the extent there are roads – are miserable. You take a dirt road West of Steamboat Springs toward Buffalo Pass. The pass winds eight miles up through shimmering Aspen groves toward the Continental Divide and Summit Lake before diving West toward and through the 12 ski resorts in the White River National Forest. Once you clear the service roads for the ski trails, a 4-wheel is the only way to go in the spring and summer, and there is no way to go in the winter and fall.

One could always go around – West to Craig, then north, east, and south to come in through Wyoming. It is a more comfortable ride, but it adds another hour to your journey. And there simply wasn't that much time.

I let Brad drive and took the time to enjoy being back in the mountains. The weather was wonderful, a cool crisp 67 degrees. The air was clean. The views were staggering. Some things never change.

If you don't love the Rockies, if they don't lift your soul, if you don't feel the inner peace that comes with the awareness of something greater than you are when you are there, there is something wrong with you. I never feel closer to God than when I am in the Rockies. No church or cathedral ever built can compare.

Brad concentrated on the road and let me have my peace. There has never been a lot of extraneous talk in my family. If you had something to say, you said it. If not, you kept your mouth shut.

There is no need to fill the air with a lot of noise and say things that don't need to be said. Brad had lived on the ranch long enough to understand that. Being married to Cheyenne undoubtedly helped. I don't think I have ever had a conversation with her longer than three sentences.

The West is a different place with a different vibe. If you are like me, when you step off Amtrak in New York City, your pulse quickens. You feel the need to move quicker, step faster, look sharper, and keep your hands in your pockets. The West slows you down and makes you more deliberate in your thoughts and movements as you adjust to a more solitary and independent environment.

"Thanks for coming, Brad," I said finally when my pulse settled and my system reset.

It was something that needed to be said. He had dropped everything when I called and driven an hour and a half to pick me up.

"No problem, Bear. What's up?"

"I have invited trouble. I want to get home in time to get the children out of harm's way."

You might think I should have said "women and children," but the women in my family can take care of themselves. Daughters and granddaughters of Denali would drop an intruder cold, chop him up and feed him to the chickens and pigs.

Cheyenne might be the fiercest of the bunch. I would put her up against a division in the woods. They would never see her.

Still, I fought my nerves all the way to the ranch. I didn't think there was any way they could get there before me, but you never know. They had a lot of resources at their command. We were coming in by land. They would almost certainly come by air.

A land approach would be too risky for them. There are no street signs in the high country. There are no power lines or traffic to follow. No roads to speak of. Take the wrong turn, and you could be wandering in the woods forever. Plus, there are too many places where someone on high ground can see you coming, wait, pick their moment, and take you out before you know what hits you.

The Everglades might be a more popular place to dump a body, but only because of its proximity to many more people. Alive or dead, you can vanish in the high country, and no one will ever know or give a damn.

As my grandfather always said, "It's so beautiful it's dangerous." Once again, I marveled at his courage and wondered how he came to find the place that was to become his home.

How could he have lived there alone when all his supplies had to be packed in, and the only way in and out was by horseback? We talk about the evolution of the species, but when I'm honest with myself, I must admit there is no way I could do what he did or live like that. On the other hand, he would probably have been equally lost in Washington or New York City.

The Land Rover began complaining when we hit the service roads. We bounced along, bracing for the inevitable potholes and holding on to the frame when we had to detour to find a road where the road had been washed out and seemed to disappear for long rocky stretches. You went where you needed to go in the West, whether there was a road or not.

Brad was too busy watching the road and dodging boulders to ask any more questions. I was grateful for that. Not that he was likely to intrude. Our family and the Baxters were, for all intents and purposes, one extended family connected by several levels of blood.

Both families, by necessity, had been raised to respect the Indian ways and follow Kaiah's example. We had all grown up the same way. You could not be around our families as long as he had without understanding the way we value our independence and privacy.

When we pulled up to the ranch, Cheyenne and her three kids were waiting. I tried to remember how old they were and how old they had been the last time I had seen them. I decided the boy, Robert Baxter IV, called Four, had to be twelve, and the girls, Parker and Shasta, had to be ten and eleven.

They were playing with the dogs, Cappy, a fearless Airedale, and Cassie, one of the best herding dogs you will ever see. As I watched them, I remembered the many times Cheyenne, her brothers, and I had played together, running wildly through these woods, chasing each other, and trying to sneak up on some real or imaginary creatures of the forest.

The kids stopped when they saw us coming up the long driveway leading to the house and barns. Cheyenne gathered them near the flowerbed mom had built at the center of the yard around our old well.

The pump was still in place, though it hadn't been used much since Dad had piped water into the house from above. Mom used the well to water her plants. It is still used almost exclusively for that purpose.

As always, I felt a small tug when I saw the sign announcing home – The White River Valley Ranch. I remember working with my father to set the posts in place and hang the sign between them.

I have lived far longer in other places, but still, whenever someone asks where I'm from, my mind always comes back to Colorado and the Rockies. Home is where the heart is, I guess. I have always felt connected to the mountains, this place, and this land. It was good to be back, breathe the air, and feel the serenity of the forest.

The house is set at the base of a hill that backs up to a mountain that backs up to an even bigger mountain, which is part of the foothills of the White Mountain range. You go from a mile high to 11,000 feet in the blink of an eye.

The barns and corrals are set to the East. The stream Kaiah, christened Bear Creek, winds around behind the west side of the house along the timberline.

Summer comes on fast in the mountains these days. I wasn't surprised to see the melt was nearly gone in the mountain tops. Ground cover was already thick and lush.

A hundred yards beyond the creek, just inside the timberline and before the pines gave way to the Aspens with their characteristic white bark and leaves that blaze like the sun in the fall, is a stand of large pines anchored by Bear's tree, the oldest and tallest. I saw them and remembered the night of the Grizzly like it was yesterday.

I felt an incomprehensible link between then and now – and perhaps, more than that. Some sense that destiny had led me to this time and this place.

The kids and the dogs gathered around as soon as we pulled up. I hugged the kids, patted the dogs, and knew I couldn't do either sufficiently or satisfactorily. I loved seeing them, but there wasn't enough time.

Cheyenne held back and watched me with wide eyes. I knew she was waiting for an explanation, but I couldn't stop to give her one. Still, she knew something odd, probably dangerous, was happening. I was sure she had talked with her husband before he set out to get me, but how much could she know? How much did Brad know to tell her?

Not much. And I didn't have time to tell her.

"You need to take the kids and leave," I said. "I'll let you know when it's safe to return."

She nodded her head in quiet acceptance. I threw my small travel bag on the kitchen floor and went directly to the gun case in the living room. Whatever else I did, I wanted to make sure I did it armed.

I pulled Dad's 30/30 out of the rack. Winchester lever action. The gun that won the West. Twenty-six-inch barrel. Eight rounds. Seven in the tube and one in the chamber.

There were several other fine weapons in the case, but this was the gun I had grown up with. I had been shooting it since the age of seven. I could drive a nail with it at 50 yards, split a cantaloupe at 100, and a watermelon at 200.

Brad came in to say they were about to leave. He saw the gun and stopped.

"You sure you don't want me to stay?" He said.

I shook my head. "The less you know about this, the better."

He didn't argue. He backed away and left me to do whatever it was I had to do.

Growing up in the West, you are taught early to clean up your mess and take care of yourself. Knives are always sharpened before being put away. Guns are cleaned and loaded, ready for use.

You are taught to be careful and take nothing for granted. But things change. There are kids around. The Winchester probably hadn't been used in a while.

Out of an abundance of caution, I checked the load and was glad I did. It was carrying .32 Specials. I wanted better carry, penetration, and a higher smash factor.

I jacked the shells out of the rifle and replaced them with Winchester's Supreme Ballistic Silvertips. Silvertips have a polymer tip and an alloyed lead coil. That provides greater penetration and rapid expansion. There isn't anything that you might care or need to shoot that it can't stop at 200 yards.

They come in 20 to a box. I loaded the rest of the cartridges in the ammo belt hanging on a peg next to the gun rack. I set two more boxes aside and went looking for a warm shirt.

I left the door open while I did so I could see the yard. The dogs were wandering in and out, looking for attention. Cap was my dog. He displayed the best features of his breed – smart, intensely loyal, and fearless.

I have seen him trail and take on a mountain lion that had been feeding on the stock, treeing her, and not backing off. He stood in the center of the room and watched me. I patted his head with affection every time I passed from closet to table.

I soon found what I needed – a Pendleton shirt, a green and blue plaid with an insulated lining, and my high-top moccasins. They are the only footwear I know that is more comfortable than my boots. Plus, they are a lot quieter in the woods.

I took off my windbreaker and put the shirt on, letting it hang over my jeans and cinching it in place with a leather belt, as was the custom of my Indian ancestors. The ammo belt went over my left shoulder.

I grabbed the two extra boxes of shells and was ready to go when Kaiah's knife caught my eye. It's a classic Bowie knife with a bone handle and a metal hasp. It was resting on the bottom shelf of the display case in its leather sheath.

The Bowie knife has been used on the frontier for 200 years. It became famous in 1827 as a close-combat weapon when its namesake used the knife in a duel with several men on a sandbar in the Mississippi River across from Natchez.

Bowie was stabbed, shot, and beaten half to death, but he managed to win the fight, largely because of the knife's unique design. It's 9.5" long with a double cutting edge on the first two inches. Bowie said he wanted a knife wide enough to use as a paddle, heavy enough to use as a hatchet, and sharp enough to shave. He got it.

The sheath for Kaiah's knife is decorated with beads she had woven in an intricate pattern with the image of her grandfather, Chief Denali, centered over the hasp. I picked up the knife and threaded the sheaf through my belt and let it come to rest over my right haunch.

Satisfied I had everything I needed, I closed the door firmly behind me and headed for the woods. By the time the sound of the Land Rover had faded, I was in position in the aspens high above.

Colorado's Aspen trees are the largest living organism in North America. Aspen's roots grow near the surface of the ground from which new trees sprout, giving us vast forests of aspen that are interconnected and genetically identical. That's why you see their leaves sprout, shine, turn, and drop as one. They are a family.

I settled in against the base of an old pine, leaned back and listened to the forest breathe. The only sound was the rustling of the leaves high above. The only movement was a gentle breeze coming from the northwest. I was in my element.

From years of hunting games with my relatives, I knew I was positioned where I could see what I needed to see and not be seen unless I moved suddenly – and only then by someone looking in the right direction.

Small pine, scrub brush and the tall grass stretched out before me, filling the distance below until yielding to the gravel of the driveway. Bear Creek cut through the grass halfway down. I settled in to wait.

It seemed appropriate somehow that I was paying a debt to one branch of my family on land that belonged to the other. It was another way to unite my mother and my father; it was time for their history, as well as their blood, to be joined.

The End of the Beginning

I knew they would come. The only question was when.

The manuals all say attack at first light. But there was also the possibility that they might have concluded they had a tactical advantage in resources and decided to try to beat me to the spot. They would have no way of knowing I was able to hitch a ride on Colgate's plane.

But one way or another, I knew they would come. I knew they would come because Chambers knew that I would come after him if they didn't come after me.

I came home because I wanted to fight on familiar ground. It would be harder to see them coming to Naples. It would also be harder to know how many I would have to deal with, what they looked like, and where to find them.

Given that uncertainty, I would only have one option. My grandmother said it best. Whenever we came across a rattlesnake near the house, she would find a sturdy branch and pin the snake to the ground. When she was sure the snake was secure, she would take out her Bowie knife and lop off its head.

"If you cut off the head," She would say, "What is the tail going to do?"

Difficult as Chambers' mopes might be to find in Naples under normal circumstances, I knew they would disappear if he disappeared. I would have to look for them in the ether of the underworld without knowing who and how many to look for – Scartizina and Wolfe for sure, but how many more?

Much as I wanted Chambers, I wanted his muscle more. They were the ones who took my uncle for a ride. They were the ones who questioned him. They were the ones who dropped him into the deep when they were done. I didn't want to risk their escape. I would deal with Chambers later. He wasn't going anywhere.

As I had many years before, I made a nest on the forest floor. I gathered leaves and branches and pulled them around me for warmth. After a few minutes, I picked up a slight sound, a rustle of grass and brush near the creek, coming my way.

Cap came slowly into view and walked up to nuzzle me with his shaggy head. He let me scratch him behind the ears before settling down to wait with me, stretching his long frame along my left side. He spent the night there. I watched the stars fill the sky over the ranch – the way they only can in the west – with his head on my knee.

In the morning, at first light, his head came up, and his

ears twitched. He heard them coming. He got up and trotted down to protect the house. That had always been his job.

I searched the sky and listened hard, trying to hear what he had heard, until a familiar sound disturbed the still mountain air. It came from the south.

I followed the sound with my eyes, but it was difficult to see through the branches of all the trees around me. They blocked the sky, filtering the light that was just beginning to shine through.

The sound – so out of place in my pristine environment – grew louder by the moment as it came closer. A loud, whirring motor. Blades chopping the air. A sound you never forget. One I'd heard too many times in too many distant places.

The chopper was coming in from Denver, 150 miles to the south. I checked my watch. It was 5:12 AM. They had timed it well. Sunrise.

I took a moment to reverse my watch, putting the crystal on my wrist as the sound grew louder and the helicopter came closer. It slowed as it broke through the cloud cover.

It was an Airbus 145. A 15-to-20-million-dollar corporate toy. Probably one of the four registered to GerriCare. Pilot and co-pilot. Up to 3700 pounds of cargo.

It hovered for a moment, trying to get the lay of the land. The side doors opened. Gun barrels protruded. I could see men searching for a target, left and right.

Finally, the chopper began to settle, kicking up dust as

it came down in the middle of the driveway. It sent the livestock scurrying. The horses circled the fence in the coral, looking for a way to escape or a place to hide. Chickens scattered. Four men in combat gear jumped out before the chopper touched the ground, fanning out around the helicopter.

It's a nice tactical move when you don't know where danger may be or how the enemy might come at you. All four men were carrying Bushmaster Carbon 15s with banana clips.

They are short ugly weapons designed for urban armies or macho shitheads. I guess the theory behind these guns is that if you can get off enough rounds fast enough, you may get lucky and hit something before something hits you. To each his own.

In the mountains, you learn that when it matters, "fast is fine, but accuracy is fatal." These guys reminded me of the California greenhorns that used to descend on the mountains like locusts come fall, outfitted head-to-toe by some Hollywood designer who thought he knew what a hunter looked like, offering big money for hunting privileges and gathering each night around the campfire to brag about how many "sound" shots they had. One could only wonder what they thought they heard and what, if anything, they hit.

Dad found one of these groups on his land the year after my Vision Quest. They were so green they didn't even know they were on private land. They had wandered up from Craig, stopping along the way and shooting at anything that might possibly be a deer.

Dad told them they were trespassing. He was furious. He told them to pack up and leave. If they fired another round before they left, he said, he would turn the dogs on them. And if he learned they had damaged any of the livestock, he would take their guns and shove them up their collective designer-dressed asses – and then turn the dogs on them.

I thought of my father as I watched my invaders. He wouldn't have thought much of these guys. Four mercenaries ill-prepared for the fight they would face in defense of the honor of a man who had none. Kaiah would have been even less impressed.

I knew these four men had to be what was left of SafeCo – the two remaining principles and two younger, greener hires. There were two more men in the chopper – a pilot and a co-pilot.

The man closest to the house appeared to be in charge. That would be Scartizina. He carried a backpack and looked a little older, a little better-fed than the others. From the way they moved, I guessed the other partner – Wolfe – was nearest the barn, top right. I took some satisfaction in the thought that Foster was probably still raining somewhere over the Everglades.

Scartizina was yelling at the two hires furthest away from him, but it was hard to hear what he was saying over the noise of the chopper. He waved his left arm at them, gesturing broadly while keeping the Bushmaster in his right hand.

They didn't quite seem to know what he wanted them to do. More evidence of how green they were. His movements told me he was trying to tell them to spread out and secure the perimeter, perhaps in the hope they had beat me there.

While they moved, the pilot and co-pilot were preparing to land. The co-pilot released his safety restraints so he could come out as soon as the chopper touched the ground.

I wondered why he had waited. He could easily have jumped out with the others. Was he waiting to see if it was safe, or was something else going on?

The dogs were barking furiously at the chopper and the invaders. Cappy was charging. Cassie kept her distance. Wolfe opened fire, burning half a clip. Cassie turned and ran, heading for the barn, but Cap was too brave to back down.

I saw him fall. As he fell, I put a bullet through Wolfe's brain. One bullet was all it took. He collapsed on himself like the air going out of one of those blow-up dolls you see in front of a used car dealer.

He seemed to dissolve into a boneless mass. If I thought he could feel it, I would have put another bullet in him out of spite. I loved that dog.

The three remaining shooters saw him fall, ducked, and ran for cover. There wasn't much.

One ran for a corner of the coral. The second tried to hide behind the coral and the chopper, now stalled in its descent. Scartizina ran to the old well pump in the center of the yard. All three heads were on swivels.

They knew I was there now, but they had no idea where "there" was. They also didn't know if I had kept my word and was truly alone or if I had done what they would have done and set them up.

I could have any number of people with me, and they could be anywhere – in the woods, the house, or the barn. They were disoriented, shocked, and confused.

Whatever training they might have had was lost in that moment. There was no chain of command. There was no control. There was no coordination. It was a free-for-all all, every man for himself.

Their lack of discipline made me wonder if they had even considered the possibility of a fight with someone who might shoot back. From what I had seen of their combat records, it occurred to me that this might be the first time they had that experience.

Or maybe they had watched too many Westerns. The latest remake of "The Gunfight at the OK Corral," perhaps, is on the way out. Maybe they thought we would meet in the street, and I would wait for them to make the first move in classic western good-guy style and then slap leather.

If that was the case, they were deluded. They had no idea who I was. I had no delusion about who they were. They were six snakes, like the rattlers Kaiah always chased out of the camp.

There was only one thing to do with them. She had taught me well. Whatever else happened, they weren't walking out. That was the one certainty. I had to make sure they couldn't fly out, either.

So, first things first. I had to cut off their means of retreat. I turned my attention to the helicopter. It was about to touch down. I didn't want it to settle. I had to do something before the rotors came to a full stop.

As long as the machine was powered up, I had something to work with. If I didn't act fast, I would probably be stuck with a 4000-pound paperweight.

It was about 75 yards from my position. I put a round just behind the pilot's head – close enough to get his attention. He got the message and quickly started to take the helicopter back up.

I encouraged him with a second shot. This time, I aimed for the fuel tank below the main rotor. I aimed low. The chopper would have burned a third to a half of a tank coming out. I wanted to make sure he had enough fuel to get away but not enough to get back.

As the chopper started to lift off, it spun around, exposing the co-pilot, who was desperately trying to unload cargo. He had a black duffle bag about halfway out of the chopper when I put a bullet in his heart. He tumbled out, pulling the bag with him. He hit the ground hard. The bag fell on top of him.

The three men on the ground saw the co-pilot fall and watched the chopper lifting off with something approaching panic. It must have dawned on them that if the chopper left, they were stuck in the mountains with no way out.

Scartizina waived frantically, shouting at the pilot. The shooter behind the chopper looked like he was hoping to find a way to get back on board. He chased it in desperation, trying to grab one of the skids as it started to pull away.

The third man seemed more concerned about the co-pilot's bag. It looked like he was thinking of making a run for it. I wasn't sure why.

Maybe he was feeling exposed and looking for

another place to hide, but my gut told me he was probably more concerned about getting what was inside the bag – probably armaments and explosives – than hiding behind it.

If so, the size of the bag suggested they had come well prepared, probably hoping to blow me, my place, and everything in it apart. That seemed like something Chambers would want to do.

I put a round in the bag as a precaution and was instantly glad I had taken the time to load the Silvertips. They are designed for rapid, controlled expansion. The jacket and core stay intact upon impact, providing great penetration, which is essential if you are hunting big game and have to penetrate the skin to reach the vital organs and deliver a quick kill.

In this case, it meant the bullet penetrated the canvas as easily as an elk's hide before expanding and smashing into something more substantial. Probably a grenade.

The bag exploded. Flames shot up, enveloping the chopper, and blackening its windshield with smoke. Shock waves bounced the chopper around like a kid's toy. The man on the skids couldn't ride it out and fell off. It was all the pilot could do to hang on and maintain control.

He rode the momentum like a racer, taking speed into a turn, accelerated, and headed back the way he had come. I think he knew he would never make it, but he had to try.

Flames covered half the chopper. I just hoped he would be off my property before he went down.

The three remaining invaders shot the woods up in

every possible direction, telling me they were angry, but they still didn't know exactly where I was. The Winchester shoots a smokeless cartridge, which makes shots hard to track.

I replaced the rounds I had fired while I watched them try to figure out what to do next. They were exposed with few places to hide, particularly when they didn't know my angle of attack.

They hugged the ground, looked around and waited. Finally, Scartizina said something to his nearest comrade. His man nodded, turned on his side, and opened fire on the horses in the corral.

His first burst shattered the boards at the bottom of the corral. The horses kicked up their heels and ran to the farthest corner, where they paced back and forth, looking for a way out.

He turned on his side and prepared to fire again. When he turned, he elevated his torso about a foot. It was all I needed. I put a round through the top of his head. He fell back, twitched once, and released his weapon, letting it fall by his side.

Scartizina had sacrificed a pawn, but he had accomplished his purpose. He knew where I was now. In the process, he had seriously pissed me off. I have no use for a man who will abuse animals. That kind of cruelty reflects a dark spot on the soul. It tells you all you need to know. A man of that sort is much smaller than the animals he tortures and kills. Those "animals" would never do to him what he would do to them.

I pulled back behind the big pine as they opened fire. It rained bullets for 10 minutes, slaughtering the trees.

Bullets bounced all around me and chewed up the vegetation like a weed-whacker, but nothing came close enough to cause concern. I was more in danger of being hit by a ricochet than a direct hit. Their bullets bounced off the trees and rocks all around me.

To the south, I heard an explosion that could only be one thing. The eagle had landed. Hard. It made me smile.

I peeked around the pine I was using for cover and saw them take notice, reload, and prepare for their next attack. Scartizina was in the center of the driveway, tromping on my mother's flowers and hiding as best he could behind the old water pump. The second man was now trying to hide behind Grandpa's beehive oven, keeping it low.

They hadn't moved much since the chopper departed. Now they did.

On Scartizina's command, the shooter by the oven did his best commando imitation, zigzagging to the south. Scartizina burned up a clip trying to provide cover. His mope dove into the bush at the edge of the clearing, thinking he had found safety.

The problem was no one told him the clothing he wore jumped out of the foliage rather than blended into it. I'm sure he felt it made him look tough back on the street, but in the high country, it provided no protection. If anything, it made him even more visible.

I let him catch his breath and think he was safe for a moment while the bullets rained around me. When he turned around to signal Scartizina, he was ready to provide cover. I made that impossible by putting a round through his middle. The gut shot was fatal, but it would take a while for him to die.

Five down. One to go. The leader of the pack.

He sprayed my position, emptying a full clip, his bullets coming closer this time. One of his rounds kicked off a branch or some bark that stuck my forehead. I didn't know how deep it was, but blood started to fall.

I folded my bandana, covered the wound, and tied it behind my head. I couldn't help but think Kaiah would have approved of the look, particularly under these circumstances.

Scartizina looked around, evaluating his options. He could run for the house, but he knew he would never make it. There was too much open ground. He could try to wait me out, but he was exposed, and I was not. If he stayed where he was, I could take my time and pick him off whenever I wanted.

I saw the moment when he made up his mind. He was an aggressive animal. He knew where I was. He had the firepower. He would bet on himself, come at me, and take me out. It was a bad bet.

Scartizina dashed, coming directly at me, emptying a clip as he came. He dropped into the brush near the creek and popped in a new clip while checking my position.

I could see him looking for me as he did a commando crawl through the brush. I stayed out of sight and let him come. I could smell his perspiration and fear when he was still 50 feet away. If he was making any attempt to be quiet, he wasn't very good at it.

He was reverting to type, trying to get in close where

he could fight the kind of fight he had always won. Point blank. Superior firepower. Guns a blazing.

From an early age, I had learned to pick up my brass. I waited for the right opportunity, a moment when he looked down to check his footing and threw a couple of shells off to his left. I was rewarded with a burst of rapid-fire as he chased the sound. I backed off, moving silently deeper into the words.

I watched him come until he found himself in a small clearing formed by three ancient pines. He walked in cautiously, put his back against the largest tree and listened.

He had no way of knowing he was leaning on Bear's tree. I threw the last of the shells I had gathered off to his right and came in around behind him from the other side, moving silently the way I had learned and practiced as a boy. I was on top of him before he realized I was there.

He turned toward me and tried to bring his gun up, but it was too late. I knocked the barrel down, blocking it with my left arm and brought the butt of the Winchester up to strike him just above the Adam's apple.

He wanted a close fight. I gave it to him, pinning his right arm between our bodies and pushed him back forcibly against the tree. I could smell his sour breath and see the panic in his eyes as I found Kaiah's knife.

I stuck it in him up to the hilt, just below the third rib, pinning him to the tree like the bug he was. He let go of his gun and sagged down against the knife. He was dead, but he didn't know it yet.

A bloody foam started to form around his lips. His hands closed around the knife and stayed frozen there.

It was impossible to know if he was shoving it in or trying to pull it out. If he had pulled it out, he would have bled out in a matter of minutes. Maybe he knew that.

I left him where he was, picked up the Bushmaster, and began to prepare to dispose of the bodies. He watched me with amber eyes, tinged with blood and full of hate. It was a look I had seen before. They were the eyes of Kaiah's coyote.

Cheyenne was the first member of the family to come out of the woods. She must have been watching from just above my position.

A few moments later, her brothers, Tuesday – called Two – and Jackson, appeared. Jackson was 100 yards to the south. Two came in from just behind the house.

They all carried Remington 700 bolt action rifles. The one Cheyenne carried had been modified for use as a sniper rifle by our Uncle Nick, the one who died in Iraq. It has a 26-inch barrel with a 1:12 rate of twist for awesome accuracy at a distance. It's all we have left to remember him by. It's not much, but it's something.

Cheyenne nodded to Jackson, her youngest brother, and he disappeared to re-emerge 10 minutes later with their horses. I waited for her near the well and greeted her without ceremony.

"What are you doing here?" I asked.

I knew the answer full well, but I also knew she wouldn't give me the satisfaction of saying it.

"I know you," She said instead.

"What does that mean?"

"You always make a mess. If someone doesn't help

you clean this up, it will be a week before the kids can come home."

She pulled out her cell while the boys and I started cleaning up. Cap was dead. There was nothing I could do for him. The horses appeared unharmed. Cass came out of the barn with her tail between her legs when I called her.

When I was sure she was all right, I got keys to the truck – our rusty, red Ford 150. The odometer has turned over, and nearly every part of the motor has been replaced, but it still runs fine. We attached the plow and dropped the tailgate before pulling out of the barn.

I picked a spot 50 yards behind the barn where the mountain began and carved a hole with the plow, taking out six feet of the side of the mountain and digging another three feet down.

Then, I put a sheet of plastic on the bed of the truck and started collecting bodies. I piled them up on top of each other and watched their blood mingle.

Cheyenne closed her cell and picked up a broom and a shovel. She said the kids would be home in time for dinner.

"Some of your junk landed near Trappers' Lake," She added. "There was an explosion and a fire. The People are there protecting the forest. When the fire burns out, they will drop what's left of that noisy thing into Craig's Canyon."

It was a good solution on several levels. We get more than 50,000 forest fires a year in the United States, four-fifths of them out west. We didn't need another one, and we both knew that if the helicopter were left where it fell, it wouldn't be long before some mope would stumble on it and make up a story about how it got there.

Soon, word would get around, and mountain guides would begin marketing excursions and hikes into the mountains to see this foreign object, feeding speculation about why it was there, how it got there, and what it was.

Was it someone scouting a movie location? Prospectors looking for the newest precious metal or a mineral source? Extreme skiers? A secret government project? Who knows? Anything but the truth.

Burying it at the bottom of Craig's Canyon seemed as good a solution as any. The brush would cover it in a week.

There was a small crater the size of a Mini Cooper where the ammo bag had exploded. What was left of the co-pilot was scattered around in pieces too small to identify. Cheyenne worked her broom and shovel, and her brothers began picking up the brass and policing the area for parts. It wouldn't do for one of the kids to find a shoe with part of a foot in it. It's been known to happen.

They pushed everything into the crater. It still left a sizeable depression. The brothers began the tedious process of filling it in, hauling dirt and gravel from beyond the barn.

Scartizina was still alive when I got back to him. I saw a dim look of recognition as I grabbed his collar and hauled him down the mountain. I left the knife in until I was ready to bury him.

Then I wiped the blade on his pant leg and put it back in its sheath. I went through his pockets and found a fat wallet. I threw that and his jewelry into a bucket by the well. The other shooters weren't carrying much, but what they had went into the bucket as well.

I threw their weapons on the bottom of the grave and piled the bodies on top of each other, crosshatching them with layers of lye in between. I would have given the guns to Cheyenne's brothers, but The People have no use for weapons of that kind.

I spread another 50 pounds of lye over the top of the shooters before covering them with the plastic sheet from the truck and pushing the dirt back on their graves. I used the truck to pack it down tight.

After I put the truck back in the barn, I took the bucket over to the well and put it near Scartizina's backpack. He had used all the munitions he carried. The only thing left in the backpack was money. It was ironic. The legacy of a mercenary. Munitions and the money that paid for it.

I put the leather – wallets and the backpack – into Grandpa's oven, spreading it out on top of the kindling that was waiting for the next fire. I didn't bother checking their identification or credit cards. It didn't matter.

I collected all the cash before setting everything else on fire. Between them, they carried four thousand three hundred in pocket money. I added that to the stack of bills I had taken from Scartizina's backpack. There were five banded stacks of $5,000 and one of $25,000.

I guess it should have been flattering. I had no idea I was worth that much.

Private jets run anywhere from $2,000 to $5,000 an hour. I saw no reason Colgate should pay for my return flight to Naples. I took out what I needed to get home and gave the rest to Cheyenne for the family.

"I want to head back to Naples tomorrow," I said. "The sooner I am seen there, the less likely they are to come looking for me here."

She nodded. We both knew this wasn't the end of it. If anything, it was only the end of the beginning.

Then I picked up a shovel. I buried Cappy near my parents and grandparents. He was part of the family. He deserved to be there.

Bury Them

Tuesday morning, June 1. I was sitting on the top deck of The Big Doll. Taylor was down below, soaking in the rays. Meyer was on the bow surrounded by a gaggle of girls, Carla and Darlene, and a couple of their friends from Momma Madeline's extended family.

It was a hot summer day. There was the promise of more to come. The clouds above were too high to do much good.

Taylor wore a yellow bikini that covered everything that needed to be covered and not much else. I was sipping Writer's Tears and enjoying the view when my cell rang. I had been waiting for the call.

"Yes, Sir?"

"Are you ok?" Colgate asked.

"Yes, Sir. Some people were upset with our last investigation. They took it personally."

"I know. I met with Chambers yesterday at the Cosmos Club."

"That must have been interesting."

"It was. He said you blew up his boat and shot down his helicopter. Cost him somewhere around $80 million."

"I'm sure he is insured. Probably overinsured. If that doesn't work out for him, he'll find a way to make Medicare pay for it."

"He also said he lost six men. Maybe more. He is not sure."

"He got off easy… They killed my dog."

"Chambers asked for the meeting because he wants me to call you off. He said our investigation did a lot of damage. He said his company is making a comeback, but they still haven't fully recovered. He doesn't think they can sustain any more bad news."

"Are we supposed to feel sorry for them?"

"Gets better. He said if I called you off, he would make it worth my while. He said he would start contributing like a relative…And you know my relatives. That's a big offer."

"Plus, he promised to start a PAC. Get the industry involved. Said he would support an exploratory committee for me down the road if and when I want to run for higher office."

"What did you say?"

"I told him I would think about it."

"And…"

"I've thought about it."

"What do you want me to do?"

There was a deliberate pause. I could almost see his jaw set before his firm, quiet response.

"Bury him."

"With pleasure."

Then, his voice rose with anger and indignation.

"Can you believe that son-of-a-bitch tried to bribe me? Who the hell does he think he is? What makes him think I would even consider something like that?"

"Not sure he thought you would. But from his point of view, it is worth an ask. They have to find out where you are. They need to know if you will play ball. It's not personal. It's just how they operate, how they live.

"They have been bribing doctors, hospitals, administrators, and regulators for years with every kind of kickback they can think of. Why should you be any different? Are you in or out? They need to know, and it costs them nothing to find out."

"Other than committing another Federal crime…Gov. Divos asked for the meeting. He said it would be good for everyone. Does that mean he is in?"

"The question probably answers itself. My guess is he has the same deal Chambers offered you."

"See if we can prove that. If so, I want to bury them both."

"Yes, sir."

"I would never tell you how to do what you do, T.J., But nothing would make me happier than to see both these clowns before the Committee with their balls on the table. I want them to know we've got them by the short hair, and the FBI and the DOJ are waiting for the handoff on the other side of the door."

"I'll see what I can do."

"I know you will."

"One more thing, if you have a moment."

"Sure."

"We should start thinking about what comes next."

"What's that?"

"What will they do once they know they can't bribe you."

There was a soft silence.

"What do you think they will do?" He said, finally.

"You are a once-in-a-generation talent. You have carved out a record as a maverick, someone who can't be influenced, someone who walks away from the herd.

"That's popular with the people, but it worries partisans. Now comes this. In their book, a man who can't be influenced and won't be bought is a dangerous man."

"How so?"

"You don't need them. Worse, you don't want them. You threaten their positions and their power. If you are not indebted to anyone, then no one has a hold on you. No one is safe."

"They haven't seen anyone like you since Kennedy – and you know what happened to him."

"Do you really think they would go that far?"

"When extraordinary things happen, you have to ask yourself – Why? Who benefits?" That's Sam Spade's first rule. The second rule comes out of the first – Follow the money.

"In the political world, those two things are almost always connected. That's the nature of the beast. It's no accident that some of the richest people in the world are politicians. It's no accident that there isn't a single member of Congress who isn't wealthier now than when he was first elected."

"There is one notable exception – You."

"To put it bluntly. That makes you a threat."

"Kennedy famously said at his inauguration that the torch had been passed to a new generation. He should have known the "old" generation wasn't going to take kindly to that. He underestimated how far they would go."

"It's worth noting the Warren Commission never tried to answer Sam Spade's questions. If they had, the answer would probably have looked like a circular firing squad."

"The same people – different names, different faces, but the same people – are going to be troubled by you. The bigger you get, the more prominent you become, and the more you are going to worry people like Divos, the money behind him, and a raft of others who are lining up to take their shot."

"You know them better than I do. Washington is a one-mouse town. There are a hundred cats, and they are all hungry."

"My gut tells me this is part of that. A beginning. A feeler. They saw the *Congressional Times*. They know you are a player now. So, they put the bait out there. They will wait and see if you take it. If you don't, they may just change the bait, or they may start considering other options."

"Like what? Trying to get me defeated next year when I am up for re-election?"

"That and anything else you can think of and a hundred things you can't. History has shown nothing is unthinkable. People will do anything to get and hold power."

"So, where does that leave us? What do you think I should do?"

"Be prepared. I'm not trying to scare you. And I'm sure as hell not telling you to back off. Just be aware they are going to come after us in every way they can, and be ready for it."

"Start by telling Mack to add another layer of security for you and the family. Use your people. People you know. Double vet every new hire at home or in the office."

"Tell M.J. what's going on and have her be careful with your schedule. Be mindful of who is asking for you, where they want you to go and what they want you to do. Fortunately, you do not need to use public transportation. That eliminates one big risk factor."

"I'll move things as fast as I can here. If we lock some of these bastards up, it might slow the others down. It helps that we have built up our own intelligence network with backdoor channels to the Agency and the Bureau. We also have eyes on the street. There is a measure of comfort there. Chambers and company have good reason to know the kind of damage we can do."

"Plus, in terms of your personal security, there is this: If they want to come after you, they know they have to take me out first. Any attempt to get at you or any member of your family will only make me come at them harder. And I won't be hampered by anybody's arbitrary rules."

"OK. Be careful, T.J. Let me know if there is anything you need."

Colgate clicked off.

I took a sip of my scotch, enjoying its mellow taste. I gazed out over the harbor with new appreciation. I was getting to like this place. The view had certainly improved, particularly to the south, where I could see a salvage crew trying to resurrect what was left of the gerriantics.

Another crew was beginning to reconstruct the dock at Port Royal. The yachts had been pulled away and repositioned in the harbor to make room. I couldn't help feeling sorry for the money men. That must have been a big inconvenience.

I thought about my conversation with Colgate, the work ahead, and the woman below and smiled. One of the greatest gifts in life is to be able to do good things in good company.

This was going to be fun.

...

Epilogue

BLOOD FALLS, coming soon:

. . .

Taylor's mother called late Wednesday morning. She wanted to know if I knew where Taylor was.

Taylor had said she was going home for a few days to see her mom, pick up some clothes, and check in with her editor. But she had never made it home, and her editor hadn't seen her. Her editor had called home looking for her. He said it was unlike her to miss an appointment.

When she hadn't appeared by Tuesday afternoon, *The Sun* ran a trace on her. GPS located her car at Miami International Airport. There was no sign of her there.

The car had been swept. Even the fast-food wrappers were gone. The only thing left in the car was a single sheet of plain paper, 8x10, folded in half and tented over the gearshift on the console.

There were three letters on the outside, my initials, broad and black and crude. They looked like they had been drawn in crayon.

There were three letters inside, written in blood, and two spots at the bottom of the page where blood had fallen on the page as the page was prepared. It said:

I. O. U.

Made in the USA
Columbia, SC
03 April 2025

56089582R00180